THE GHOST

FROM THE SEA

HAUNTING DANIELLE

HAUNTING DANIELLE - BOOK 8

THE GHOST
FROM THE SEA

BOBBI HOLMES

The Ghost from the Sea
(Haunting Danielle, Book 8)
A Novel
By Bobbi Holmes
Cover Design: Elizabeth Mackey

Large Print

ISBN-13: 978-1-949977-26-4

Dedicated to three of my author friends:
Randall Morris, Nick Russell, and Billy Kring.
For all the crazy questions you answer.

ONE

Jack imagined Thelma's vacant eye cavities watched him as her skull rolled around under his feet. What little remained of Thelma did not remotely resemble the skeleton Doc Clemens had proudly hung in his office.

A school of fish meandered by, taking a detour through what was left of Howard's rib cage. Jack tried initiating a conversation. Like all the rest, the fish ignored him. The only ones who seemed interested in conversing were the dolphins, yet they never came inside. Jack made his way to the upper deck—or what was left of it. He often wondered what Walt would think of the *Eva Aphrodite* now.

Shafts of early morning sunlight streamed through the seawater above. It glistened and sparkled as it showered his world and made him again crave what once was. He should have left when the others had, he told himself. Yet something kept him here—tied for eternity to the *Eva Aphrodite*—or at least until he figured out how he had arrived on the boat.

Jack was about to return to the lower deck when something blocked the sunlight. He looked up and saw the bottom of a boat's hull come to a stop; it rocked gently from side to side. A few moments later, someone from the boat jumped into the water and started swimming toward him. The diver's finned feet kicked furiously.

When the interloper reached the sunken craft, Jack recognized him. It was not his first trip to the *Eva Aphrodite*; he had come once before. He carried a light to help him see. He also carried a small box in his arms.

Jack followed the visitor to the lower deck, to the cabin Thelma and Howard had occupied.

The diver deposited the box in one corner and then swam toward the exit, but paused a moment to inspect Thelma's skull. He picked it up briefly, turning it from side to side. For a moment, Jack thought the diver intended to take her with him, and he didn't think he could let that happen. Thelma and the rest had been with him since the beginning, and it didn't seem right to let the stranger defile her in this manner.

Unfortunately, Jack had no way to prevent the diver from taking off with Thelma's skull, not unless he could convince a dolphin to intervene on his behalf, and he hadn't seen any dolphins around for some time. In the next moment, the diver abandoned his find. The skull made a sluggish descent to the cabin's floor as the man exited the ship.

Relieved that problem was diverted, Jack followed the diver to the upper deck and watched as he swam back up to the awaiting craft. Jack wasn't sure how long he stood there, but finally the boat moved away, no longer blocking the sunlight. It was in that moment a thought occurred to Jack—*Could I have gone with him? Could I have followed him back to his boat, stowed away? Returned to shore? Would that have been possible?*

Jack continued to stand on the upper deck until it went dark again. Nighttime had fallen. He was still standing there the next morning when the sun began to shine, teasing the depths with its brightness.

Visions of departure consumed his thoughts. Jack closed his eyes and imagined the *Eva Aphrodite* on the water's surface. Lost in keen desire, he didn't notice the hull's gentle rocking along the ocean's floor was somehow different from normal. But when he opened his eyes a moment later and looked upwards, he realized the water's surface was fast approaching. The moment he questioned the turn of events, the deck below him dropped, and the *Eva Aphrodite* plummeted back to the ocean's floor, sending a cloud of silt billowing upwards.

"What just happened?" Standing on the deck, he watched as nearby fish hastily moved away from the unsteady wreckage. After a moment of reflection, Jack asked aloud, "Is it possible? Did I do that?"

With a renewed sense of power, Jack

stretched out his arms and willed the ship upwards to the light. It didn't happen instantly. First, there was a gentle rumbling from below, a shifting of the boat's hull against the ocean floor. It then rocked slightly, sending more silt ballooning upwards, but then the ship seemed to unseat itself, and to Jack's delight it began to rise, slowly at first and then picking up speed, scattering the sea life above from its path.

Unable to contain his delight, Jack began to laugh, the intensity of his laughter in sync with the rise of the downed ship. At last the once defeated wreckage broke through the surface, sending sprays of seawater in every direction. Jack saw, for the first time in what seemed like an eternity, blue sky—unfiltered sky. He knew then it was only the beginning.

"Home, *Eva Aphrodite*! Let's go home!" he roared.

The motorless ship, powered only by Jack's determination, headed east toward the rising sun. It was only when the shoreline came in view did he begin to lose confidence. Nothing was as he remembered. For a brief moment the ship slowed and began to fall back into the sea, yet Jack had waited too long to quit now. Focusing his energy, he lifted the *Eva Aphrodite* up above the water and moved it swiftly toward land.

Instead of searching for the once familiar harbor, he concentrated all his energy on the swiftly approaching wide stretch of pale sand. As he neared the shore, the *Eva Aphrodite* took flight, hovering like a seagull over the water's surface, until at last it reached the beach and settled itself a good distance from where the waves met the sand.

It took a few moments before the ship settled itself comfortably on the beach. Looking out from the top deck, Jack surveyed his surroundings.

"Where am I?" he asked aloud. "Am I even in Oregon?"

Making his way off the boat, the soles of Jack's dress shoes landed on the beach. He took a moment to wipe imaginary sand from his slacks before heading south. He had almost convinced himself he had arrived somewhere other than Frederickport when he saw a familiar building—it was George Hemming's house. With an excited grin, Jack raced toward George's back porch.

Normally, he would just walk in; after all, this had been his home. Yet Jack wasn't sure how long he had been gone, and he imagined George had long since rented out his room. He started to knock on the back door. Instead of his knuckles making a sound against the wooden door, they moved effortlessly through it. Without thought, Jack followed his hand into the house, his body moving through the solid door.

Once inside, he looked around. Nothing was as he remembered. Confused, he stepped back outside again and took another look at the rear of the building.

"I'm sure this is George Hemming's house," Jack muttered. Moving back inside, Jack surveyed his surroundings. If he imagined the space without the furniture or any of the wall hangings and other items scattered around, it was as he remembered George Hemming's home to be. Jack had been gone a long time—how long exactly he wasn't sure—but he was certain if George was still around, he would probably have new furniture by now.

When Jack walked into the kitchen, he was surprised to find a large yellow dog sitting in the middle of the room, watching him, its tail wagging.

"When did George get a dog?" Jack asked aloud.

The dog cocked its head, tail still wagging. Jack frowned. He could swear he'd just heard the dog ask, "Who's George?"

Confused, Jack felt the sudden urge to go back to the boat. Abruptly, he turned to go. The dog barked and rushed toward him. Startled, Jack took off in a run, heading for the back door. The dog, at a full gallop, ran through his body, reaching the back door before him. Still barking, the dog stood guard, facing Jack, daring him to come closer. Wanting nothing more than to be on the outside again, Jack made a dash to the dog's right and effortlessly moved through the back wall, landing once again on the porch facing the ocean.

He could hear the dog still barking inside, her paws now up on the windowsill as her nose attempted to push aside the curtain so she could get a look outside. It was then he heard a man's voice yell out, "Sadie!" It didn't sound like George's voice, so Jack ran off the porch and headed north, back toward the *Eva Aphrodite*.

Once he reached the boat, Jack entered the lower deck, curious to see how it had fared in the voyage. The first thing he noticed was that water no longer filled the lower cabins.

"Where did it go?" he asked aloud. The disappearance of the seawater confounded him, so he moved to the upper deck, hoping to get a clearer picture of his surroundings and a possible answer to the mystery.

Standing at the stern, Jack gazed out to sea. The sand from where the breakers touched the beach to where the *Eva Aphrodite* settled appeared to be dry. The only conclusion he could arrive at was that the water had somehow spilled out while the ship made its way toward shore. He remembered that for at least a portion of the journey the boat was completely out of the water. He then remembered the gaping hole in the hull and imagined all the seawater spilling out while the boat made its way to shore.

Satisfied with his conclusion, Jack moved from the stern to the ship's bow. Gazing down the beach, he could see the rooftop of George Hemming's house. Jack smiled. Walt Marlow's house was just across the street from George's. He couldn't see it from where he stood on the upper deck of the ship, but he knew it was there. Jack had no idea what he would find at Walt's house.

Just as Jack was about to leave the ship for a second time, he glanced down the beach and noticed something coming toward him from the direction of George's house. Leaning over the side of the ship, he narrowed his eyes and watched the curious sight.

He assumed it was a woman, considering the long black pigtails flopping up and down as she made her way toward him. Dressed all in purple like a giant plum, her arms, bent at the elbows, swung dramatically up and down, reminding him of a milkmaid preparing to torture some poor dairy cow. Her knees lifted dramatically with each step, faster than a walk yet not quite a run.

As she got closer, he realized her eyes were closed. If she continued on blindly, she would run straight into the side of the *Eva Aphrodite*. Considering the speed of her jaunt, he winced. *It's going to hurt.*

He was about to shout out to her when he noticed something hanging from her ears—wires. From each of her ears there was a wire; the opposite end of each wire ran into the side pocket of her purple pants.

TWO

Music blared through the headphones. Heather Donovan continued on her morning run, despite the chilly damp drizzle. The soles of her jogging shoes pounded against the sand, one after another, never stopping. She fisted her hands and pumped her arms to maximize her workout. With eyes closed, she blindly jogged down the empty beach, aiming to where the damp sand met the dry.

Since moving out of Marlow House and back into her own place, Heather had taken up jogging. She ran this way every morning, starting at the pier, and she told herself she could do the entire run with her eyes closed. It was a personal dare she decided to accept. The worst thing that could happen, Heather told herself, was that she might run into another jogger.

It wasn't a straight run, as the shoreline curved slightly near Ian Bartley's house. She allowed herself to cheat and opened her eyes for a moment. Yet instead of looking up, she kept her gaze down, just to make sure she continued to follow the shoreline's curve and didn't run into the ocean.

A few houses past Ian's, the shoreline no longer curved, and Heather felt confident she could blindly continue down a straight path. Lifting her head, her eyes tightly closed, she breathed deeply and relished the sensation of her heart bounding in her chest as music filled her head.

A few moments later, Heather came to an abrupt halt and opened her eyes. She didn't have time to ask herself why she had stopped so unexpectedly or why she opened her eyes. Instead, she stood stunned and stared at what appeared to be the wreckage of a beached ship less than one hundred yards from her, perched stranded on the sand like a gutted whale.

Dazed, Heather pulled the headphones from her ears, letting them dangle from her hand, as she tried to comprehend the scene before her.

"What is that?" Heather heard a voice shout. She looked over to see one of her neighbors rushing toward her.

HANDS ON HIPS, Sergeant Joe Morelli stood on the boardwalk at the edge of the sand, next to his partner, Brian Henderson. They stared in awe at the unexpected sight not far from the water's edge. "I'll be damned, we have our own *Peter Iredale*," Joe murmured.

Removing his cap briefly before fitting it back onto his head, Brian stepped off the sidewalk onto the sand. "Where in the hell did it come from?"

Instead of following Brian onto the beach and toward the mysterious boat, Joe paused a moment and watched as two of the local residents approached them from the wreckage: Heather Donovan and Pete Rogers.

When the pair was within hearing distance, Pete shouted, "I told you!"

Joe started walking, following Brian. When Pete and Heather were a few feet away, Joe responded with, "You said a boat washed up, but I didn't imagine anything like this."

Now walking alongside the two officers, Pete said in a breathless voice, "It wasn't even stormy last night! How did it ever get up on the beach like that?"

With a shake of his head, Joe continued to follow Brian. "The tide must have brought her in."

Trailing beside them, Pete asked, "Where did it come from?"

"Also looks like it's been under the water for some time," Brian said when they reached the wreckage.

Joe walked around the battered hull, attempting to make sense of the scene. "I suppose we need to call the Coast Guard."

"What's the Coast Guard supposed to do?" Heather asked.

"Well, for one thing, it might be a hazard,

especially if the tide takes it back into the ocean and it stays afloat. They might decide to haul it off and sink it," Brian said. "But first, we need to figure out where it came from."

MIDWEEK IN MARCH, it was especially quiet at Marlow House. The last two guests had checked out on Monday morning. Joanne had cleaned the house on Tuesday and wouldn't be returning until Friday morning, when the next round of guests would check in.

Lily refilled her coffee cup and joined Danielle at the kitchen table. She briefly glanced up to the ceiling before sitting down. "Is Walt in the attic?"

Danielle poured extra cream into her coffee and said, "I think so. I noticed Max slinking up there when I came downstairs."

"I never thought I'd say this, but it seems a little strange without Heather here."

Danielle glanced over at Lily and smiled. "Strange?"

Lily giggled. "Strange in a good way, I suppose. It's not that I miss her exactly; she could be awful bitchy at times. But it's so quiet around here when we don't have any guests."

"Sometimes I wonder if Heather is a little bipolar, the way she runs hot and cold."

Lily considered Danielle's suggestion for a moment before responding. "Bipolar? You know, you might be onto something."

Danielle shrugged and took a sip of her coffee.

Lily set her cup back onto the table and looked at Danielle. "So tell me, how long is Chris going to be in Chicago? At first I heard him say he was going to be gone a week, and then Ian said it was two weeks."

"He'd like to be back in a week, but he doesn't think he'll be able to get everything done by then. So it looks like two weeks. Not sure."

"I guess that means he didn't make his return reservation yet."

Danielle shook her head. "Nope."

"I was about to ask you why he didn't just have his own jet—considering how much money he has. But then I remembered he doesn't even own a car."

Danielle laughed. "Well, according to Chris, when he gets back from Chicago, he's buying a car in Portland, which means I won't have to pick him up at the airport."

Narrowing her eyes, Lily studied Danielle a moment before asking, "So what's up with you two?"

Danielle shrugged nonchalantly and sipped her coffee before asking, "What do you mean?"

"You know what I mean. How long is this good-buddy act gunna go on? You two have known each other for almost three months now. The guy is hot, and I can tell he's attracted to you. I mean, you two haven't even kissed…" Lily paused a moment and stared at Danielle. Her eyes widened. With a gasp she said, "You guys have kissed! Haven't you? And you didn't tell me!"

Danielle briefly glanced up to the ceiling. In a whisper she said, "Quiet, it's not a big deal."

"Not a big deal? I want details," Lily teased. She noticed Danielle's gaze flash up to the ceiling again. "Ahh…Walt. You don't want him to know. Hmm…interesting…"

Danielle shifted uncomfortably in her chair. "It's not that."

"Not what?" Lily asked smugly.

"Like I said, it was no big deal. I just don't see the point in saying anything to Walt and having to endure his commentary on the subject."

"If it's not a big deal, then why the secrecy?"

"Can we take this conversation outside?" Danielle suggested.

Lily stood up. "I suppose so. Looks like that's the only way I'll get any details."

Five minutes later, Lily sat with Danielle on the porch swing in front of Marlow House. Before going outside, each woman had slipped on a light jacket.

Cradling the warm coffee mug in her hands, Danielle looked down into the cup. "Like I said, it really isn't a big deal. It happened so quick and was over in a second."

"Well, *that* sounds exciting," Lily quipped dryly. "I expected something more from Chris."

"It was at the airport, right when he was about to go through security. He was saying goodbye, and then all of a sudden he grabs me, gives me a kiss, looks at me a moment without saying anything, and then rushes through security."

"That was it?"

"Well…" Danielle looked off into space and smiled softly. "It might have been brief and sudden…but it was nice. I rather liked it."

"Hmm…interesting."

Danielle looked to Lily and frowned. "Anyway, technically it was our second kiss. You are forgetting New Year's Eve."

Lily rolled her eyes. "A quick New Year's kiss in front of a roomful of people isn't a real kiss. Which makes it stranger that he took this long to kiss you again."

"Why?"

"These days it seems like everyone kisses before the first date. But look at you. How many times did you go out with Joe Morelli? He never kissed you once. And look at Chris; he's been hanging around you for three months now, stayed under the same roof as you for most of that time and even bought a house on our street. And what, you've only kissed once?"

"Twice. And are you trying to make me feel like a prude or what?"

"Just the opposite. I'm starting to feel a bit like a ho," Lily said glumly.

"Ho?" Danielle laughed. "Why do you say that?"

"Well, if I find a guy attractive, and we're going out, I sure as heck won't wait three months to kiss him. Even if I have to be the one to instigate it. But look at you; these guys obviously adore you. Yet it's almost like they placed you on some pedestal."

"You're being silly. Anyway, Joe no longer adores me. He and Kelly seem to be going strong."

Lily sighed. "Yeah, I suppose."

"What's wrong? You don't like Kelly with Joe?"

"It just feels weird when we do the double-date thing with them. Ever since all that stuff between you and Joe, how he treated you."

"Joe's not a bad guy. I consider him a

friend. I think he and Kelly are good together. What does Ian think?"

"Ian likes Joe okay, as long as he makes his sister happy." Lily shrugged. "But between you and me, he calls Joe the Clueless Boy Scout."

The nickname made Danielle laugh; she choked on her coffee. Once she regained her normal breathing, she said, "That does kinda fit. He didn't tell Kelly that, did he?"

"No way!" Lily started to laugh but stopped when she noticed two police cars drive by. Putting her foot down to stop the swing, she stood up and stepped toward the road, looking down the street.

"They're stopping near Chris's house," Lily told Danielle.

"HOLY CRAP, WHAT'S THAT?" Lily exclaimed when they reached the sidewalk just beyond Chris's house and looked out to the ocean.

"Looks like a shipwreck," Danielle muttered. She was relieved to discover the four police cars, now parked near Chris's house, were obviously not here because of a break-in at his property. The real reason seemed far more interesting to Danielle.

Together, Danielle and Lily stepped off the sidewalk and made their way down the beach, heading to the wreckage, where the police officers gathered around.

Heather greeted them before they reached the officers. "I found it during my morning jog!"

Lily and Danielle stared at the battered hull. "What is it?" Lily asked.

"Obviously it's a shipwreck," Heather snapped.

Lily let out a sigh. "Yeah, I see that. But I mean where did it come from?"

"No one knows. It just showed up on the beach like that. It almost looks like someone just dropped it there. The sand between the wreckage and ocean doesn't even look as if it's been disturbed," Heather explained.

"I imagine the tide washed out evidence of tracks," Danielle suggested.

"No," Heather said emphatically. "Brian and Joe are totally confused."

"Joe and Brian are always confused," Lily muttered under her breath.

Ignoring the exchange, Danielle stared at the mysterious wreckage. Motion on the front of the hull caught her attention. Silently, she walked toward it, leaving Lily and Heather behind her, talking amongst themselves. After walking some ten feet, she paused; her eyes widened in surprise. Standing atop the wreckage, looking down at the police officers on the beach, was a man dressed in vintage clothing of the 1920s.

THREE

Danielle continued to stare at the apparition atop the wreckage when she heard someone shout out, "I guess I can't blame this one on you."

She looked to the right and saw Brian Henderson walking in her direction, a cocky grin on his face. He boasted a full head of shortly cropped gray hair and had a stocky build. Danielle guessed Brian was only a few years younger than her father—if her father were still alive.

Dressed in his Frederickport police uniform and wearing a baseball cap with the department's insignia on its front panel, Brian stopped when he reached Danielle and then glanced over at the wreckage. "It's something, isn't it?"

"Any idea where it came from?" She tucked her fingertips into the back pockets of her jeans as she kept an eye on the apparition. The morning breeze loosened strands of her dark hair from her once neat fishtail braid, sending them whipping into her eyes. Removing one hand from a pocket, she brushed back the hair, tucking it behind one ear.

Brian shook his head. "Not a clue. We're waiting for someone from the Coast Guard to show up, and we have a call in to the coroner's office."

"Coroner's office?" Danielle's gaze darted briefly to Brian and then back to the apparent ghost, who remained standing atop the wreckage, watching the people on the beach.

Lowering his voice, Brian said, "Joe managed to get into the lower cabin. He found skeletal remains inside."

Danielle frowned. "Isn't that dangerous? Shouldn't he have waited for the Coast Guard or someone?"

Brian shrugged. "He was careful. It's not going anywhere."

After a few moments of silence, Danielle said, "By the looks of that ship, I'd say its passengers have been dead a long time."

"By the look of the passengers, I'd have to agree with you."

Danielle glanced back at Heather, who stood a distance away, chatting with Lily. "Heather didn't say anything to us about finding remains."

"We didn't say anything to Heather."

Danielle studied Brian for a moment. She thought his expression seemed friendlier than normal. "Why tell me?"

Brian shrugged. "I imagine it'll be in the paper. Anyway, figure the chief will tell you when you see him." Brian nodded toward Chris's house. "So why isn't your friend out here checking this out?"

Danielle glanced briefly in the direction of Brian's gaze. "You mean Chris?"

"Obviously."

"He's in Chicago on business."

"Business? I didn't know he had a job."

Danielle smiled. "He's busy giving away a couple of million or something like that."

"Of course he is," Brian muttered under his breath. He looked back at the wreckage.

"Any idea where the ship might have originated?" she asked.

"We called the local historical society, and they're sending someone who's familiar with the Marlow line."

"You think it's one of theirs?" Danielle asked.

"Not really, but at least it's someone local who knows a little about maritime history."

"Any idea how you're going to get rid of it?" The moment Danielle asked the question, the apparition on the ship vanished.

"We may not," Brian told her.

"Are you saying you might just leave it there? On the beach?"

"If the Coast Guard feels it's a hazard, they might drag it off and sink it. If not, look at the *Peter Iredale*."

"You're talking about the old sailboat at Fort Stevens State Park?"

Brian nodded. "What's left of it."

Danielle glanced from Brian to the wreckage. "I've never been there—just seen the pictures."

"Not that far from here."

"Does that mean this will turn into some tourist attraction?"

Brian shrugged. "I imagine it would be good for your business."

"I suppose. But is that thing safe? Kids start climbing around on it. Doesn't seem very safe to me."

"Let's see what the Coast Guard says." Brian paused a moment when he noticed new arrivals walking from the direction of the street to the wreckage. "Looks like someone from the coroner's office is here. Talk to you later."

Danielle gave Brian a parting nod and watched him walk away. The next moment she heard Heather shout out a goodbye, and when she turned around, Lily was walking toward her.

"I thought she was never going to shut up," Lily said under her breath.

"And weren't you just saying you missed her?"

"I'm over it."

Danielle smiled at Lily, noting the way her rusty-colored hair seemed far curlier than it had been when they were inside less than an hour earlier. It had grown considerably since it had been cut short in the fall and now reached past her shoulders, falling midway down her back, where it curled wildly. Danielle always felt tall standing next to petite Lily—and Danielle was not a particularly tall woman. At one time, Danielle had been envious of Lily's full bustline, especially considering Lily's otherwise trim figure. Yet Danielle had come to accept her own body—even with the extra fifteen pounds she was unable to lose.

Danielle glanced down the beach and watched Heather jog in the direction of the pier. "What did she say about the ship?"

"Just how she found it this morning when she was jogging. Did you know Heather jogs an hour every morning?"

"She never did when she was staying with us."

"I guess it's her new thing. Anyway, she's all concerned about the bad vibes this is going to bring our neighborhood."

Danielle frowned. "Bad vibes?"

"According to Heather, the ship probably sank with people on board who are now restless spirits, and they will undoubtedly disrupt the harmony along this stretch of beach… and blah, blah, blah. Ever since her experience with Harvey, Heather imagines herself to be some sort of expert on spirits. I keep waiting for her to publish that book she says she's writing, but I'm beginning to think she's one of those people who talks more about writing than actually does it."

"She may have a point about the spirits," Danielle whispered. "At least one of them."

Narrowing her eyes, Lily studied Danielle. "What do you mean? Do you see something?"

"Not now, but I did. There was a man standing on top of the ship…or at least what's left of it."

"What do you mean a man?"

"A man. Well, not a man man. A man like Walt."

"You're talking about a ghost?" Lily asked.

"I assume so. I certainly don't think it was a flesh and blood man. He was just standing there, watching all the activity. And then when I looked again, he was gone."

"Standing where?"

Danielle pointed to the far right of the wreckage. "On the very top, over there."

Lily cringed. "That's creepy."

"According to Brian, they found skeletal remains on board."

Lily stared at the ship and the activity of the responders gathering around its hull. "I suppose that's to be expected. But where did the ship come from? It had to have been somewhere."

"I'm not an expert, but it looks like it's been under water. Look at all that crap covering its hull."

"If that's true, Dani, how did it float to the surface and end up here? We haven't even had any storms lately."

"An earthquake perhaps," Danielle suggested.

"I don't know. Wouldn't we have felt something?" Lily asked.

"Who knows where it drifted in from. Maybe that ghost ship has been sailing all over the ocean."

"Maybe it's not even that old. After all, the salt air—not to mention the salt water—can do a lot of damage," Lily suggested. "Who knows, maybe those bones they found on board are from recent victims."

"I don't think so. You forget the spirit I saw. I have to assume he came with the ship."

"What does that have to do with anything?"

"If his clothes are any indication of his era, my guess is he's from the twenties."

"That's rather specific. Why do you say that?"

Danielle looked at Lily. "Because he was wearing a suit exactly like one Walt has."

Lily frowned. "I can't imagine it's exactly like Walt's."

"It darn sure looked like it. That dark blue pin-striped one he likes to wear."

"Can't say I remember that particular suit. It's been a while since I actually saw Walt, aside from in a dream hop. What does Brian say about it?"

"Not much, really. Said they called the Coast Guard and the coroner's office."

"I was watching him talk to you, seemed awful friendly." Lily chuckled.

"Yeah, I have to agree with you. He has been pretty friendly lately."

"So what's up with that?" Lily asked.

Danielle shrugged. "Who knows? Let's take a closer look."

Cautiously, the two approached the ship. Police tape, already circling the wreckage, prevented them from getting too close. As they walked the perimeter of the corded-off area, the yellow tape draped along the sand gently fluttered, held down by strategically placed rocks.

When they reached the front of the ship, Danielle looked up, using one palm to shield her eyes from the sun. Squinting, she pointed toward the ship's bow and said, "I see its name."

Lily looked up to where Danielle pointed. Lily tried to make out the faded letters. "—*va Aphrodite*? What does that mean?"

Danielle shook her head. "No, I think it says *Eva Aphrodite*."

FLASHLIGHT IN HAND, the coroner followed Joe through the lower deck of the wreckage. Behind them was the coroner's assistant. When they reached the first evidence of remains, they paused, kneeling down by what appeared to be a pile of bones.

"There's more over there," Joe explained, pointing his flashlight to the left.

With a gloved hand, the coroner reached out and picked up a skull. Gently turning it in his hand from side to side, the light of the flashlight illuminated the object. The coroner paused a moment, briefly tucking the end of the flashlight under his chin to free up a hand. While one hand held the skull, the other brushed over the side of it, examining a foreign object protruding from the skull's base.

After silently examining it for a moment, the coroner announced, "Whoever he was, he didn't drown."

"What are you saying?" Joe asked.

"This is a bullet."

Joe leaned closer. "Murder?"

"It looks like it." He handed the skull to his assistant. "Let's have a look at the others."

Together the three made their way

through the lower deck, examining the skeletal remains of those who had been either passengers or crew of the ship. When they were finished, they counted seven skulls. Yet it was possible there were more in other parts of the hull; they couldn't do a more thorough search without bringing in additional lighting.

With his flashlight back in his hand, the coroner stood up and looked at Joe. "I don't know what the hell happened here, but every one of them was murdered. Whoever did it shot each one in the head."

"Where's the rest of them? I don't think we found enough human bones to make an entire skeleton, much less account for seven people."

"I assume they've decomposed, especially considering the condition of the skulls. But I'm going to need some help on this one."

FOUR

The crowd surrounding the mysterious wreckage had grown considerably since Danielle and Lily had first shown up on the scene an hour earlier. Ian arrived before Lily got around to calling him. A reporter from the *Frederickport Press* was busy taking photographs and asking questions. Danielle guessed most of her neighbors were now on the beach, along with numerous townspeople.

Lily and Ian were busy talking to one of the local business owners when Danielle interrupted them. "I'm going back to the house."

In response, Lily excused herself from the conversation for a moment and pulled

Danielle to the side, out of earshot of the others. She asked in a whisper, "Did you see him again?"

Danielle glanced over to the wreckage. "I assume you mean the ghost. No."

"I guess even if you did, it would be impossible to talk to him."

"Yeah, pretty much. I want to tell Walt about all this, see what he thinks."

"Okay. I'm going to stay here with Ian."

WHEN DANIELLE RETURNED to Marlow House, she raced through the front doorway, down the entry hall, and up the stairs, heading to the attic. She found Walt standing at the window, looking out through the spotting scope, while Max slept peacefully on the arm of the nearby sofa bed.

Walt turned to face Danielle, who was now breathless from her run up the stairs. "What's going on out there? I've been watching for the last hour. Never seen so many cars on this street. I tried to convince Max to go check out the commotion, but his desire to nap won over helping me. I'm starting to think cats are useless."

From the sofa, Max lifted his head and looked at Walt. Yawning, he closed his eyes again and rested the right side of his face back on his front paws.

"A ship washed up on the shore, a few houses down from Chris's place."

"Ship?"

"Or really big boat. At least what's left of it."

"And its passengers, crew?"

"Looks like they've been dead for years." Danielle walked over to the sofa bed and sat down, sitting next to Max. She reached over and stroked his neck.

"What do you mean dead for years?"

"By the looks of the wreckage, it's been out there for decades. No one knows where it came from. By all the barnacles on the hull, I almost think it had to have been under water. Oh, and it came with a ghost."

Walt walked to Danielle. "You saw a ghost?"

"Yep. Sitting on top of the thing, watching all the commotion."

"And you're sure it was a ghost?"

"No one else seemed to see him. And then he just vanished."

Walt sat down on the sofa arm, on the opposite end from where Max perched. "Perhaps it's just your overactive imagination?"

Danielle arched her brows at him. "Am I imagining you?"

Walt smiled and then said, "Tell me about this ghost ship."

Danielle chuckled. "That's just what I called it. Maybe we're hanging out too much together."

"Perhaps." Walt smiled softly. "So tell me about this mysterious ghost ship."

"From what I overheard from the Coast Guard—"

"The Coast Guard was there?"

Danielle nodded. "Brian said something about them towing it out and sinking it if they deem it a hazard. Although, it looks too big to tow. I heard one of the Coast Guard guys say it was a yacht. Or at least, once was."

"Sailing yacht?" Walt asked.

"Hard to tell; it was only the hull, with a lower and upper deck, and parts of the top of the boat were missing. I didn't hear what they said about any of that."

"How big was this yacht?" Walt asked.

"My guess, a couple hundred feet long. Oh, and according to Brian, they found the skeletal remains of the crew—or passengers—inside the hull. Which probably explains the ghost I saw. Makes me wonder if there'll be more than just him."

"And they've no idea where it came from?"

Danielle shook her head. "Not yet. At least, I didn't hear anything to the contrary. But I imagine they'll be able to easily figure out where it came from."

"It does seem as if you can find out anything with your computers."

"There's probably some expert somewhere who knows who built the ship or when a ship like that went missing. Plus, its name is visible on the hull. That should be an excellent clue."

"What's the name of this mystery ship?"

"*Eva Aphrodite*."

Walt stared at Danielle for a moment before asking, "What did you say?"

"*Eva Aphrodite*. From what I recall from my Greek mythology class, Aphrodite represented love and beauty and was considered the goddess of the sea."

Walt stood up. "Yes, she was." He walked back to the window and looked outside. While still looking out, he said, "Tell me more about this ghost you saw."

"Hard to tell his age—had he been alive. Not a kid or teenager—and not an old man. What I found most interesting, he was wearing a suit exactly like your dark blue pinstripe."

Walt turned to Danielle with a frown. "My dark blue pinstripe?"

"Yes. Did you have a suit like that when you were alive?"

Walt nodded. "Yes. Yes, I did." He turned back to the window and looked out.

"Which is why I suspect this new spirit came from your era. Unless he died while attending a twenties theme party."

"Twenties theme party?" Walt asked.

"Sure. Like a fifties party where women wear poodle skirts and ponytails, and guys wear leather jackets and pompadours, or a sixties party with tied-dyed shirts and love beads."

Turning back to Danielle, Walt looked sincerely confused. "I have no idea what you're talking about."

"I've seen you watch *Happy Days* on television."

Walt frowned. He still did not comprehend.

Danielle sighed and explained, "A theme party. Maybe the ghost went to a 1920s theme party where the women dressed up as flappers and men wore...well, dark blue pin-striped suits."

"You think that's what happened?"

"No. I'm just saying if he isn't from your era, that might explain his choice of clothing. Or maybe he just likes to dress retro."

"Retro?"

Danielle sighed again. "Never mind."

Once again looking out the window, his hands resting on the windowsill, Walt said in a quiet voice, "Perhaps it would be best if the Coast Guard simply towed it back out to sea and let it sink."

"Why do you say that? Aren't you curious about its history?"

"Dredging up old history often does nothing more than stir up unpleasant memories, and for what purpose?"

"I can't imagine there's anyone still around who'd be hurt by learning more about the ship. In fact, it's entirely possible there are people out there still wondering what happened to a grandparent or parent. I just find the entire thing fascinating. I thought you would too."

Walt shrugged indifferently. "Ships have been sinking since man took to the sea."

"Well, you're no fun." Danielle stood up. "I think I'll walk back down there and see if they've figured anything out."

Walt continued to stare out the window, withholding comment and not bidding Danielle farewell as she made her way from the attic. A few minutes later, he watched as she walked down the street, back to the wreckage.

"Well, Max," Walt said with a heavy sigh when Danielle was no longer in view. "It looks as if the *Eva Aphrodite* has come home at last."

Lifting his chin from his paws, Max looked at Walt, silently blinking his golden eyes.

"I can't really explain," Walt told Max. "Maybe later. But now…now I need to think about it."

Turning from the window, Walt walked toward the doorway, vanishing before he reached it. A moment later, he was downstairs in the parlor, peering out the window. A thorny rosebush just outside the glass pane was severely overgrown and in need of pruning, obstructing some of his view. He was about to move to another window when a familiar face appeared on the other side of the glass, looking in at him. Walt took several abrupt steps back, and the man moved from outside the glass to inside the parlor, standing just a few feet from Walt. The two men stared into each other's eyes.

"Jack?" Walt said in surprise. "I certainly wasn't expecting to see you."

"Walt, is that all you can say? How long has it been?" Jack asked.

Walt's gaze swept over the apparition,

noting the dark blue pin-striped suit. "Ninety-two years."

Jack walked past Walt and looked around the parlor. "It's almost like I remember." He paused at the desk and looked at the unfamiliar object sitting there. "What's that?"

"A laptop computer," Walt explained.

Jack frowned and then moved on, continuing with his inspection of the room. He stopped at the flat-screen television on the wall and pointed to it. "What's that?"

Walt smiled and said, "A television." The next moment it turned on, its sound blaring as bloodied zombies marched across the screen. Jack jumped back from the television and Walt chuckled; the set turned off.

Confused, Jack looked at Walt.

"A lot has changed in the last ninety-two years," Walt explained. "Are you here because of the *Eva Aphrodite*?"

Jack took a seat on one of the chairs facing the sofa. He looked up at Walt. "So you know about that."

"I know it washed up on shore this morning. Or maybe last night."

"I wouldn't say it washed up exactly." Jack chuckled.

"What do you have to do with it being here?"

Jack raised his brows. "You don't know?"

Walt took a seat on the sofa. "How would I know?" With a wave of his hand, a lit cigar appeared. He took a puff.

Jack stared at the cigar, momentarily mesmerized. "How did you do that?"

"How do you think?" Walt took another puff.

"You aren't alive, are you?" Jack asked.

Walt laughed. "What did you think, that I'm well preserved for being over a hundred?"

Jack shook his head. "It's all bushwa. I feel like I don't know from nothing anymore."

"Why did you come here? Why now?"

Jack stood up. "It's hard to explain." He glanced around the room. "Everything looked so different when I got here. I wasn't expecting that. But I recognized Hemming's house. Went there first. Was a big dog there. I swear, I could tell what it was thinking."

"Sadie," Walt said.

"Sadie?"

"The dog. Her name is Sadie."

"Are you saying George is still there? He has a dog named Sadie?"

Walt shook his head. "No. George Hemming has moved on. At least I assume he has. Someone else lives in George's old house now. Hell, lots of people have lived there since George moved on."

"Where did George move on to? Is that where the rest of them went?"

"Rest of who?" Walt asked.

"Everyone from the *Eva Aphrodite*."

"I assume so. It's been a long time, almost a hundred years. They all should have moved on by now."

"But you're still here, why?"

"That's really none of your concern. Jack, it's been a long time. I wish I could say I was glad to see you. But I'm not."

"I can't believe you're saying that, Walt. We were friends. Best friends. I wasn't sure if I'd find you here when I looked in the window. But there you were. I thought for a moment maybe that's why I was able to get here."

"Jack, you burned that bridge a long time ago. I'm over it now. Move on."

"Over it? You don't care I died?"

Walt laughed. "Jack, we've both been dead for years. I assume practically everyone I once knew is probably dead. Why should that bother me now?"

"Considering everything, didn't you at least feel bad at the time?" Jack asked.

"Bad? You mean because you betrayed me?" Walt roared.

"What are you talking about? I never betrayed you!"

"Tell that to Sweeny!" Walt yelled back.

The next moment the front door opened and they could hear voices and a dog bark. Sadie raced into the parlor, her tail wagging. Jack disappeared.

FIVE

Whoever was playing the xylophone, Danielle wanted them to stop. They kept repeating the same tune over and over and over again.

Finally opening her eyes, she blinked twice and yawned. She heard it again. Sitting up in her bed, Danielle sleepily reached for her phone, picking it up from the nightstand. Before answering, she looked to see who was calling. It was Adam Nichols. Reluctantly, she answered, letting her head drop back down to the pillow.

"Do you have any idea what time it is?" She stared up at the ceiling.

"It's after eight. Don't tell me you're still asleep."

"Well, not now."

Adam laughed. "Sorry. But it's my grandmother. She insisted I call you."

Still holding the cellphone to one ear, Danielle sat back up in the bed and rubbed sleep from her eyes. "Is she okay?"

"Yeah. But she insisted I call you this morning before she goes to the police."

Turning in the bed, Danielle sat up completely and put her feet on the floor. "What do you mean, before she goes to the police?"

"It's about that ship that washed up yesterday. I assume you know about it, since it was on your street. Grandma read about it in the paper."

"Adam, I need more information. I still don't understand why your grandmother needs to talk to me, or the police for that matter. Why didn't she just call me?"

"She misplaced your phone number. Again."

"So what about the ship?"

"She thinks she knows where it came

from, and she wants you to know about it before she goes to the police."

Danielle got out of the bed. "Why's that?"

"Because, according to Grandma, the *Eva Aphrodite* belonged to Walt Marlow."

Danielle paused a moment and glanced up to the ceiling. "*Eva Aphrodite?*" she mumbled.

"Yeah, according to the article in the paper, they have no idea where the boat came from. Called it a wreckage of a yacht, but one clue is its name. The *Eva Aphrodite.*"

"*Eva Aphrodite,*" Danielle repeated in a low whisper.

"According to Grandma, that was the name of Walt Marlow's yacht. Apparently, he named it after Eva Thorndike. I imagine you recall that name. By the way, you still have the Missing Thorndike, don't you?"

Instead of responding to Adam's question, Danielle stood silently by the side of the bed. Again, she glanced up at the ceiling, expecting Walt to pop in at any moment.

"Danielle, are you still there?"

"Umm…yeah, Adam. I was just thinking."

"Hey, I was just teasing about the Missing Thorndike. I know you still have it…you do still have it, don't you?"

"Umm…yeah. I haven't found a buyer for it yet. It's still at the bank," she muttered, her gaze still on the ceiling. "When does your grandmother want to see me?"

"She's hoping you'll come over this morning."

"Okay. Let me get dressed and then—"

"Hey, don't get dressed on my account. Want me to pick you up?" Adam snickered.

"Cute, Adam," Danielle said dryly. "Tell her I'll be there within an hour. Is that okay?"

"I'll see you then."

"You're going to be there?" she asked.

"Stop making me feel unwanted," Adam teased.

BEFORE GETTING DRESSED, Danielle slipped on her robe and went out into the hall to see if Lily was up. She found her in the bathroom, putting on her makeup.

"Morning, Dani!" Lily greeted her when

Danielle looked into the open bathroom doorway. "You slept in this morning." Lily leaned closer to the mirror as she penciled liner over her eyebrows.

"I'm going to Marie's house this morning. I was hoping you'd go with me."

Lily turned from the mirror and faced Danielle. "Marie's? What for?"

"I'll explain in the car." Danielle gestured to the attic.

"Hmm…" Lily glanced up at the ceiling. "Okay, sounds interesting. Umm…where is Walt, by the way?"

"The attic maybe. I haven't seen him this morning."

"AND WALT NEVER SAID ANYTHING?" Lily asked as she snapped on her seat belt. She sat in the passenger seat of the red Ford Flex as Danielle backed the vehicle down the driveway.

"Yesterday, when I told him about the wreckage, I mentioned its name. He said nothing."

"Maybe he didn't make the connection? It has been almost a hundred years," Lily suggested.

"Oh, come on. Like Walt isn't going to remember the name of his yacht, one he named for the love of his life?"

Lily stared at Marlow House as Danielle pulled out onto the street. "I just can't figure out why he'd lie about something like this."

"He was interested when I first told him what had washed up on the beach. In fact, when I got to the attic, he was watching all the commotion through his spotting scope and was trying to get Max to go see what was going on. But the moment I mention the name of the boat, he loses all interest—or so it seemed. Even said something about it not being necessary to dredge up old memories."

"Well, there you have it. Something about *Eva Aphrodite* is too painful for him to think about. And didn't you tell me they found human remains on board?"

"According to Brian, they were skeletal remains, which leads one to believe they've been on the boat since—since it obviously went missing."

"Those were probably people Walt knew."

"Then, Lily, wouldn't that make Walt more curious about the wreckage?"

"ADAM BROUGHT THE CINNAMON ROLLS. Wasn't that sweet of him?" Marie explained as she set a plate of pastries on the center of the kitchen table and passed napkins to Lily and Danielle.

Danielle gazed longingly at the frosted rolls. "Not from Old Salts Bakery?"

"Where else?" Adam said with a grin as he snatched one from the plate and took a bite. He sat at the kitchen table with Lily, Danielle, and his grandmother.

Succumbing to temptation, Danielle took a roll. "My scale hates you," she grumbled.

Adam laughed and took another bite. "I think you can afford a few extra calories."

Chewing slowly, Danielle closed her eyes for a moment, savoring the treat. "They really do bake the best cinnamon rolls."

"Yes, they do," Marie agreed.

"So what is this about that boat belonging to Walt Marlow?" Lily asked.

Marie took a sip of her coffee before answering. "He had it built before he sold his grandfather's shipping company and they moved everything out of Frederickport. He named it for Eva Thorndike. Of course, she had already died by then."

"Doesn't the Frederickport police department already know this?" Danielle asked. "Adam said you wanted to talk to me about it before you went to the police department."

"Why would they? The *Eva Aphrodite* sank almost a hundred years ago; or at least, everyone assumed it sank, considering the storm."

"It went down in a storm?" Lily asked.

"Oh yes." Marie nodded. "According to my father, it was one of the worst storms he could remember. Came out of nowhere. They never found any wreckage of the ship. At least, not until yesterday. Everyone always assumed it went down in the storm."

"I suppose that explains the human remains they found on board," Danielle said.

Marie picked up a roll and tore it in half. "Yes, I read that in the paper."

"Why wasn't Walt Marlow on board?" Lily asked. "If it was his yacht."

Marie chuckled. "It was all part of Marlow's moonshine enterprise."

"Moonshine?" Lily asked curiously.

"I remember you mentioning that once," Danielle said. "When we first met, you said something about Walt running moonshine."

Marie leaned across the table and patted Danielle's hand. "That's so sweet how you call him Walt. As if you really knew him."

Adam eyed Danielle critically as he chewed another bite of his roll. "Yeah, you do act like you knew him," he mumbled under his breath.

Danielle shrugged. "It's just that I live in his house—where he lived—where he died."

"I want to hear more about this moonshining," Lily said.

"This was during prohibition," Marie explained. "Actually, Oregon went dry before the Eighteenth Amendment became law."

"I didn't realize that," Danielle said.

"You can thank women for the passage of

prohibition," Adam grumbled. "That's what happens when you let women vote."

Marie playfully batted her grandson's arm. "Oh hush, Adam."

"It's true, you told me yourself. If women hadn't won the right to vote, prohibition would never have been passed," Adam reminded her.

"Technically speaking, the Eighteenth Amendment bringing prohibition was passed before women got the right to vote," Lily said with a cheeky grin. "You know, eighteen comes before nineteen."

"You're only talking about nationally. Women could already vote in Oregon, and if it wasn't for them, prohibition probably wouldn't have been passed," Adam reminded her.

Lily tore a roll in half. "Pesky details."

"I remember when I first heard that," Danielle began. "I thought, gee, makes women look bad, pushing through something like prohibition that just created more problems and ended up getting repealed. But then I looked at the big picture."

"What's that?" Adam asked.

"Back then, a married woman really had no rights—no protection from her husband. It was probably much worse for a poor woman saddled with a drunk. He could freely spend all their money tying one on, then come home and beat the crap out of her. Divorce wasn't an easy option. I imagine suddenly having the power to close the saloons—by simply casting a ballot—was empowering for those women," Danielle explained.

"So true," Marie agreed. "Young women these days have no idea how lucky they now have it."

"And it wasn't just women voters," Lily spoke up. "From what I learned when Ian was researching the Emma Jackson story, the KKK was a big supporter of prohibition."

"Why was that?" Adam asked.

"It was because of the Catholics, Irish, and Italians," Marie told Adam. "The KKK didn't just target blacks, they went after other minorities."

"True," Danielle agreed. "It was a way to target certain groups."

"I want to know what any of this has to do with the *Eva Aphrodite*," Lily said.

"It's quite simple, really," Marie explained. "The *Eva Aphrodite* was often used to transport Walt's friends—and customers—out to the booze ships."

"What's a booze ship?" Danielle asked.

"My father would call them party ships; mother called them booze ships. They would come down from Canada and park in international waters."

"Ahh…and people could drink on them," Danielle said. "I think I've heard about that."

Adam chuckled. "Floating nightclubs."

"Exactly." Marie nodded. "According to my father, Walt Marlow would occasionally host private parties aboard his yacht, where he would supply the liquor. But mostly he would use the *Eva Aphrodite* to ferry his clients out to the larger ships that would come down from Canada."

"When it sank, was that what it was doing, taking passengers out to international waters to meet up with a booze ship?" Danielle asked.

"According to my father, yes."

"Wouldn't the local museum have information on this?" Lily asked.

"Hardly." Marie snorted. "They have a lot on the Marlow Shipping line, but not much about the grandson. And if you ask me, Walt Marlow was a more colorful character."

"He didn't have such a terrific end," Adam reminded her as he wiped his sticky hands off on a napkin.

"So what all did your father tell you about Walt's yacht going down?" Danielle asked.

"I just remember my father saying it was a bad time for Walt. The passengers were friends of his, quite prominent members of the community. And then his best friend and business partner stole all that money and just took off."

"What best friend and business partner?" Danielle asked.

"Oh, I didn't tell you about that?" Marie asked.

SIX

A previous customer had abandoned the morning newspaper on the empty chair next to Kurt Jefferson. He didn't notice it until after the waitress had taken his lunch order. Alone at the diner's table, he picked up the newspaper and skimmed through it while waiting for his food. The photograph accompanying the front-page article caught his eye. Something about it looked familiar. Curious, he read the paper.

Finishing the article, he gripped the edges of the newspaper, crushing it. Taking a deep breath, he reread the article. *This is impossible*, he told himself. After reading the article two more times, he set the newspaper on the tabletop, picked up his cellphone, and made a call.

"Hey," came the female voice on the other end of the line.

"Do you know anything about that wreckage that washed up in Frederickport?" he asked.

"Yes, I was just getting ready to call you," she told him.

"This is bizarre. According to the article, the boat's name is *Eva Aphrodite*. And I swear, looking at this picture, it could almost be the same one."

"I think it is," she told him.

"That's impossible. That boat wasn't going anywhere."

"I saw it, Kurt. I was down at the beach yesterday morning. Hell, I think half of Frederickport was down there. I'm sure it's the same one."

"How would you know? You never saw it."

"It's just a gut feeling I have. And didn't you just say it looked like it could be the same one?" she asked.

"I just think it's a bizarre coincidence," he told her. "Because of the name."

"I was going to call you because I wanted you to look at the photograph, see what you thought. I couldn't really go by the wreckage since I never actually saw it."

"Even if it has the same name, how could you even jump to that conclusion it's the same boat—especially if, as you say, you never saw the other one?"

"Like I said, a gut feeling."

With a snort he said, "I know all about your gut feelings."

"Hey, you called me about it," she reminded him.

"I admit it looks like it could be the same boat, and the name…well, that's just freaking bizarre. But I don't see how it's even possible."

"Stranger things have happened, Kurt."

"You certainly don't seem upset. I figured you'd be upset, especially if you think it could be the same boat—which I'm not convinced it is. I think it's just some freaking coincidence."

"Why should I be upset?"

"Considering all the trouble we went to."

"If you read the article, I guess you know they found the bodies. Or what was left of them."

"I have to admit—that does make it look like it could be the same boat."

"I think it is," she said calmly.

"Let's assume you're right. How did it get to Frederickport?"

"I think it's what we did," she said.

"Now you're just being crazy."

"Doesn't mean I'm not right."

DANIELLE FOUND Walt in the attic when she returned home from Marie's house. She had dropped Lily off at Ian's before pulling into the driveway, just minutes earlier.

"Why didn't you tell me?" she asked.

He turned from the spotting scope and looked at her. "Tell you what?"

"That the boat was yours."

With a sigh, Walt walked to the sofa and sat down. He looked over at Danielle. "Where were you this morning?"

"Marie's house. She called, wanted to talk to me about the wreckage."

With a wave of his hand, Walt summoned a lit cigar. He took a drag and then said, "I tend to forget what a busybody Little Marie grew up to be."

Danielle walked to the sofa and sat next to Walt. With a concerned frown she asked, "Why wouldn't you tell me? What's the big secret?"

Walt shrugged. "It was just a time in my life I'd rather forget."

"Were they your friends?" Danielle asked. "Or customers?"

Walt cocked his brow and studied Danielle. "So she told you about that too."

"That you used your boat to ferry people out to the booze ships? Yeah."

"People needed a little fun after all that had happened." Walt puffed on his cigar.

"What do you mean, what had happened?"

"I always thought it ironic federal prohibition went into effect a year after the war ended—and just months after people stopped dying from influenza. If anyone needed a drink, this country did. Of course, Oregon went dry a few years before the rest of the country. I think I was around sixteen at the time."

"That's right, World War One…*the war to end all wars*," Danielle quipped.

Walt let out a sardonic chuckle. "According to your *History* channel I've been watching, that obviously didn't work out."

"Were you in the war?" Danielle silently waited for his answer. She wondered why they had never discussed this before.

"Eva died in April, a couple weeks after the country entered the war," Walt explained. "1917. I was determined to enlist. Looking back, it had nothing to do with being patriotic."

"Your heart was broken, losing Eva," she whispered.

Walt smiled softly. "I suppose I was. Of course, Grandfather wouldn't hear of it. Insisted he needed me to help him with the shipping company, especially with the war going on and new demands placed on the family business."

"Didn't they have the draft?" Danielle

asked. "Did your grandfather fix it so you didn't have to serve?"

"About a month after we entered the war, they passed the Selective Service Act. Of course, that didn't apply to me; I was only eighteen at the time."

"I thought the draft applied to eighteen-year-old males."

Walt shook his head. "Initially it only applied to men twenty-one to thirty-one. There was a third registration the following year, where it would have applied to me. But that was in the fall, and by that time I was already sick with influenza."

"You're not talking about the pandemic I've read about?" Danielle asked.

"It's interesting, watching documentaries about all that now—almost a hundred years later. But yes, the same one. I became ill in September of 1918. Although, most people didn't even realize there was an epidemic here. Reports started coming in the following month. I almost died—I was sick for quite a while."

"Walt, I never knew. I always heard the pandemic was especially hard on healthy males; you were lucky."

"Unfortunately, my grandfather wasn't."

"Are you saying your grandfather died during the pandemic?"

Walt nodded. "The war had ended, I was starting to feel better, my grandfather got sick, and within hours he was gone. I always thought it so strange, considering he was around me during my illness and seemed fine through it."

"What about your grandmother?" Danielle asked.

"She was already gone. And here I was, barely twenty-one, the sole owner of a shipping company—and all alone."

"That must have been terrifying."

Walt shrugged. "I decided to sell the company—which didn't make me especially popular at the time, since they moved the entire company out of Frederickport, and with it, jobs. But I didn't want to run the shipping company. I'd already lost the woman I loved, my last family member, and almost lost my own life. I decided time on this earth was short—and I was determined to enjoy it. Plus, they offered me a considerable sum to sell."

"So you got involved with party boats?"

Walt smiled at Danielle. "Not right away. After I sold the company, I wasn't sure what I wanted to do. Money wasn't an issue. Traveled abroad for about a year, and when I came home, I found the brown they were peddling was barely worth drinking."

Danielle frowned. "Brown?"

"Whisky. Anyway, I was getting bored about that time, so a friend and I worked out a deal with a couple fellows we knew from Canada. I still owned the *Eva Aphrodite*, so we used her to import some first-class moonshine. One thing led to another, and I started hosting parties on the boat."

"Weren't you afraid of getting arrested?" Danielle asked.

"We were okay as long as we were in international waters. But that didn't protect us when transporting the hooch from Frederickport. Got boarded one time, but managed to toss the booze before they got too close. After that, Jack and I decided to stick more to ferrying our customers out to the party boats rather than hosting parties ourselves."

"Jack? Who's Jack?"

"Someone who I thought was my best friend, but turned out to be nothing but a piker."

"Marie mentioned something about a friend of yours taking off with some money around the same time that the *Eva Aphrodite* went down."

Walt stood up and shook his head, a fresh cigar appearing in his hand. "I can't believe her father told her all that."

"Is Jack the one she's talking about?"

Walt nodded and walked to the window. "We had a nice little thing going on." Placing his hands on the windowsill, he gazed outside. "If he needed the money, all he had to do was ask me. It's not like I was doing it for the kale."

"Kale?"

Walt chuckled. "Money. I wasn't doing it for the money."

"Why were you doing it?" she asked in a soft voice.

He shrugged. "For the hell of it, I suppose."

"How much did Jack take off with?"

"It was a couple thousand, from what I

recall. I let Jack handle the money. My first mistake."

"Marie said something about Jack staying with her parents at the time."

Walt turned from the window and faced Danielle. "Yeah. Jack was renting a room from George. He was keeping our money over there, and I told him he needed to move it. I didn't think it was safe to keep it there."

"You didn't trust Marie's dad?"

"Just the opposite. People knew what was going on. It was an open secret. If someone realized Jack was keeping the money at George's, it wouldn't be safe for George and his family. I told Jack to bring it over to Marlow House. He gave me some excuse, promised he'd bring it over. And the next thing I know, he's vanished from George's— along with the money."

"Did you try looking for him?"

"He was seeing this little Sheba from town. She lived with her aunt and uncle in a broken-down motel that used to be on the south side of town. I checked there, but she was gone too. Pretty obvious to me the two had taken off together. But then I got news the *Eva Aphrodite* had never arrived at the party ship. It was no longer important to look for Jack. Figured I really didn't want to find him."

"Marie said there had been a bad storm that night."

"Yes. But there had been storms before, and she was seaworthy and had a good crew. But we sent out rescue boats—never found a trace of her. At least, not until yesterday."

"Do you have any idea who the spirit I saw might have been?"

Walt faced Danielle; his cigar disappeared. He crossed his arms over his chest. "I know exactly who it was. It was Jack."

Danielle frowned. "Jack? Why do you say that?"

"For one reason, he paid me a visit yesterday."

"Jack? Your friend that double-crossed you, he was here? Yesterday?"

"At least his ghost was."

"Okay, maybe you did see Jack, but what makes you think that's the spirit I saw?"

"Jack was wearing a dark blue pin-striped suit."

Danielle stared at Walt for a moment before responding. "If you're right, why was he with the wreckage? Didn't you just say he took off with his girlfriend? Are you saying you now think he might have been on the boat instead?"

Walt shook his head. "No. Jack wasn't on that boat. But considering what can bind spirits to this realm—my dear wife at the local cemetery, Darlene at Pilgrim's Point, that annoying little twerp at Presley House. Perhaps Jack's eternity is in some way tied to the *Eva Aphrodite*—the ship he profited and stole from."

SEVEN

Danielle silently considered all that Walt had told her. Finally, she asked, "Do you know why he's here?"

"I don't care why he's here. I told him to leave." Walt turned back to the window.

"What about the people who died on the boat? You never answered my question. Were they friends of yours?"

Walt sighed wearily. "Some were. But what does that have to do with anything?"

"There must be some reason your boat washed up on shore. Some reason Jack showed up when he did."

"What do you want me to do?"

"I don't know. Maybe listen to Jack the next time you see him. Find out what he has to say."

"I doubt I'll see him again."

Danielle studied Walt for a moment. "If he came back, would you talk to him? See what he has to say?"

Walt shrugged. "I suppose. Perhaps I shouldn't have been so abrupt with him. It was just a shock. He was the last one I expected to see."

"Okay then." Danielle started walking toward the door.

"Where are you going?"

"Where do you think? Back to the beach, of course. If he's still lingering around, my bet is he's down by the boat."

MAX WAS WALKING toward the attic stairs when Danielle reached the second-floor landing. She paused a moment and picked up the cat, giving him an affectionate snuggle.

"Where've you been hiding out?" Danielle rubbed the side of her face against Max's fur.

She could hear his loud purr. After giving the top of his head a quick kiss, she set him on the floor and told him, "Walt's in the attic." With a swish of his tail, the black cat sauntered up the attic stairs, not looking back. Danielle watched him for a moment, noticing the way the white tips of his ears twitched slightly.

Danielle continued on her way downstairs. She stopped at the coatrack in the front hall and grabbed a light jacket, slipping it on. Just as she opened the front door, her cellphone began to ring. She pulled it from her pocket and looked at it. Chris was calling.

Before answering the phone, she glanced up at the ceiling, wondering if Walt was still standing at the attic window, waiting to watch her walk down the street. Answering the phone, she stepped outside, closing the door behind her.

"How's Chicago?" she asked as she started down the walkway toward the street.

"Hectic. I was wondering, find out anything about the mystery boat?" Chris asked. The night before Danielle had talked to Chris on the phone, telling him about the wreckage not far from his house and about the spirit she had seen.

"You could say that." Holding the phone to her ear, she glanced up at the attic. Walt stood by the window, watching her.

Continuing down the street, Danielle turned her back to Walt and proceeded to tell Chris all that she had learned about the *Eva Aphrodite*.

"I wish I was there to help you," Chris said after she finished.

"I wish you were too."

"Do you?"

Danielle could imagine Chris's teasing grin as he asked the question.

"I could always use help with this new spirit."

"You could ask Heather for help," Chris suggested.

"Now you're just being mean. She was down there, by the way."

"Yeah, you mentioned she was there."

"As was everyone from our street. Almost looked like a block party."

Danielle heard another voice on the phone. Someone was calling for Chris.

"I'm sorry, Danielle; I have to cut this short. The meeting is about to start; they need me in there."

"Next time, why don't you just send them a check?" she suggested.

Chris laughed again. "That might be a good idea."

By the time Danielle was off the phone, she was by Chris's house. She noticed there were two police cars parked on the side of the road. When she stepped onto the beach, she saw Joe Morelli, Brian Henderson, and Police Chief MacDonald. She also noticed the crime tape continued to encircle the yacht.

Joe's and MacDonald's backs were to her, but Brian saw her coming.

"Office meeting at the beach?" Danielle called out. Joe and the chief turned toward her.

"Afternoon, Danielle," the chief greeted her.

"Did you talk to Marie yet?" Danielle asked when she reached them.

"Yes. I was just telling Joe and Brian about it," MacDonald explained.

"So I guess this boat is your problem." Brian chuckled.

Danielle frowned. "My problem? How do you figure?"

"You're basically Walt Marlow's heir. So it stands to reason his yacht now belongs to you—along with the cost of hauling it off."

Danielle looked at the chief. "Is that true?"

MacDonald shrugged and flashed her a grin. "I've no idea. But it makes for interesting speculation."

"And then there's the matter of the human remains," Brian went on.

"Now wait a minute!" Danielle started to laugh. "I knew you'd find some way to drag me into this!"

"Considering your history, can you really blame me?" Brian teased.

"I don't know why any of you find this funny," Joe snapped.

"Oh, lighten up, Joe," Brian told him. "You have to admit it's rather amusing."

"I don't think those poor people found it terribly amusing being executed," Joe snapped.

"How long ago, almost a hundred years?" Brian countered. "Even if they all died of old age, they'd be dead by now."

"What are you talking about?" Danielle interrupted. "Who was executed?"

The three officers exchanged knowing glances.

The chief sighed and said, "We'd rather this not get out right now."

"What are you talking about?" Danielle asked.

"The people we found, who died on that boat—"

"What's left of them," Brian interrupted the chief.

"True," the chief continued. "But they didn't drown. They were murdered."

"How could you tell that? If there's only skeletal remains, you can't do an autopsy, can you?" Danielle asked.

"We haven't gone through the entire boat yet, but yesterday we removed what remains we found, which mostly amounted to seven skulls. Each one had a bullet lodged in it," the chief told her.

Danielle frowned. "That's impossible. According to Wa—Marie…the boat went down in a storm. Everyone drowned."

Brian shook his head. "Maybe there was a storm, but the remains we took off that boat —those people were murdered."

"What are you going to do now?" she asked.

"We're making arrangements to have some lighting brought down so we can do a more thorough search. In the meantime, we're going to have another look inside to see what we're going to need," the chief explained.

Danielle looked at the wreckage. "Is it safe?"

"I think so." The chief looked at Brian and Joe. "Why don't you two go ahead and start without me. I'd like to talk to Danielle alone."

"I expected to find half of Frederickport crawling all over the boat when I got down here," Danielle told the chief when they were alone on the beach.

"We had a guard on the boat all night."

"Guard?"

"We didn't want anyone tampering with

the evidence. A few people showed up this morning, but after they realized they couldn't go beyond the tape, most just took a few pictures before moving on."

"Evidence?"

"Technically speaking, it's a crime scene."

"You think I might really be responsible for hauling that thing off?" Danielle asked.

"Don't worry about that now. I'm more concerned about you living in the same house with Walt."

"Walt? What are you talking about?"

"After Marie called, I went down to the museum and had a little talk with Ben Smith and looked through some of the old Frederickport papers they have on file for that era."

"What does this have to do with Walt?"

"Smith seems to think Walt Marlow may have had those people killed."

"What are you talking about?" Danielle asked angrily.

"Obviously, Walt is dead. You might say out of my jurisdiction. But that doesn't mean I can't be worried about you living under the same roof with his spirit."

"Chief, you know Walt; he's a good guy."

"I can't say I know Walt. I've been witness to his levitations—"

Danielle couldn't resist giggling. "You saying you've seen him fly?"

The chief flashed her a rebuking frown. "I meant the way he skillfully levitates objects. I'm concerned for your safety. When Stoddard decided to haunt you, he wanted nothing more than to physically harm you, but thankfully he hadn't been able to—what is it you call it? Harness his energy. But Walt, he's rather adept at harnessing his energy. I remember how he almost killed Renton."

"Yes, to save my life."

"But what happens if something provokes him? Jealousy, perhaps?"

"Jealousy?"

"From how Chris talks, I get the impression he and Walt tend to compete for your attention."

"This is ridiculous," Danielle said impatiently.

"Is it? If Walt Marlow was capable of executing those people—or having them executed—who's to say he might not do something like that again? What happens if he gets jealous of Chris and decides to bring you to his side?"

"Are you suggesting Walt might kill me—so I can join him as a ghost?" Danielle didn't know if she should laugh or get angry at the chief's suggestion.

"I just think you and Lily should consider staying somewhere else until we figure this thing out. For your own protection."

"How is that going to help?"

"You told me yourself Walt can't leave Marlow House. And once you suggested if he ever managed to, he probably wouldn't be able to harness his energy as he can there. So what would it hurt? You can afford it. Stay somewhere else while we investigate the murders."

"I don't believe for a moment Walt killed those people. I know Walt. I trust him. And I know he cares about me…about Lily."

"Then you won't even consider my suggestion?"

"No."

"Don't you think you at least owe it to Lily to give her the option to stay at a safe place while we investigate the murder? She could stay with Ian."

"Why would Walt hurt Lily? I thought you just said I was in danger because he might go into a jealous rage over Chris," she snapped.

The chief wore an expression devoid of humor. "If he was capable of executing those people—he is capable of anything."

Angry, Danielle turned from the chief and looked at the wreckage. Walking on the top deck of the *Eva Aphrodite* was Walt's old friend Jack.

"There's someone who might be able to shed some light on the situation," Danielle said angrily.

The chief looked at the ship. He didn't see anyone. Joe and Brian were already inside the boat, out of sight. "What are you talking about?"

EIGHT

"The *Eva Aphrodite* came with a ghost," Danielle explained.

"You see something?" the chief asked.

Danielle pointed to the top deck. "He's up there. Of course, I don't expect you to see him. But he's wearing a dark blue pin-striped suit, circa 1920. His name is Jack."

"You've already talked to him?"

Danielle shook her head. "No. I noticed him yesterday morning when I first saw the boat. He was up where he is now and then vanished. According to Walt, he was at the house yesterday. They talked briefly, and then he disappeared."

"I wonder if other spirits are here, considering the remains we found on board. Or perhaps they went to the coroner's office," MacDonald suggested.

"According to Walt, Jack wasn't aboard the *Eva Aphrodite* when it went down. He and Walt were partners in a business venture. They used the yacht to ferry people out to the booze ships during prohibition. Jack took off around the time the ship went down—taking all the money from their business venture with them. Walt believes Jack's spirit is drawn to the *Eva Aphrodite*. When the boat landed onshore, it might have lured Jack's spirit out from wherever he was previously haunting."

"Perhaps Jack was the one who did the hits for Walt?"

"Would you stop saying that!" Danielle snapped. "Walt didn't kill those people. And as far as I know, Jack's only crimes were embezzlement and betraying his best friend."

"I'd rather you communicate with the spirits of those poor souls who were murdered on that boat. I imagine they'd be able to tell you what really happened out there and who was responsible."

"I don't believe they're here. I think I would have seen something already. And since I don't do séances, Jack will have to do."

"As long as Joe and Brian are on the boat, you can't very well go up there and introduce yourself."

Looking back up to the upper portion of the wreckage, Danielle narrowed her eyes and studied Jack. He paced the upper deck as if agitated. For a brief moment, she contemplated waving at him, seeing if she could coax him off the boat and onto the beach with her. Then she thought of Brian and Joe and feared they'd exit the boat at an inconvenient time.

"How long do you think Brian and Joe will be in there?" Danielle asked.

"You want to wait until they leave so you can talk to your ghost?"

"His name is Jack. And he's not my ghost. But yeah, I'd like to do that."

"I tell you what. Why don't you go home and let me get to work. When we're done, I'll send Joe and Brian back to the station. I'll give you a call, let you know when they're gone. It will be at least an hour."

"Are you planning to leave anyone down here to keep guarding this thing?"

"Until we're done, yes. But I'll make some excuse and stay down here while you have your conversation."

Danielle glanced briefly back to the upper deck of the wreckage and at the ghost now looking down at her. "Okay. I just hope he's still there when I come back."

When Danielle started to walk away, the chief called out, "Danielle, please be careful."

Pausing a moment, she looked back at the chief and flashed him a frown. "I'll be fine. I don't know what Ben told you, but he was wrong about Walt."

GRIPPING THE FLASHLIGHT, MacDonald moved its beam along the interior of the dismal cabin. The scent of seawater and rotting wood filled his nostrils. Joe explored the adjacent cabin while Brian stood just a few feet from MacDonald.

"None of the theories on this thing make any sense," Brian said.

"What do you mean?" the chief asked.

"According to one of the guys I talked to from the Coast Guard, this thing was probably a ghost ship, floating around for almost a hundred years until it landed back here."

The chief continued to move his light around the small space. "I've heard of ghost ships."

"What about that hole in the stern? Looks like someone took an axe to it. I don't see how water wouldn't have come in that way. And where are the rest of the skeletal remains? I would assume being under water and exposed to sea life would assist in their decomposition, but would that be the case for a ship floating around for almost a hundred years?" Brian asked.

Focusing his light on a brass lamp still attached to the wall, the chief said, "By the looks of those barnacles, I'd have to agree with you. I'm no expert, but it seems as if this ship was once under water and for a long time."

"I suppose it could have landed somewhere and been swamped, virtually under water, and then somehow got unstuck and ended up here. But that still doesn't explain that hole."

Before the chief could respond, they heard Joe shout out from the adjoining cabin, "I found something!"

When Brian and MacDonald joined Joe, they found him kneeling on the floor, shining a light on what appeared to be a metal box. What they didn't see was Jack, who leaned against the side wall, his arms casually crossed, watching the three officers.

"You going to open that thing?" Jack asked. "I've been wondering what was in it." He watched as Brian and MacDonald gathered around Joe while Joe fumbled with the box's latch.

"I sure would like a cigarette." Jack groaned. "I wish I knew how Walt did that. I'm not much for cigars, but I'd even take one of those."

"Is it locked?" Brian asked.

Joe's fingers persistently worked on the latch. "I don't think so." The next moment its lid popped open, and Joe redirected the beam of his flashlight into the box's interior. To his surprise, its contents glittered and sparkled.

Jack leaned toward the now open box. "What do we have here?"

"Damn," Joe muttered as he reached inside and pulled out what appeared to be a diamond necklace. He handed the necklace to MacDonald and then reached into the box and pulled out a pearl necklace, which he then handed to Brian.

Brian began to laugh.

Jack stared at the diamond necklace. "I recognize that."

Joe paused and looked up to Brian. "What's so funny?"

"Danielle Boatman, every time she turns around, she either trips over a dead body or falls into a pot of money."

Jack leaned closer to the open box, his body moving through Joe's. Peering into the metal container, he spied more treasure—precious gemstones and gold.

Joe shook his head, looking seriously at Brian. "I don't get it."

The chief began to chuckle. "I see what you mean. If Danielle is Walt's heir—through her aunt's will—then this boat would belong to her."

Jack jerked his head up and looked at the chief. "Who is Danielle? Why would she own the *Eva Aphrodite?*"

Brian handed the pearl necklace back to Joe and stood up, no longer kneeling by the metal box. "You have to admit it's pretty damn funny."

"There's no reason to believe this treasure belonged to Walt Marlow," Joe said. "It probably belonged to the passengers, and they put it in the box for safekeeping."

"What, right before someone blew their brains out?" Brian asked.

Jack stepped away from the three men.

MacDonald handed the diamond necklace to Joe. "Put it back in the box and let's take this to the station so we can have a better look. Impossible to see anything in here."

Thirty minutes later, the chief sat alone in his squad car, calling Danielle on his cellphone.

"Can I come down now?" Danielle asked when she answered the call.

"I'm sorry; your talk with the ghost will

have to wait. Something came up, and I want to head back to the station with Brian and Joe. I'm waiting for someone to get here to keep an eye on the wreckage."

WITH THE BACK of his hand, MacDonald swept the pile of papers and random pens and paperclips to one side of his desk, making room for the metal box they had brought back from the *Eva Aphrodite*. Joe set the box on the cleared space as MacDonald took a seat behind the desk. For a few moments, the three men—Joe and Brian standing—MacDonald sitting, stared at the metal box.

MacDonald spoke first. "What's the first thing you notice?"

"Looks pretty good for being in that boat for such a long time," Joe said.

"Not a single barnacle," Brian noted.

"Something else. I didn't notice it until Joe set the box down." MacDonald pointed to the cabinet in the corner of his office. "Joe, on the bottom shelf of the cabinet, bring me the metal box."

Joe frowned, but did as the chief instructed. He walked to the cabinet, opened it, and then looked on its bottom shelf. To his surprise, there was a metal box—it appeared to be identical to the one they had found on the boat. He reached down and picked it up, bringing it to the chief. He set it on the desk next to its twin.

"Damn, you have a box just like it!" Brian said in surprise.

"I picked it up a few weeks ago at Walmart." The papers stored inside the chief's box shifted to one side as he turned the box upside down, making a rustling sound. On the bottom of the box the words "Made in China" were stamped into the metal, and next to them was the Walmart price sticker. It hadn't been removed.

After setting the box aside, the chief retrieved a pair of latex gloves from a drawer and slipped them on. Joe and Brian watched as he opened the box Joe had found. Gingerly, the chief removed the items from the container, setting them on the desktop. There were four necklaces, which included the diamond and pearl ones they had seen while still on the boat. There was also a pair of diamond cuff links, a woman's ruby ring, and a man's ring. After placing all the items on the desktop, the chief picked up the man's ring again and had a closer look.

"It's a wedding ring," he said. Tilting it to one side, he studied it for a moment. "Looks like initials and a date engraved inside. But I'll need a magnifying glass." Setting the ring back on the desktop, he turned his attention to the metal box.

After closing the box's lid, MacDonald turned it upside down. His attention riveted on the bottom of the box, he said nothing. Also speechless were Joe and Brian, who each moved to the desk to have a closer look.

"I guess this means Danielle doesn't necessarily have a claim to this particular treasure," Brian muttered.

"What does this mean?" Joe asked. Simultaneously, he and Brian stood straight, no longer hovering over the desk.

MacDonald leaned back and studied the upside-down metal box. "I'd like to know how this got on board that boat."

Brian sat down. "For a brief moment I started to wonder if maybe the remains we found weren't the original passengers and crew of the *Eva Aphrodite*, but considering the level of decomposition, I'd have to say what was in that box has nothing to do with the human remains we found on board."

"We need to get someone in here to look at this," the chief said. He looked up at Joe. "Maybe that jeweler we brought from Astoria who looked at the Missing Thorndike?"

"You mean the Fake Thorndike," Joe corrected.

"Good bet this is stolen," Brian said.

"Makes me wonder," Joe pondered. "Is it possible the *Eva Aphrodite* was brought to shore by whoever left this box on board? And for whatever reason was forced to leave the box behind?"

"Not sure how, since it doesn't have a working engine," Brian reminded him.

The chief leaned forward, studying the metal container. "We know one thing. Whoever left this on board didn't do it back in Walt Marlow's day." MacDonald reached for the box they had found on the *Eva Aphrodite*, his fingertips lightly touching what remained of the water-faded Walmart price sticker still affixed next to the "Made in China" stamped into the metal.

NINE

Danielle sat in the parking lot of the Frederickport Museum. Ever since MacDonald had suggested that Walt might have been responsible for murdering those people, she wondered what Ben from the museum had told the chief.

When she returned to Marlow House after leaving the beach, Danielle didn't mention anything to Walt about what the police had discovered after examining the skeletal remains removed from the *Eva Aphrodite*. She couldn't believe Walt was responsible for murdering those people—which also meant she didn't believe he knew they had been murdered.

Before sharing with Walt what she had learned at the beach, she wanted to find out what Ben had told MacDonald. It wasn't as if she didn't trust Walt, but he had already withheld information about the *Eva Aphrodite*, and she wondered why.

Getting out of her Ford Flex, Danielle slammed the car door shut and made her way to the front door of the museum. En route there, she remotely locked her car and then dropped her key into the front pocket of her purse. Pushing her way through the front doorway of the museum, she was greeted by a familiar docent, Millie Samson.

"I was hoping to find Ben here," Danielle said after saying hello and following Millie into the museum gift shop.

"Sorry, Ben won't be in today."

"Drat. Do you know if he's at home?" Danielle asked.

Millie shook her head. "I doubt it. He mentioned something yesterday about going to Portland."

Danielle let out a disappointed sigh and leaned against the counter.

"Maybe I could help you with something?"

"I just wanted to ask Ben about that boat that washed up over on our side of town."

"Oh, the *Eva Aphrodite!*" Millie said excitedly.

"Have you seen it yet?" Danielle asked.

"Yes, I stopped by on the way here this morning. So exciting. I can't imagine where it's been all this time."

"So you knew about the boat? I mean, before it washed up on shore?"

"Why certainly!" Millie frowned as if Danielle had asked a silly question.

"I sort of got the impression no one at the museum would remember the *Eva Aphrodite.*"

"Where did you get that notion?" Millie asked. Before Danielle could answer, Millie said with a snide smirk, "Oh, I know, Marie Nichols."

"Excuse me?" Danielle feigned ignorance. The last thing she wanted to do was get in the middle of whatever issue Marie had with the museum and its board of directors.

"Marie is a friend of mine, but she likes to remind everyone how hers is the oldest family in Frederickport. Which isn't true, of course. Ben's family has been here a long time too. Sure, not as long as the Hemmings, but almost."

"I'm not really sure what that has to do with the *Eva Aphrodite*."

"Well, Marie likes to imagine she has the inside scoop on all that went on back then—you know, since her family used to live across the street from Marlow House. But she was a baby when Walt Marlow killed himself and—"

"Walt Marlow was murdered," Danielle corrected.

"Oh, that's right. I know you believe that, but I'm not really convinced."

Danielle frowned. "Are you serious? I thought we all went over that. The old autopsy reports. What Emma Jackson told us. Certainly you aren't telling visitors to the museum Walt Marlow killed himself."

"I think our visitors should be given all the information."

"Given all what information?"

Millie reached over and patted Danielle's hand. "Don't look so vexed, dear. Walt Marlow has been dead for a hundred years—"

"Ninety years," Danielle corrected.

"Okay, ninety years. All I'm saying, I don't think he'll really care what we say at this point."

"Maybe he won't, but I will," Danielle snapped. "And as a member of the historical society, I assumed the museum gave out factual information."

"Certainly we do! I didn't mean to imply we make up stories. I'm just saying we feel it's important to give our visitors all the information."

"Which is?"

"That for the last hundred—I mean ninety years—it was believed Walt Marlow hanged himself in the attic of Marlow House. Yet some people seem to believe that he may have been murdered by his brother-in-law."

"I think it's a little more than some people believe. I'd say it's been proven."

Millie shook her head. "I don't know how you can say that, Danielle. Perhaps you should attend a few of our meetings—after all, you are a member. A few months ago, we had the most interesting debate about Walt Marlow's death, and most of those in attendance disagreed with your assertion."

"They're wrong." Danielle could feel her blood pressure rising.

"It all makes for an interesting debate, and really, dear, you should be more willing to listen to opposing views."

Danielle suddenly regretted coming to the museum. She felt a headache coming on.

"As for the *Eva Aphrodite*, a few of us were discussing that just last month. Ben was digging into our archives when he came across some information about Walt Marlow's yacht and how it supposedly went down in a storm."

"Supposedly? According to Marie's father, there was a terrible storm that night."

"True. But I guess there's more to the story than a bad storm. The passenger list, for example, included one of the wealthiest men in Portland. And his wife—according to rumors, Walt Marlow's mistress."

Danielle stared at Millie, dazed. "Are you suggesting Walt was having an affair with a married woman?"

"Not just any married woman. But I don't have all the details. Ben is the one who's been doing the research."

"What kind of research?" Danielle asked.

"I know he went through the old newspapers—the ones we have from that period, when the *Eva Aphrodite* went down. And then he has the diary that was donated a few months back."

"What diary?"

"It was from an estate sale in Portland," Millie explained. "When they were going through the items to sell, they came across a diary written by a Frederickport resident, from the 1920s. They donated it to the museum, and Ben's been reading it, cross-referencing the information."

"This diary—that's where this information is coming from about Walt Marlow and a married woman?"

Marie nodded. "He managed to verify

much of the information by old newspaper articles. Did you know at the time the *Eva Aphrodite* disappeared, Walt Marlow's business partner took off with a fortune?"

"Fortune?" Danielle remembered what Walt had said about Jack's theft, yet she didn't consider a couple thousand dollars a fortune.

"Yes. The two ran a moonshine operation. In fact, we plan to devote an entire section of the museum to Walt Marlow's dark past."

"Dark past?" Danielle frowned.

"He was a bit like a pirate, don't you think? It will be wonderful for the museum. Such a colorful attraction!"

"Not sure I see Walt Marlow as some sort of pirate. And according to Marie, Walt's partner did take off with some money, but hardly a fortune. From what I understand, it was about a couple thousand dollars. I imagine back then it might have been considered a fortune, but not now."

"Is that what Marie told you?" Millie chuckled. "I guess she doesn't know as much about Marlow history as she thinks."

No, Marie didn't tell me that—Walt Marlow did. "Why do you assume it was a fortune?"

"Because it was all gold coins."

"Gold coins? From what I understand about Walt's illicit venture, he ferried people out to the party boats during prohibition. I can't see what that has to do with some treasure of gold coins."

"Dear, back in Walt Marlow's day, our currency included gold coins. Real gold. Until 1933 when we went off the gold standard and the government recalled all the gold and it was melted down. Admission to Walt Marlow's party boats was paid in gold coin—and the money his partner stole would be worth millions today."

"Millions?"

Marie nodded. "Of course, that money was spent years ago and, I imagine, recalled with the rest of the gold in 1933. So it would only be worth millions if still intact—and it isn't."

"What else do you know about the *Eva Aphrodite*?"

"Probably no more than you do, since you obviously talked to Marie. Although, I doubt Marie knows about Walt Marlow's mistress unless her father told her. Which I suppose is possible. But if you want details, you'll have to talk to Ben. He's the one who's been reading the diary and cross-referencing the events mentioned with old newspaper articles. Of course, you could look at the old newspapers yourself."

"Are there many missing issues from that time period?" Danielle remembered how the newspaper office had burned down years before, destroying all their past issues. The only pre-fire editions in Frederickport were old issues donated to the museum by past subscribers.

"I'm pretty sure we have most of them. Here, let's go see."

Danielle followed Millie to the back of the museum, where the old newspapers were kept chronologically, bound in large binders. Danielle sat at the table while Millie explained what years she needed to research. Before Danielle opened the first book, a new visitor arrived at the museum, calling Millie back to the entrance, and leaving Danielle alone to skim through the old newspapers.

Midway through the first binder, she found a front-page article on the missing *Eva*

Aphrodite. The article included photographs of the missing passengers, along with a group shot of the crew. Danielle couldn't help but wonder which one of these women was supposedly Walt's mistress. The notion that he would have an affair with a married woman troubled her. She couldn't help but think of how hurt she had been when she discovered her own husband had been unfaithful. Danielle told herself not to be judgmental.

She flipped through the pages of the newspapers. As she got to the end of that year, she found it curious that even three months after the boat went missing, the newspaper ran articles speculating on the possibility those on board were still alive— somewhere. After all, the boat was never found. Yet it was found now, and according to Chief MacDonald, those on board had died long ago, each shot in the head.

She turned back several pages, coming to another article on the missing boat, along with a large photograph of three of the women who, according to the story, had been on the *Eva Aphrodite* when it went missing. Danielle had seen their pictures in several of the other articles, yet this was the first one where all three women were in the same photograph—smiling happily into the camera's lens, unaware that in just a few weeks, their young lives would meet such tragedy. The photograph was apparently taken at a charity event just a month prior to the fateful voyage.

Danielle stared at the image; each woman was dressed in her best finery. Silently, Danielle ran a fingertip over the picture, wondering what it had been like for the women— had their spirits lingered on the boat after they were killed, or had they quickly moved on?

Taking a deep breath, Danielle stood up and took her iPhone out of her purse. Turning on the desk lamp, she positioned the open book to maximize the lighting. Tapping the camera app on her phone, she looked through the iPhone and snapped a picture, capturing the image of the three women. After checking the results, she turned the page and took another picture—and then another.

Danielle spent the next thirty minutes patiently taking pictures of the various articles and photographs on the missing *Eva Aphrodite*.

She was about to close the book when she noticed another article. This one wasn't on the missing boat, but on Walt's missing friend— Jack Winters. Danielle took a moment to read the article before taking its picture.

TEN

Instead of going straight home, Danielle stopped at the police station. She wanted to initiate a conversation with Jack's ghost but knew that would be impossible with someone from the department standing guard by the wreckage. She hoped the chief was ready to go back to the beach and relieve whatever officer he had assigned to the duty.

She had just entered the hallway leading to the inner offices when she spied Joe and Brian standing a few feet from the closed door of Chief MacDonald's office. They seemed to be deep in conversation.

Joe noticed her first, heading for Mac-Donald's office. "The chief's on the phone."

"Well, nice to see you too, Joe," Danielle quipped. She glanced at his partner and said, "Afternoon, Brian."

"The chief is on the phone," Brian said.

"Yes, I know. He was talking to me." Flashing them a parting grin, she opened the chief's door and entered the office, without another comment.

Joe stared at the now closed door. "He didn't say it was Danielle on the phone."

"No, but he did make it clear he wanted to take the call in private." Brian chuckled.

"Don't go there. You keep trying to imply there's something going on with those two."

Brian shrugged. "And if there is, why do you care? I thought you were with Kelly."

"Doesn't mean Danielle isn't still my friend."

"You two didn't seem very friendly a moment ago. And if you are friends, why would you be opposed to her being with someone like the chief? I'd think you'd see it as an improvement over Glandon. That guy might have money, but I'm still not convinced he didn't have something to do with that woman's disappearance."

"I just thought she should know he was on the phone, that's all. How did I know she was the one he was talking to?"

"SO WHAT CAME UP?" Danielle asked the chief as she sat down in a chair facing the desk. "Why'd you have to come back here right away?"

"We found something interesting on the boat. I'd like to get you down to the beach, see what you can find out from your ghost."

"I said he isn't my ghost."

"Yeah, yeah." The chief waved his hand dismissively. "You know what I mean. But I'd love to see what he knows about this." Mac-Donald pointed to a metal box sitting on the center of his desk. Danielle then noticed there were two metal boxes sitting side by side. Next to them was what appeared to be a handkerchief spread out and draped over something lumpy.

"You found that in the boat?"

"One of them anyway." He pointed to the other box. "This one is mine. I bought it not long ago at Walmart. The other one, we found in the boat this morning. According to the sticker still affixed to the bottom of the box, it's also from Walmart."

"Are you saying someone recently put that on the boat?"

The chief nodded.

"What's in it?"

The chief reached for the handkerchief and lifted it from the desk. "This was."

Danielle's eyes widened. She stood up and took a closer look at the vintage jewelry arranged on the desk. "Is it real?"

"I don't think it's costume jewelry. Joe's giving that jeweler from Astoria a call, to see if he can come appraise this stuff and help us figure out where it may have come from. I have to assume it's stolen. But how it got on that boat, that's the mystery. I didn't notice right away, but there was a little salt water in the bottom of the box. Makes me think it was submerged for a while and a little water leaked in. The lid fits tightly, but I wouldn't call it watertight."

Danielle pulled her iPhone out of her purse. "Do you mind if I take pictures of it?"

"Go ahead, but I'd prefer you keep this between us for right now."

Danielle gave him a nod and then proceeded to photograph the jewelry. When she was done, she kept her attention on the phone's screen while she sat back down. She opened her picture app to see how the photographs had turned out.

Danielle stood abruptly, her eyes still on her iPhone as she flipped through the photos stored on the device. "I don't believe this!"

MacDonald frowned. "What?"

She looked up at MacDonald, her heart now racing. "Before I came over here, I went to the museum to see if Ben was there."

MacDonald leaned back in his chair and studied Danielle. "You wanted to talk to Ben yourself?"

"Ben wasn't there, so I looked through the old newspapers."

"And?"

"There was a picture of three women who'd been on the boat when it disappeared. The photograph was taken at some charity event a few weeks before the *Eva Aphrodite* went missing. They were all dressed up."

"I remember seeing that photograph. I looked through the newspapers too."

"And you don't remember anything…interesting?" Danielle practically smirked.

He leaned forward, studying Danielle's curious expression. "Interesting how?"

"Here, you look again." Adeptly, Danielle's fingers located the photograph of the three women. She enlarged it and handed the phone to the chief.

Holding the cellphone by its edge so as not to accidentally touch the screen and close the window, he studied the picture. For a moment, he stared at it, wondering what Danielle could possibly be seeing. Letting out a bored sigh, he continued to study the picture when suddenly he saw what she was talking about.

Abruptly, he stood up, looking from the iPhone in his hand to the necklaces arranged on his desktop. "No, that's impossible."

"If nothing else, a bizarre coincidence."

"How could it be the same jewelry?" he muttered.

"The necklaces those women are wearing in that photograph certainly look exactly like what you found on the boat. Now, if it was just the pearl necklace, well, maybe I'd think it was just two similar-looking pearl necklaces. But those other two—especially the cameo…" Danielle shook her head in disbelief.

The chief looked again from the phone to the jewelry. After a moment, he handed Danielle her phone and then sat back down. "Finding their necklaces on that boat would not be unusual—considering that's the last place those women were seen alive. Yet finding the jewelry stored in a box purchased from Walmart—that makes no sense."

"What, no Walmart in the 1920s?" Danielle teased. "Maybe Jack can shed a little light on all this."

MacDonald glanced at his watch. "I can't leave right now."

Danielle stood up. "Then I guess I'll have to go down to the beach and see if there's some way I can talk to Jack's spirit without looking insane."

"Or you can wait for me."

"What if Jack decides it's time to move on before you can get down there and tell your officer he can leave?"

MacDonald nodded. "Okay. I suppose if another one of my officers thinks you're a little crazy, no harm."

"Ha-ha. Funny."

He leaned back in his chair again and looked up at Danielle, who stood before his desk, prepared to leave. "You know, if it wasn't for that metal box, you might have some more jewelry to sell."

Danielle frowned. "What do you mean?"

"For all intents and purposes, you're Walt Marlow's heir."

"I was my aunt's heir."

"And if Renton hadn't been caught embezzling from her estate, it may never have been established that you were her sole heir except for several specific donations to charity."

"I still don't see where you're going with this or what it has to do with the box."

"Your aunt, through her mother, was Marlow's sole heir. That inheritance was passed to you. Therefore, technically speaking, the *Eva Aphrodite* belongs to you."

"Yes, I know. You mentioned I might be responsible for hauling it off."

The chief chuckled. "One might argue anything left on the boat would belong to you. It's not like the boat was discovered on the bottom of the ocean—so not sure how marine salvage laws would apply. Now, had someone else discovered the jewelry, they might be able to claim it under treasure trove laws, which in Oregon are more generous towards trespassers."

"Trespassers?" Danielle asked.

"Take, for example, the Missing Thorndike. Had someone like Joanne found the necklace when she was cleaning the house, or even Adam or Bill when they pulled that stunt and broke in, they may have had a legitimate claim to the necklace under Oregon law."

Danielle shook her head. "That doesn't seem right."

"If Ian hadn't uncovered that old will showing Walt had been the legal owner of the necklace, and since there doesn't seem to be anyone from the Thorndike family still around, it's entirely possible the courts would have awarded the Missing Thorndike to whoever found it. And that could have included Adam and Bill."

Danielle considered his words for a moment. Finally, she said, "Hmm, interesting. So what about this treasure? Not that I'm staking any claim to it. As it is, I already have a ridiculously expensive necklace sitting in my safety deposit box."

"Considering what we found it stashed in, I don't believe the jewelry falls under treasure trove laws. My guess, we're looking at stolen property."

"How did it get on that boat?" she asked.

"I've been thinking about that. I know by the condition of the boat's interior, one would think it had been under water. But I don't think that means sitting on the bottom of the ocean somewhere. That doesn't make sense. A sunken ship doesn't just float to the top and then find its way home after a hundred years."

"So what happened?"

"Most likely scenario, it was a ghost ship.

We know the people on board were murdered, and it didn't go down in the storm. So it could have been floating around on the ocean all these years. I've heard of that happening before. Maybe along the way it settled in some hidden cove and was discovered by modern-day pirates, who stashed their loot there. Maybe the tide took it back out to sea, and it eventually ended up here."

"I noticed a pretty big hole in its stern."

"Which could have happened when it was beached somewhere, hitting against the rocks. Could also explain the water damage inside, which makes it look like it had been under water for years."

"All good theories, but tell me, Chief, how is it your modern-day pirates got ahold of jewelry belonging to the passengers of the *Eva Aphrodite*?"

The chief considered the question for a moment, and then smiled. "Perhaps these pirates didn't have to look far to find their treasure."

"What are you suggesting?" Danielle asked.

"Perhaps our ghost ship was tucked away

in some hidden cove somewhere and was discovered by someone who explored the ship—and found the jewelry."

"And they just left it there?" Danielle asked.

"Maybe they weren't done exploring the ship and didn't think it was going anywhere. So they stored their found loot in a metal box they brought down to the ship and intended to remove it later."

Danielle considered the chief's suggestion. Before responding, she studied the jewelry laid out on the desk. "There is just one problem with that scenario."

"What's that?"

"Look at that jewelry. It certainly doesn't look as if it's been exposed to the elements for almost a century—and it definitely hasn't been under water."

ELEVEN

Danielle parked her car in the side drive at Marlow House. Turning off the ignition, she glanced up toward the attic. Walt was probably waiting for her, she thought, wondering where she had been all this time.

Just as she got out of the car, she heard Lily call her name.

Danielle looked down the drive, toward the street. She saw Lily walking in her direction; she assumed from Ian's house.

"Where've you been?" Lily asked when she reached the car. Danielle continued to stand by the Ford Flex, her keys in one hand and the strap of her purse draped over one shoulder. She was trying to decide if she should go into the house first and let Walt know what was going on or head straight to the beach.

"Stopped at the beach, over by Chris's house. The chief was at the wreckage with Joe and Brian. Then I went to the museum and stopped at the police station."

"Wow, you've been all over the place. What's up?"

Danielle glanced at the kitchen door and then decided what she wanted to do next. Dropping her keys into the front pocket of her purse, she looked at Lily and asked, "Would you walk down to the beach with me?"

"Sure, what for?"

"I'll explain on the way."

Together Lily and Danielle headed down the driveway to the street. As they walked, Danielle told Lily about her day since the two had returned from Marie Nichol's house.

"So what do you want me to do?" Lily asked.

"I never got around to asking the chief who he has watching the *Eva Aphrodite*. But whoever it is, I was hoping you'd help distract him, keep him busy—strike up a conversation, ask questions, whatever—while I try to get Jack's attention. I'd like to convince him to come back to Marlow House with me. I have some questions for him, and I think Walt needs to talk to him. I keep thinking of me and Lucas."

"You and Lucas?"

"Sure. We had unresolved issues. When Lucas first showed up, I didn't want to talk to him. But Walt and Chris convinced me I needed to see what he had to say. They were right. As for Jack and Walt, there must be some reason Jack showed up at Marlow House yesterday."

"I still can't believe the chief thinks Walt is dangerous."

"Something about what Ben told him made him wonder if Walt was responsible for those murders."

"That's another thing; I can't believe those poor people were all murdered like that." Lily cringed.

"Hey, remember, you can't say anything to

anyone, not even Ian. I promised MacDonald."

Lily chuckled. "Did he say you could tell me?"

"No. But I tell you everything." Danielle flashed Lily a guilty yet not remorseful grin.

"Foolish man," Lily said with a laugh.

Just as they got to Chris's house, a police car passed them and pulled behind the other Frederickport squad car already parked down the street.

"It's Joe," Lily said when she saw him get out of his car.

"What's he doing here?" Danielle groaned. "Why would the chief send him down here? He knew I was going to try to talk to Jack. How does he expect me to do it with Joe here too?"

By the time they reached the squad cars, the officer who had been watching the wreckage climbed into one of the vehicles and drove off.

"Hi, Joe. What are you doing here?" Danielle asked when she and Lily reached him.

"Eddie's wife called. Their kid broke his

leg, and she had to take him to the hospital. I came to tell him."

"Does this mean you'll be standing guard?" Lily asked.

Joe smiled. "Not a bad way to spend the afternoon. But it could be a little warmer. So why are you two back down here?"

"Thought we'd come have another look," Lily told him.

Joe nodded toward Danielle. "Danielle was down here a couple hours ago."

"This is practically my backyard. Plus, I wanted to check on Chris's house," Danielle lied.

Joe shrugged, turned to the beach, and started walking toward the wreckage. Lily and Danielle followed alongside him.

"So how's Chris? You said he was in Chicago?" Joe asked.

"Yeah. He'll be there for a couple of weeks." Danielle fixed her gaze on the upper deck of the *Eva Aphrodite*. She didn't see Jack.

Stopping a few feet from the yellow tape, Joe turned to face Danielle. "I guess the *Eva Aphrodite* is technically yours. Any plans?" he asked with a grin.

Before Danielle had a chance to answer, Jack appeared—not on the upper deck of the *Eva Aphrodite*, but standing between Joe and her.

"What do you mean it's hers?" Jack asked Joe. He then turned abruptly and faced Danielle. His nose was just inches from hers. "Are you Danielle?"

Joe asked Danielle another question, and when she did not respond, Lily looked at her curiously. She noted the way Danielle's eyes had widened and the way she seemed to focus on the empty space between them and Joe.

But it's not empty space, Lily thought. *I bet Jack is standing there.*

Abruptly stepping toward Joe, Lily inadvertently walked through Jack.

"Hey, watch it!" Jack shouted.

Lily grabbed Joe's right hand and said, "Joe, I wanted to ask you something about this..." She then pulled him away from Danielle, leading him to the boat. Danielle could hear Lily chattering away a mile a minute, yet what she was actually saying, Danielle had no idea. Instead, the spirit standing before Danielle had captured her attention.

"I know you can't see or hear me, but I'm getting tired of this. All these people coming and going. They just walk right through me. What am I supposed to do? Why am I here? Why doesn't Walt want to see me?"

Danielle pulled her cellphone from her back pocket and put it to her ear, pretending to take a call. Her eyes darted to Lily and Joe and back to the apparition. "Jack, if you come with me, we can discuss it," Danielle said in a low voice.

"Did you just call me Jack? Can you see me?"

"Yes, I can see and hear you. But they can't."

"Are you dead too?" he asked.

Danielle smiled. "No. I'm alive. But I can see people like you."

"Dead people?"

Danielle smiled again.

"I'm a ghost, aren't I?"

"Walt prefers spirit," Danielle said.

"You know Walt?"

"Yes, I live at Marlow House."

"What are you to Walt?" Jack looked Danielle up and down with curiosity. "You aren't really his type."

Danielle arched her brows. "His type?"

"It's those bloomers. You some sort of farmer? Never knew Walt to go for the country girl. At least not one wearing men's clothing. Pretty face though. I bet you'd be a hotsy totsy all dolled up. Anyone ever tell you that?"

Danielle smiled. She remembered Walt once saying something like that to her when they had first met. She recalled Walt used to call her jeans farmer pants. "Will you come back to Marlow House with me?"

Jack considered her question a moment and then shook his head. "I don't think so."

"Don't you want some answers?"

He narrowed his eyes and studied her. "What do you mean, answers?"

"I'm pretty good at helping people like you. If you come back to Marlow House, where we can talk alone, I can help you."

"I don't need any help. And I don't want to see Walt. He doesn't want to see me. He made that perfectly clear earlier."

"You have to understand, he was surprised to see you. It has been a long time."

"No reason for him to accuse me of betraying him. After all I've been through! That certainly isn't the welcome I expected."

Danielle glanced over her shoulder. She could see Joe was inching back in her direction in spite of Lily's enthusiastic attempt to keep him away from her.

"Jack, the police removed a metal box from the *Eva Aphrodite* this morning. Did you see them take it?"

"Yeah, I did. Don't know what business they have taking things off the boat." Folding his arms across his chest, he stared past Danielle, looking at the wreckage.

"Did you know what was in it?"

"Not until they opened it."

"You mean the police?"

Jack nodded.

"Do you know how the box got on the boat?"

"Sure. Some guy left it there."

"What guy?" Danielle asked in a whisper.

Jack shrugged. "I don't know. He came around a few times. Never would talk to me."

"When was this?"

"I don't know. Before I came here."

"Are you saying you were on the boat before it arrived back at Frederickport yesterday?"

Uncrossing his arms, Jack propped his balled hands on his hips and looked Danielle up and down. "How do you think I got here?"

"Are you saying you arrived here on the *Eva Aphrodite*?"

"Yes."

"Did Walt lie to me?" Danielle muttered under her breath.

"Lie about what?"

"He said you weren't on the boat when it went out that last time."

Jack sighed and looked momentarily confused. "I don't think I was."

"Are you saying you weren't on the boat?" Danielle asked.

Jack looked out to sea and scratched his head in confusion. "I haven't figured it out. I don't remember getting on the boat. I just remember being there. And…everyone was dead."

Danielle studied Jack a moment. "Were

you dead? When you first remember being there?"

Jack shrugged. "I must have been. I don't think I could live under water."

"Under water?"

"Yes. We were under water."

"Is that the first thing you remember about being on the boat?"

Jack nodded.

"Was anyone else there?"

"Yes, but they were arguing, shouting at each other."

"Was this when you were under the water?" Danielle asked.

"Yes. And then they all left me. All alone. I wasn't even supposed to be there."

"Tell me about that box, the one the police removed today."

"Like I said, some guy put it there. He didn't say why."

"Who was he?"

Jack shrugged. "How am I supposed to know?"

"Well, what did he look like?"

"Hard to tell with that mask on."

"He had a mask on?"

"Certainly. How else could he breathe under water?"

"Are you saying he had a diver's mask on?"

"I suppose that's what it was. And fins on his feet. Had some sort of tank on his back. Never seen a contraption quite like that one before, but it seemed to work for him."

"Where was the boat when he left the box on it?"

Jack let out a sigh and turned back to face Danielle. "Where do you think? On the bottom of the ocean, of course."

Her conversation with Jack was cut short when Joe returned with Lily. Still holding the phone to her ear, she looked from Lily and Joe to Jack. "I have to go now. Lily and I are going back to Marlow House; we're hoping Jack will be there." Danielle smiled and then tucked her phone back into her back pocket.

"Is Jack one of your guests?" Joe asked.

"More of a friend of a friend."

TWELVE

J ack followed Lily and Danielle, who crossed the street and started walking down the sidewalk toward Marlow House. Instead of trailing behind them, he stayed to Danielle's right, on the road.

"Your friend can't see me, but she knows I'm here, doesn't she?" Jack asked.

Briefly glancing over her right shoulder, Danielle saw Joe standing on the sidewalk across the street, watching them return to Marlow House.

"Yes," Danielle said after she looked back down the street.

"Is Jack with us?" Lily asked in a whisper.

"Yes, Lily, he's on my right."

Lily leaned back and looked to her right behind Danielle, at where she imagined Jack was probably walking. "Hello, Jack, nice to meet you."

"I thought you said she can't see me."

"She can't. Lily, Joe is probably wondering what you're looking at," Danielle reminded her.

Lily looked behind her. Joe was still watching. She gave him a friendly wave goodbye and then looked back to Marlow House. "I imagine you're right."

Danielle glanced over to Jack. "I have questions for you, but I might as well wait until we get back to Marlow House. Walt will probably want to hear the answers too—no reason to ask everything twice."

Jack responded with a nod and kept walking. From the corner of her eye, Danielle studied him. She wondered how old he had been when he had died. He looked to be around her age, early thirties. She hadn't noticed before, but he wore a thin mustache. Had his hair been dark like Walt's, it might have looked attractive. However, with his sandy-colored hair it practically disappeared on his face. At first glance, one might think he needed to wash above his upper lip.

It was a nice enough face, but Danielle thought he needed to tone down the men's hair oil. She could only imagine the stain that hair had left on a pillow. However, since he was no longer alive, and his body—along with his head of hair—was only an illusion, it was no longer an issue.

She assumed his death was around the time the *Eva Aphrodite* went down, because he mentioned the spirits of the murdered passengers and crew were still there when he had arrived—they were arguing. However, it was entirely possible his death occurred a few years later, and the spirits had lingered. Perhaps they had made the decision to depart after Jack had shown up. His arrival might have served as the catalyst to help them come to terms with their new reality. She thought of Lucas and how he had lingered for months in a building not far from the site of his death before he continued on his journey.

They were halfway down the street when they noticed a Frederickport police car driving toward them. Danielle assumed it was on its way to the wreckage site. She was surprised when it pulled over beside them, causing Jack to leap out of its way, onto the sidewalk behind Lily and herself.

With its engine still running, the vehicle parked and the passenger-side window rolled down. Danielle peeked into the car. It was Chief MacDonald.

"I was just heading down to the beach to tell Joe he can leave. You can come with me and see if you can find your ghost," he told her.

Danielle leaned into the open window, resting her elbows on the car door. "I don't need to now." She nodded toward Jack. "He's here. He's going back to Marlow House with us. You almost ran over him."

The chief turned off his engine and moved closer toward the open passenger window. "He's with you now?"

"Yes. He's agreed to go back to Marlow House with me and talk to Walt."

"Why did he call me your ghost?" Jack sounded annoyed.

Danielle looked over to Jack. "Don't let

the chief bother you, Jack. He doesn't understand."

"I don't understand what?" MacDonald asked.

Danielle looked back at the chief. "How some things you say might be offensive to someone in the spirit realm."

The chief let out a sigh. "I guess this means you'd rather I not come with you."

"I don't think that would be a terrific idea. But I can tell you what I learned about that metal box you found on the boat."

"What's that?"

"According to Jack, the *Eva Aphrodite* was under water. A diver visited the boat. That's who left the box."

"Does he know who killed the passengers and crew?" the chief asked.

Danielle glanced at Jack, who shook his head no. She looked back to the chief. "No, Chief. I get the impression his spirit showed up on the boat after everyone was killed."

"So he wasn't killed there with the rest of them?"

"I don't think so."

The chief didn't respond immediately. Finally, he said, "You be careful, Danielle. If it wasn't Walt, maybe it was him."

After the chief drove away, Jack asked, "What did he mean? *If it wasn't Walt, maybe it was him?*"

Danielle shook her head. "It's not important." She started back down the street again.

"Does everyone these days know about people like me?" Jack asked.

"What do you mean?"

"When I was alive, if I started having conversations with someone other people couldn't see, I'd be called crazy."

Danielle laughed. "Trust me; I've been called that often enough."

"Called what?" Lily asked.

"Crazy," Danielle told her.

"But your friend seems to accept that I'm here even though she can't see me. And that cop who just drove away, he did too."

"There are three people in my life who accept my ability to communicate with spirits. You've met two of them."

"He didn't meet the chief," Lily reminded her. "You didn't actually introduce them."

"I suppose you have a point," Danielle conceded.

"Who's the third person?" Jack asked.

"A friend of mine, who's out of town at the moment and who, by the way, can also communicate with spirits."

They paused a moment when they reached the sidewalk in front of Marlow House. Danielle looked up to the attic window. She didn't see Walt there, but Max sat in the window, watching them.

"It looks just as I remember," Jack said. "Although, that police car your friend was driving looks nothing like the cars back in my day."

Danielle looked over to Jack, who stared up at the house. He didn't appear to be in a hurry to go inside. "I understand you were over here yesterday."

"Yes. I saw Walt. He told me he doesn't want to see me."

"He's changed his mind," Danielle assured him. "You have to understand, seeing you after all this time came as quite a shock to him."

"I think I'll go back to Ian's house," Lily

announced. "You know how I hate these one-sided conversations. Anyway, you don't want Ian and Sadie coming over here, interrupting the reunion."

"I suppose that would be for the best," Danielle agreed.

When Lily crossed the street and headed for Ian's house, Jack turned around and watched her. "She's rather a doll, even if she does dress like a boy. Is she going to George Hemming's house?"

"Yes. Her boyfriend lives there now."

"And George?"

"Well, George has been gone for years. But his daughter still owns the house."

Jack looked at Danielle. "George had a daughter?"

"Oh, that's right, I don't imagine Marie was born when you lived there."

He shook his head. "No, George didn't have any children when I knew him."

They watched Lily disappear into the house.

"Your friend's boyfriend, he has a dog, doesn't he?"

"Yes, he does. How did you know that?"

"I went to George's house first. After I got here. The dog was in the kitchen. Walt called it Sadie."

Danielle smiled at Jack. "Yes. Sadie and Walt are old friends."

"I could swear I heard the dog ask me a question."

"It works like that for spirits—being able to communicate with living animals."

Jack looked at Danielle and smiled, as if he had just figured out a mystery. "You mean like the dolphins!"

"The dolphins?"

"Yes, they'd come by the boat sometimes, and we'd talk. It scared me at first, but I found it comforting, having someone I could talk with. Although, they didn't speak in words, exactly. It's hard to explain."

Danielle nodded. "I think I understand. Was the boat always under water—I mean when you were on it?"

"Yes. As far as I can remember."

"How did the boat get here?"

Jack smiled again. He looked up the street, toward the beach where the *Eva*

Aphrodite had landed. "I believe I brought it here."

"How did you do that?"

"That diver—the one who left the box—had just gone back to his boat. I watched him. After the boat disappeared, I started wondering, could I have gone with him? Had I missed my chance to leave?"

"Couldn't you just leave without a boat?"

Jack turned to Danielle. By his expression, it was obvious he thought her question absurd. "How would I do that? I was on the bottom of the ocean."

Danielle shrugged. "I don't know. You got there some way."

"Well, I didn't know how to do that," he said, sounding annoyed. "But when the sun came up the next morning, I imagined the *Eva Aphrodite* afloat again—back on top of the water—taking me home."

"You harnessed your energy?"

"What does that mean?"

"Spirits can sometimes harness their energy and move objects. You obviously moved the boat from the bottom of the ocean and brought her here."

Jack let out a sigh. "Perhaps, but when I was on the boat, I could never get anything to move. And since I've arrived back at Frederickport, nothing—I haven't been able to move a speck of sand."

"I imagine you used up your reserve. Getting that boat up off the bottom of the ocean and then bringing it here, it probably required all the energy you amassed in the last ninety years."

IAN STOOD at the living room window, staring across the street at Marlow House. Lily had arrived a few minutes earlier, but had immediately excused herself to use the bathroom.

"You want to go get something to eat?" Lily asked when she entered the living room a few minutes later.

Ian turned from the window and faced her. "Who in the world is Danielle talking to?"

Lily frowned. "What do you mean?"

"She's been standing across the street, talking to herself for the last five minutes."

Lily walked to Ian and looked out the window. "Umm, she's probably on the phone."

Ian shook his head. "No, she isn't. She's not holding her cellphone. And the way she keeps moving her hands around, it's like she's talking to someone."

"Because she is," Lily insisted. "She's talking to someone on the phone. She obviously has earphones on."

Ian looked again and shook his head. "No, she doesn't. I don't see any wires."

Lily grabbed Ian's hand and pulled him away from the window. "Oh, you're just being silly. Of course she's on the phone. She's using one of those wireless earphone thingies."

"When did she get one of those?"

Lily shrugged. "I don't remember. Sheesh, Ian, you think Danielle has finally gone over the edge?"

"You're right. She probably is on the phone. But considering all the crap she's been through this last year, I wouldn't blame her."

Lily stood on her tiptoes and brushed a kiss over Ian's cheek.

He smiled down at her. "Let me go change and we can go grab something to eat."

"Okay, sounds good."

Ian headed for the hallway and then paused. He looked back to Lily. "Do you think we should ask Danielle to go with us?"

"Oh, heck no. That girl is nuts."

Ian just laughed and continued to the hall.

After Lily heard Ian shut his bedroom door, she pulled her cellphone from her pocket and sent Danielle a quick text message: *Go into the house. You look crazy talking to yourself. People can see you!*

THIRTEEN

When Danielle and Jack entered the front door of Marlow House a few minutes later, Walt was standing in the entry hall, waiting for them. Jack froze the moment he saw Walt.

"I see he agreed to come back with you." Walt's expression was no friendlier than it had been the last time Jack had come to Marlow House.

"Walt doesn't seem happy to see me."

Danielle shut the front door. "That's not true; Walt wanted a chance to talk to you again."

"If that was true, why didn't Walt just come down to the beach and get me himself?"

Danielle glanced from Jack to Walt, reluctant to tell Jack that Walt was confined to Marlow House. She knew nothing about this new spirit's character, aside from the fact that he had embezzled from his supposed best friend. Knowledge was power, and handing Jack power over Walt was not something she was willing to do.

"Walt's just a little reclusive, that's all," Danielle said. "He prefers to stay at home."

"Reclusive?" Jack laughed, taking a step toward Walt, who stood quietly, watching him. "That's not the Walt I remember."

"A great deal has changed since you left Frederickport," Walt told him.

"Why don't we take this conversation in the parlor, where we can have a civil discussion," Danielle suggested.

Eyeing each other suspiciously, Walt and Jack reluctantly followed Danielle into the parlor. Once they moved into the room, Walt took a seat on the sofa while Jack sat on a chair facing him. Danielle leaned back along the edge of the desk, her arms crossed over her chest, observing the two spirits.

"Jack tells me he's the one who brought the *Eva Aphrodite* here," Danielle began. "He harnessed his energy."

Walt arched his brows and eyed Jack. "Impressive." With a wave of his hand, a lit cigar appeared. He took a puff.

Jack leaned forward and stared. "How did you do that? I haven't had a cigarette…well, for almost a hundred years."

Danielle wrinkled her nose and shook her head. "I really don't allow anyone to smoke cigarettes in the house. Not even spirits."

Jack pointed to Walt. "What about him?"

Walt laughed. "You forget, it's my house."

"Plus, the brand he smokes isn't quite as offensive as the stench of cigarettes." Danielle wrinkled her nose again.

Jack slumped back in the chair. "Fine, I'll take a cigar. How do I do it?"

Walt leisurely inhaled and then released several smoke rings, watching them rise and disappear. He smiled smugly at Jack. "I would imagine someone capable of lifting the *Eva Aphrodite* from the bottom of the ocean and bringing her here would be quite capable of conjuring up a simple cigar." Walt leaned back, casually crossing his legs.

Jack frowned and waved his right hand, attempting to imitate Walt. Nothing happened. He waved it again, the gold from his ring capturing Danielle's attention.

She stood up straight and approached Jack, looking at his right hand. "Is that a Masonic ring?"

Jack paused and looked at his ring and then glanced up to Danielle. "Yes, why?"

"Were you a Mason?"

"I *am* a Mason," he corrected.

"Really?" Danielle took a seat on the sofa next to Walt. "My mother's father was a Mason. I never knew him, but I have his ring." She looked to Walt. "Were you a Mason?"

He shook his head no.

"Why do you seem so surprised?" Jack asked.

Danielle shrugged. "I don't know. I just never thought of bootleggers as Masons."

Walt let out a sigh and waved his hand. The cigar vanished. He looked across the room at the other spirit. "Why are you here, Jack?"

Jack considered the question for a moment. "I suppose I got tired of being confined to the bottom of the ocean."

"Why did you steal that money?"

Jack frowned. "What are you talking about? What money?"

"Your bootleg money," Danielle interjected.

Walt flashed Danielle a reproving glare. "I don't believe bootleg money is an accurate description of our enterprise. We provided a transportation service."

Danielle rolled her eyes. "Yeah, right."

"You think I stole from you?" Jack snapped.

"Technically speaking, some of the money was yours," Walt corrected. "If you needed money, why didn't you just ask? I never understood why you did it."

Jack stood up. "I didn't just take off! How could you even imagine I'd do something like that?"

"I didn't at first. I hoped I was wrong."

Jack sat back down again and stared at Walt.

"Perhaps we should start at the beginning," Danielle suggested.

"Where would that beginning be?" Jack asked.

"I suppose you could start with where did you go? From what Walt tells me, you were keeping the money over at George's house, and he was worried it wasn't safe, so you agreed to bring it here, but didn't. You disappeared."

Walt stared at his once best friend, waiting for his answer.

Jack pondered the question, a quizzical expression on his face. "I forgot about that. You're right. I remember that conversation now."

"The conversation about moving the money here?" Danielle asked.

"Yes. I haven't thought about that since—well, since before. Walt was concerned about keeping the money at George's house. He wanted me to bring it here."

"Then what happened?" Danielle asked.

Jack shook his head. "I…I don't really remember. Those last weeks—they're a blur."

"Sure they are." Walt rolled his eyes.

"Perhaps start with when you arrived on the *Eva Aphrodite* and then move backwards," Danielle suggested.

Folding his hands together on his lap, Jack looked down and nodded. Closing his eyes, he attempted to recall what had happened those many years ago. "I remember standing in one of the cabins in the lower deck of the *Eva Aphrodite*. I couldn't understand how I had gotten there, but I was. And then I heard Thelma yelling at Howard."

"Thelma…Howard?" Danielle remembered one of the women in the photograph she had shown the chief was named Thelma. "Friends of yours?"

"Not friends, really. Customers. Howard was Thelma's husband. He told her it was all her fault. That none of it would have happened if it hadn't been for her."

"I'm assuming they were dead?" Danielle asked.

Jack opened his eyes and looked at her. "Yes,

but I didn't know that at first. I was confused and couldn't understand why I was in the cabin with them. I felt uncomfortable, awkward; after all, the last thing I wanted to do was get in the middle of a married couple's argument."

Danielle wondered if Thelma was the one Walt reportedly had an affair with.

"They weren't paying any attention to me, and I figured they didn't even realize I was there, so I decided to slip out of the room, leave them to their argument, and try to figure out how I got there. But when I turned to leave, I practically tripped over Thelma."

"You mean Thelma's body?"

Jack nodded. He closed his eyes briefly and then continued. "She was there on the floor, her eyes open, staring up at me. She had been shot in the head; there was blood every-where. And then I saw Howard. He was dead too."

"Did they tell you what had happened?"

Jack shook his head. "No. I was terrified, so confused, and ran from the cabin. I found the rest of them—and everyone was shouting, arguing; everyone was so angry."

"When you say everyone, are you talking

about spirits, like you and Walt, or people who were still alive?"

Jack stood up and shook his head. He walked to the window and looked outside. "They were all dead. It took me a while to figure that out. But it was the water—that's how I knew. They were dead. I was dead. I really didn't know at the time. I kept asking them how I had gotten there, and no one would answer me. They just kept arguing amongst themselves, ignoring me."

"What do you mean the water?" Danielle asked.

"I was in a panic, moving from cabin to cabin. Everywhere I turned someone was yelling, there were bodies—and the boat started to fill with water. The boat was going down, but I couldn't feel anything. I panicked at first, afraid that I was going to drown. But then nothing happened." Jack turned to face Danielle and Walt.

"What do you mean nothing happened?" Walt asked.

"Water filled the cabin and nothing happened to me. I wasn't gasping for air. My body wasn't being moved around the cabin like the bodies I had almost tripped over were."

"I thought you said the boat was already under water when you first remember being there?" Danielle asked.

"I…I must have forgot. It filled with water after I got there. I just remembered." Jack shook his head, a look of confusion on his face.

"If the boat hadn't yet filled with water when you first arrived on the *Eva Aphrodite*, and the bodies you saw hadn't yet—umm—decomposed—it's a safe bet to assume you arrived on the boat shortly after their deaths," Danielle suggested.

"Did something happen when you ran off with our money?" Walt asked. "Did that little Sheba you took off with double-cross you? Was being sent to the *Eva Aphrodite* your penance?"

"I didn't run off with anything!"

"Why don't you back it up a bit?" Danielle suggested. "Try to remember where you were right before you found yourself standing in the cabin with Thelma and Howard."

"I said it was a blur."

"You have to remember something," Danielle urged. "Think back. What was the last thing you remember doing right before you found yourself in the cabin with Thelma and Howard?"

Jack closed his eyes for a moment and took a deep breath. When he opened his eyes again, he looked at Danielle and Walt. "I was going to pick up Sally. That's all I can remember."

"Who's Sally?" she asked.

"His little Sheba," Walt said with a snort.

"You say you were going to pick her up, were you in a car? Walking somewhere? Where were you?"

"I was walking to her place."

"Walt said she lived at a motel in town."

"Yes. Her aunt and uncle have a motel on the south side of town. They live in a house in the back, and Sally moved in with them after she left home. I remember walking up to their house—but that's all I can really remember clearly."

"What about the money? The missing money?" Danielle asked.

"Are you talking about the money Walt claims I stole?" Jack asked angrily.

"Obviously," Walt snapped.

Jack frowned and rubbed his right temple. "I might have moved the money, but I didn't steal it."

Walt stood abruptly. "Maybe you've forgotten what you've done, but I haven't. We argued about the money being kept at George's; then you agreed to bring it over here. The next day when you didn't show up, I went across the street to get the money myself. But you weren't there. George and his wife were out of town that week; they had gone to Portland to visit family. Your car wasn't there, and I was pretty angry by that time, so I used the key George had given me and let myself into the house."

"I told you I was going to bring it over."

"But you didn't, did you? You weren't there, and neither was the money. I looked under the bed where you kept it."

"You kept the money under the bed?" Danielle asked.

"Yes. Brilliant hiding place," Walt scoffed.

"I don't remember any of that, but I swear I didn't steal anything."

"You say you moved the money, do you remember where you moved it to?" Danielle asked.

Jack shook his head. "Like I said, that time is a blur. I didn't even remember that conversation Walt and I had about moving it until you mentioned it."

"Did you move it from under the bed?" Walt asked.

"I'm sure I did. I feel it. I just…can't remember…"

"Sometimes it happens like that. The memory of what occurred during your final hours can be blurred…confused," Danielle explained. "It doesn't mean those memories are lost forever. It just might take you a little time before things come in focus. Maybe it would help if you try to remember anything you learned after you found yourself on the *Eva Aphrodite*."

"What I learned?" Jack frowned.

"Sure. There must be a reason your spirit ended up on that sinking boat. Did anyone say anything before they left that you can remember?"

Narrowing his eyes, Jack looked off into blank space for a moment, thinking back to when he first found himself aboard the yacht. Finally, he blinked his eyes and looked over at Danielle.

"There's one thing Howard said…" Jack looked uneasily from Danielle to Walt.

"Which was?" Danielle asked.

Jack shook his head. "No, it was just crazy talk. I figured Howard didn't know what he was talking about."

"Tell us," Danielle urged.

Jack glanced to Walt, who gave him a nod. "Go ahead. Tell us what Howard said," Walt urged.

Jack let out a deep sigh and said, "After the boat filled up with water, I came to the realization I was already dead. They started leaving. One by one, they vanished."

"I assume you're talking about the spirits?" Danielle asked.

Jack nodded. "Yes. They had stopped screaming at each other—it was so quiet on board, even though I could still see them all, watching each other, no longer saying anything. Silently—one by one—they vanished. The bodies, which had been on the floor, began to bloat and rise to the ceiling. I thought they'd all left. I panicked and ran back into the first cabin I had been in. Howard was still there."

"Howard's spirit?" Danielle asked.

"Yes. Thelma was gone, but Howard was still there. Right before he vanished, he looked at me and said, *I wonder what Marlow had to pay to kill us all.*"

FOURTEEN

Adam had just sat down in a seat across from Bill Jones at Pier Café when he heard someone shout, "If it belongs to Boatman, I say she can haul it off!"

Adam craned out from the booth to see who was doing all the shouting. The voice was coming from two booths down. He could see the back of one man's head, but the one who was doing all the animated ranting faced Adam. It was Pete Rogers.

Settling back in his seat, Adam looked at Bill, who just shook his head and took a sip of his coffee.

"What's Rogers's problem?" Adam asked

Bill just as Carla approached their table with a pot of coffee.

"They've been going at it all morning," Carla explained as she filled Adam's cup.

"Do you know what they're arguing about? I heard them mention Boatman. Are they talking about Danielle?"

"Isn't Frederickport drama normally centered on Boatman?" Bill asked.

Carla leaned down, her nose just inches from Adam. In a loud whisper she said, "It's that ghost ship that washed up by Danielle's house." Carla gave a nod and stood back up straight again.

Adam picked up his coffee cup. "Pete expects Danielle to move it?"

"The historical society had an emergency meeting last night," Carla said in an excited whisper. "When the police finish with the boat, they want it turned over to the historical society."

Adam frowned. "What for?"

Bill chuckled. "Those idiots want to make some historical exhibit out of it. But Pete's not thrilled with the idea since it's not that far from his back patio. Can't say I blame him."

"What does that have to do with Danielle?" Adam asked.

"She inherited the Marlow estate," Carla explained. "According to this morning's paper, that boat belonged to Walt Marlow."

"Yeah, I know about that." Adam sipped his coffee. "So the historical society wants the boat left there?"

"Have you seen it yet?" Bill asked.

"Yeah. I don't see how it'd do much for local property values. The thing's an eyesore," Adam said.

Carla topped off Bill's cup and set the coffee pot on the table. "I just know Pete's not happy about it." She pulled her order pad and pen from her apron's pocket. "You guys ready to order yet?"

After Carla took their order and left the table, Bill said, "I sure as hell wouldn't want to be responsible for hauling that monstrosity off. I wonder where it's been."

"It must have been at sea all this time."

Bill grabbed a sugar packet from the end of the table and tore it open. As he dumped it into his cup, he said, "Can you imagine coming across something like that while out fishing?"

"Have you seen it yet?"

"Yeah, I stopped by this morning. It's all taped off, can't get close to it. I guess they've had a cop down there twenty-four seven." Bill picked up a spoon and stirred his coffee.

"Considering they found human bones on board, I imagine they want to see if there're more."

"I don't think that's why they won't let anyone near it. Probably has something to do with what they found yesterday."

"What are you talking about?"

Bill tossed the spoon aside and picked up his mug. "I guess it hasn't been on the radio yet. I imagine they're keeping tight-lipped about it."

"Tight-lipped about what?"

"The cops found a treasure on board."

Adam perked up. "A treasure? What kind of treasure?"

"A freaking fortune in jewelry. Maybe not worth as much as the Missing Thorndike, but close."

"Jewelry?"

"Vintage stuff, all in pristine condition. They called in a jeweler from Astoria to have a look at it. He was there last night. A freaking fortune."

"I'm surprised there wasn't anything in the newspaper about it."

"They probably consider this an ongoing investigation. Maybe they don't want the public to know yet. My friend wasn't supposed to say anything. So keep this between us."

"Ongoing investigation? What for?"

"They think it might be stolen," Bill explained.

"Stolen? Why would they think that? It probably belonged to some passenger on board the ship when it went down."

Bill shook his head. "Nope. The metal box it was in was fairly new. From Walmart. It still had a price sticker on the bottom. While I said it was vintage jewelry, I also said it was in pristine condition. According to my friend, the jeweler said there was no way it had been on that boat all those years."

Adam considered the scenario a moment and then let out a chuckle. "Can you imagine pulling off some jewel heist and then stashing your loot on an old boat and to have not only the loot disappear, but the entire damn boat!"

"I suppose this means that boat must have been washed up somewhere all these years, but where?"

"I have no idea." Adams sipped his coffee. "And now that it's here, I can't believe anyone would want to keep it."

"If I had a house along that stretch of beach, I wouldn't be too thrilled either."

"What's the historical society thinking? They don't seriously want to take responsibility for that thing? Can you imagine the liability?"

Bill shrugged. "I doubt they've gotten that far."

"Obviously not."

"That reminds me, is it true about Boatman donating an emerald to the museum?"

"Didn't you read the article in the newspaper?" Adam asked.

"Yes, but it didn't make any sense. Something about an emerald from the Missing

Thorndike. Why would she take one of the emeralds out of the necklace?"

Adam leaned back in his seat. "She's not taking one of the emeralds out of the necklace. That would be crazy, considering what that thing's worth."

Bill frowned, shaking his head. "Then why did they say she was donating an emerald from it?"

"Don't you ever read?"

"Obviously I didn't read about this. Are you going to tell me, or are you just going to be a jerk?" Bill snapped.

"The original diamonds and emeralds were stolen from the necklace before it went missing and were replaced with fakes. Eva Thorndike's parents found out and had the fakes replaced before Walt Marlow stole it."

"Yeah, yeah, I remember all that. But what does it have to do with the emerald Boatman's giving to the museum?"

"You know who Heather Donovan is?" Adam asked.

"The woman with the mold?"

"Yeah. She's also the one who inherited Presley House. I guess her great-grandfather

—the one who built Presley House—was involved in the original Thorndike jewel heist. One of the missing emeralds was passed down in her family."

"So why does Boatman have it?"

"Heather returned the emerald to Danielle."

"Returned it to Boatman? Why in the hell would she do that?"

Adam shrugged. "I guess she figured the emerald belonged to her."

"Why? She's not related to Eva Thorndike. Why would Donovan give Boatman the emerald? Hell, it's not as if she needs the money. Danielle Boatman is loaded. And from what I know about Heather Donovan, she can't afford to be giving away precious gems."

"If it was me, I wouldn't have given it to Danielle."

Bill laughed. "And you consider yourself Danielle's friend."

Adam smiled. "True. But as you said, it isn't as if Danielle needs the money, and I doubt she cares that much about the emerald. Hell, she's donating it to the museum."

"I still don't get why Donovan gave it to her."

"Because Walt Marlow inherited the Missing Thorndike, and Danielle inherited his estate through her aunt. I guess Heather considered Danielle the rightful owner."

Bill silently fidgeted with the handle of his coffee mug as he considered the facts of the Missing Thorndike. Finally, he looked up at Adam and said, "Donavon was a fool; that emerald didn't belong to Marlow, so there was no reason to give it to Boatman, even if she was the rightful owner of the Missing Thorndike."

"Why do you say that?"

"Think about it. The Thorndike necklace had three sets of stones: real diamonds and emeralds, fake stones, and a second set of diamonds and emeralds. The first set of real gems was stolen. That's where Donovan's emerald came from. The fakes were removed and given to the jeweler. We know that, because Hayman had them."

"So?"

"The second set of diamonds and emeralds are in the necklace today. The original setting and the second set of precious stones is what Walt Marlow inherited. The stolen stones, if they belong to anyone else, would belong to the Thorndike family, or their heir. Marlow just inherited the necklace with the second set of stones. He didn't inherit the first set of stones, the ones that were originally stolen."

Adam stared at Bill a moment, a blank expression on his face. He then started to laugh. "Damn, you're right. I wonder if Heather will ever realize she gave the emerald to the wrong person."

"Considering how she was bitching about what it was going to cost to get rid of the mold in her house, I have a feeling she's already regretted her generosity." Bill reached for the pack of cigarettes in his blue work shirt pocket and stood up.

"You can't sit for fifteen minutes without a smoke?"

"I'm just having a quick one before Carla brings our breakfast. Stupid smoking laws." Bill walked outside to have a cigarette, leaving Adam alone.

In the adjacent booth, Kurt Jefferson sat

alone, quietly finishing his breakfast while processing the conversation he had just over-heard. The urge to hit someone—anyone—was overwhelming.

After washing down the last of his bacon and eggs with the now cold cup of coffee, he shoved his mug and plate aside and stood. Digging one hand into a front pocket of his jeans, he pulled out several bills and angrily tossed them onto the table.

FIFTEEN

Kurt Jefferson hadn't planned to spend his fortieth birthday in Frederickport. Last year, his ex-wife had invited him over for a birthday breakfast so he could spend the morning with his son. It was a gracious offer, yet one she hadn't extended for this year. They were no longer on the best of terms, which was partially attributed to the fact that his last two child support payments had been late.

He pulled his Jeep up behind the squad car and parked. He sat there a moment, still thinking of what he had overheard at the diner. Pulling his key from the ignition and grabbing his cellphone from the center console, he exited the vehicle. It was breezy out, with temperatures in the mid-fifties. He had dressed casually that day, denims, long-sleeved T-shirt, and his windbreaker with the name of his company embossed on the back: *Jefferson Diving and Salvage.*

Stuffing the keys in his front pocket and the phone in his back one, he made his way to the beach. Once he reached the sidewalk, he paused and looked out toward the ocean. There it was, the *Eva Aphrodite*. He couldn't tell from this angle if it was indeed the same boat, but considering what he had just overheard at the diner, he was fairly certain it was.

Stepping onto the sand, he walked toward the boat. It looked larger somehow, perched up on the beach, crowding the area. Space seemed greater on the bottom of the ocean, and the boat smaller. Silently, he approached, looking up at the name on the boat's bow. *Eva Aphrodite*—the lettering was the same. Yet he couldn't even imagine how the yacht—or what was left of it—got here.

"That's far enough," Kurt heard someone

yell out. Looking to his left, he watched as a police officer walked in his direction.

"I'm just looking," Kurt called back.

The cop pointed down to the portion of yellow tape under Kurt's feet. Looking down, Kurt abruptly stepped back. He hadn't even noticed the tape surrounding the boat or the fact he was standing on it. On closer inspection, he realized one reason he hadn't noticed: much of the tape was covered by sand.

When the officer reached him, Kurt read his name tag. "Sorry, Officer...Henderson. I didn't even notice the tape."

"No problem." Officer Brian Henderson turned to face the boat. "It's really something, isn't it?"

"Any idea how it got here?" Kurt asked.

Brian shook his head. "That's the current mystery." Under his breath he added, "One of them."

"I'd love to have a closer look. Do you think it would be possible for me to take a look inside?"

"Sorry. We can't let anyone on her just yet."

"What are the plans for it?"

Brian shrugged. "I know there're some who'd like her to stay here."

"Like the *Peter Iredale?*" Kurt asked.

"Exactly. But I've been hearing from a few of the local property owners. They aren't thrilled with the idea."

Kurt stared up at the wreckage. "No. I can't imagine they are."

"Is this your first time seeing it?"

"Yes. I'm from Astoria. I own a diving and salvaging company, heard about this on the news, and was curious to see it in person."

"Any chance you've ever seen this before?" Brian asked with a chuckle. "We'd sure like to figure out where she came from."

"Sorry, I can't help you there."

"Well, go have a look around. Just stay on this side of the tape. I have to go make a call."

"Sure. No problem." Kurt stood silently, looking up at the *Eva Aphrodite* as the officer walked toward the street. After a moment, Kurt began walking the boat's perimeter. He had never seen it from this angle before— looking up at it as opposed to looking down from the upper deck. He studied the wreck- age. When he came to its stern and the gaping hole, Kurt froze. There was no mistake —it was the same boat.

He could feel his hand tremble as he pulled the cellphone from his back pocket to make the call. After two rings, she answered.

"Hey, what's going on?"

"I'm down here," Kurt told her.

"Down here where?" she asked.

"Standing on the beach, looking up at the *Eva Aphrodite*. It's the same boat."

"I told you it was."

"This is impossible."

"Anything's possible," she countered.

Holding the cellphone by his ear, Kurt walked slowly around the boat as he talked on the phone. "I found out something interesting this morning."

"What was that?"

"I know what was in the box."

Silence.

"Why did you do it?" he asked.

"That's really none of your business."

"What do you mean it's none of my business? You do know the cops have it now, don't you?"

"That doesn't surprise me, considering

they've been going through the boat since it washed up on shore."

"Is this what you wanted, for them to find it?"

She laughed before saying, "Don't be ridiculous. How did I know the damn boat was going to find its way back here?"

"You don't sound very upset."

"What am I going to do about it now?"

"You put a fortune in that damn box. How do you plan to get it back?" he asked.

"I don't plan to get it back."

"This is insane."

"What do you expect me to do? March up to the cops and say, *excuse me, I left a little something on that boat, and I want to pick it up.*"

He didn't think she sounded upset. "If you'll remember, I'm the one who put that box on the boat."

"It's not yours," she reminded him. "This is for the best. It's not what I originally planned, but perhaps this is how it's supposed to be."

"Listen, maybe you can walk away from a fortune like that, but I can't. I need the money."

"We had a deal, Kurt. You were paid well."

"Not well enough to walk away from this," he hissed.

"There's nothing you can do now."

"If you can afford to just walk away from a fortune, then you can afford to pay me more."

"Fortune? Who said it was worth a fortune?" she asked.

"That's what the guy said."

"What guy? Where are you getting all this, Kurt?"

"When I went to breakfast this morning. I heard some guys talking. One of them knew all about the vintage jewelry you stashed in that box. They even had some jeweler from Astoria come check it out."

She laughed. "So now you're picking up your intel at the local diner?"

"Was it wrong?"

"I can't give you any more money." She was no longer laughing.

"Yes, you can. Or I go to the police."

"We have a contract. You signed a confidentiality agreement. If you tell anyone, I'll sue you."

JACK THOUGHT there was something familiar about the man. It wasn't until he said, *"I'm the one who put that box on the boat,"* did he know who he was. He was about the right height and size. Of course, the more he thought about it, he wondered why he hadn't figured it out sooner. After all, it had been almost a hundred years since he had seen anyone, and everyone he once knew had long since died. In his defense, he had never seen the man's face.

Jack had returned to the beach the night before, after meeting with Walt for the second time since his return to Frederickport. The meeting had not ended well. After telling Danielle and Walt what Howard had said before leaving the ship, Walt called him a liar and vanished. Danielle wanted him to stay; she had more questions. Jack had nothing else he wanted to say to Danielle, so he followed Walt's cue and vanished. He didn't go far, just up the street, back to the *Eva Aphrodite*.

The man he recognized carried a telephone in his hand and continued to talk into it. Jack couldn't understand how the phone worked without a cord. So much had changed in the last ninety plus years.

When Danielle had taken him over to Marlow House the previous day, she had pulled one of those gadgets from her pocket and looked at it. When he had asked her what she was doing, she explained she was reading a text message on her cellphone.

"What's a cellphone?" he had asked.

"It's a telephone, but unlike the phone from your era, it does more and it doesn't need to be plugged in. Lily just sent me a message, and I guess we should stop talking out here. People are starting to watch."

Jack had a few questions of his own for Danielle. There was so much about this new world he didn't understand. Yet he was anxious to leave Marlow House and put some distance between him and Walt. Perhaps if Jack could remember what had happened those many years ago, he would be more willing to stick around and convince his old friend to listen to him. Unfortunately, he couldn't remember, and it was entirely possible Walt was right. Perhaps he had stolen the money.

Jack remembered he had moved the money from its hiding place in his room at George's—but it wasn't to take it to Marlow House. Back then, perhaps he should have talked to Walt, explained what was going on, that he was in trouble. But he had wanted to handle it himself. What he had finally decided to do, Jack couldn't quite wrap his mind around. Those last days were lost in a distant fog.

Focusing his attention back on the man talking on the cellphone, Jack moved closer to him. Maybe he couldn't remember what had happened during his final days, but that didn't mean he couldn't try to figure out why this man had left the box on the boat and what it all meant—if it meant anything at all.

KURT STOOD by the stern of the wreckage and shoved his cellphone into his back pocket.

He could see the police officer walking toward the other side of the boat, talking into his cellphone.

Turning from the ship, Kurt walked toward the ocean, stopping just a few feet from where the waves washed up on shore. He looked out, wondering how the *Eva Aphrodite* managed to get from its former home to this site. None of it made sense.

He felt a hand touch his shoulder, startling him. Turning abruptly to face whoever it was, he was surprised to discover he was still alone. The officer remained a good distance from him, still talking on his cellphone. Reaching up and touching his right shoulder, Kurt glanced around quickly.

"I could swear someone just touched me," he muttered.

Shaking it off, he turned back to face the ocean. He felt it again, yet this time it felt more like a finger poking his right shoulder.

"What the…" Kurt said with a shout as he abruptly swung around to face whoever was playing tricks on him. Yet he was still alone. Again, he looked up and down the beach. Still holding his shoulder, he absently massaged it and glanced around nervously.

After a few moments, Kurt convinced himself it must have been the wind, or perhaps a seagull dive-bombed him and escaped undetected. No longer rubbing his shoulder, he dropped his hand to his side and was about to leave when something abruptly shoved him in the back. Again turning and finding nothing, Kurt let out a curse and took off in a run, heading for his Jeep.

JACK STOOD ON THE BEACH, laughing. *When was the last time I've laughed like this?* Jack asked himself. A broad smile on his face, Jack watched the man run from the beach. "Damn, that was fun!"

SIXTEEN

Joanne Johnson, Marlow House's housekeeper and occasional cook, unpacked the groceries Lily had picked up that morning, putting them away in the refrigerator and pantry. It was mid-morning on Friday. Guests were arriving that afternoon, one couple from Portland and a writer from Washington State. Joanne had already prepared the rooms, putting clean linens on the beds and setting out the towels.

The writer from Washington would be staying upstairs in the Red Room, and a couple from Portland would be staying in the downstairs bedroom, as the husband had a problem navigating the stairs. Danielle was still contemplating renaming the rooms. Initially she had named the upstairs bedrooms by color, eventually regretting her decision. However, she hadn't yet decided on new names, so for now, rooms on the second floor were by color, while the downstairs bedroom was simply called the downstairs bedroom, and the attic room—a room which had only been used by one guest—was called the attic room.

While Joanne organized the kitchen and prepped the food for Saturday's breakfast, Lily was in the side yard, instructing the gardener on a few changes they wanted to make in the landscaping. Upstairs, Danielle sat alone in her bedroom, trying to decide if she should sit down with Walt and tell him everything she knew about the *Eva Aphrodite*. They hadn't yet discussed what Jack had said before Walt's hasty departure, nor the murdered passengers and crew, and Walt knew nothing about the mysterious jewelry found on board.

Walt normally came to her room each

evening, and the two would discuss the day's events or simply say goodnight. Yet Walt hadn't shown himself last night—or this morning. Taking a deep breath, Danielle stood up and decided to talk to him.

Just as she stepped out of her bedroom, she heard Sadie racing up the stairs, the nails of the dog's paws scraping against the wood steps as she made her ascent. The sound of the front door slamming shut could be heard, along with Ian's voice calling out an unenthusiastic, "Sadie," never really imagining the dog would listen to him. Under most conditions, Sadie was a perfectly behaved, well-trained golden retriever, who listened and obeyed her master's commands. At Marlow House, not so much. Ian had come to accept his dog's peculiar behavior when visiting his neighbor's house. Since Danielle didn't mind Sadie's obsession with Marlow House's attic, Ian had given up trying to keep Sadie downstairs.

"Hey, girl," Danielle called out to Sadie, who had just reached the second-floor landing.

Wagging her tail, Sadie briefly turned Danielle's way, let out a short bark, and then continued on, charging up the attic stairs to Walt.

Danielle glanced briefly back into her room. Max, who had been sleeping soundly on the end of her bed, had just lifted his head, the dog's noisy arrival disturbing the cat's slumber. Closing his eyes and letting out a lazy yawn—displaying his razor-sharp feline teeth—Max dropped his chin back onto his front paws and went back to sleep.

Smiling at Max, Danielle pulled her bedroom door almost shut, leaving it open several inches so that Max could get out later when he finished napping.

Danielle found Walt upstairs in the attic, sitting on the sofa bed, while Sadie danced around on his lap, paws disappearing through Walt's thighs while the dog's tail swished back and forth unencumbered.

"Sadie, off the sofa," Danielle ordered as she approached them.

"Spoilsport," Walt teased while he instructed Sadie to do as Danielle commanded.

The dog jumped to the floor and curled up on Walt's feet.

"You've been making yourself scarce," Danielle said as she took a place on the sofa.

"I've been doing a lot of thinking." He glanced down at Sadie. "I take it Ian is here?"

"I would have assumed you saw him walk over."

Walt shrugged. "I've been sitting here. I haven't been looking out the window."

"I heard him come in downstairs a minute ago, and Sadie is here, so yeah, I guess he is."

"Where's Jack?" Walt asked.

"Unless he's moved on, I assume down with the *Eva Aphrodite*. He took off right after you disappeared last night."

"I had nothing more to say to him, especially after all that nonsense he spouted about Howard. Does he really expect me to believe Howard blamed me for the storm? Exactly how does one pay to rustle up a storm?"

Danielle turned to face Walt, resting her left elbow on the back cushion. "I don't think Howard was talking about a storm."

"I doubt Howard said anything. Jack is just trying to deflect. He took that money. He betrayed me, and the powers that be sent him to the *Eva Aphrodite* to serve out his penance."

"Actually, Walt, there's a few things I haven't told you."

Walt studied Danielle. "What few things?"

"Maybe a storm took your yacht down, but it didn't kill the passengers and crew. They were already dead."

"Don't be absurd; what do you mean already dead?"

"The chief and his men have been going through the boat. They found human remains. Well, not a lot, actually. Being under the ocean for that long has a way of making all signs of life—or death—disappear. But they did find skulls."

Walt cringed. "I would prefer not to think of my old friends in that way." He stood up.

"But we have to talk about it."

Walt walked to the window and looked outside. "What's the point? They've been dead for almost a hundred years."

"They were murdered, Walt. Each skull came with its own bullet."

Walt turned from the window and stared

at Danielle. "Are you telling me they were shot?"

"According to the chief, each skull they found had a bullet lodged in it. Those people were executed. Someone murdered them. Their deaths had nothing to do with a storm."

His expression unreadable, Walt made his way back to the sofa and sat down. Staring ahead blankly, he shook his head. "I don't believe this."

"It's true. And I'll be honest with you; the chief believes you might have been involved."

With a quick jerk of his head, Walt faced Danielle. Narrowing his eyes, he said, "He believes I killed those people?"

"Or paid to have someone do it. Which apparently is something Howard wondered before his spirit decided to move on."

"You certainly don't believe that, do you?"

Danielle smiled at Walt. "If I did, I wouldn't be telling you this. The chief wanted me and Lily to move out of Marlow House while he investigates the murders."

"Investigates the murders? From over

ninety years ago? I imagine the responsible party has long been dead."

Danielle shrugged. "True. But the chief knows your spirit is here, that you're capable of harnessing energy, and if you had those people killed, he's afraid of what you might be capable of doing if provoked."

Walt stood angrily and shouted, "I'll show him exactly what I'm capable of doing!"

Danielle chuckled. "Seriously, Walt, you're angry at the chief for worrying about Lily and me? Remember how you felt about Harvey?"

"That was different! I had good reason to be worried! Harvey could have gotten you killed."

"The chief doesn't know you. He's never met you. Put yourself in his shoes. He knows you're confined to Marlow House—that your powers don't extend beyond these walls. So naturally, he would feel more comfortable having us somewhere where you can't reach us. After all, it's not like he can come in and arrest you."

Letting out a sigh, Walt plopped back down on the sofa. Sadie looked up at him and let out a short bark.

"Fine, Sadie. You don't need to nag," Walt grumbled.

Danielle glanced down at the dog. "What did she say?"

"It doesn't matter. Just that she agrees with you."

Reaching down, Danielle ruffled Sadie's fur. "Good girl. Smart dog."

Walt leaned back and closed his eyes. "Does Lily know about any of this?"

"Yes. She knows the chief wanted us to stay somewhere else until he could learn more."

Walt opened his eyes and looked at Danielle. "Is Lily afraid to stay here?"

"Obviously not. She's still here. I don't believe you had anything to do with those people's deaths."

"I didn't. But what I don't understand, why in the world would the chief imagine for a moment I did? I know we've never actually met, but what motive would I have to murder my crew and customers—many who were personal friends—aboard my yacht."

"Well…umm…I think it had something to do with what Ben told him."

"Ben?"

"Ben Smith, from the museum."

"What could he have possibly said?" Walt asked.

"Well, I haven't actually talked to Ben yet." Danielle stood up. "But apparently, there's an old rumor about you and one of the passengers—a married woman—something about an affair between you two."

Walt stared at Danielle. Waving a hand, he summoned a lit cigar and took a puff. Leaning back in the sofa, one leg propped over the opposing knee, Walt studied Danielle. "If I was having an affair with a married woman, and for whatever reason found it inconvenient and wanted to get rid of her, don't you think it would be a bit—overkill—literally—to massacre everyone on board?"

Still standing, Danielle faced Walt. "I didn't say you did it. But you asked why the chief suspected you had something to do with it."

"Then you can ask the chief the same question I just asked you."

"I think there was more to it than you

being intimately involved with one of the passengers."

"More, how?"

Danielle shrugged. "I don't know. Like I said, I haven't been able to see Ben yet to find out all that he told the chief, and the chief seems reluctant to tell me everything Ben said."

"I thought you and the chief were good friends? That you shared this kind of information with each other."

"He doesn't tell me everything. And you know I don't tell him everything."

"True." Walt took another puff off his cigar.

"There's something else. Not sure what it has to do with the murders, but it's bizarre." Danielle pulled her iPhone out of her back pocket.

"Bizarre how?"

"Joe found a box on board the *Eva Aphrodite*. It was filled with old jewelry." Danielle looked at her phone and opened her photo app, locating the pictures she had taken.

"Old jewelry?"

"Yes. I took these pictures at the chief's office." Danielle showed Walt the photographs on the iPhone, scrolling through each one.

Walt leaned close to the phone, studying the images. "I recognize those pieces."

"You should." Danielle opened the photograph of the three women and showed it to Walt. He studied it for a moment, let out a sigh, and then leaned back in the sofa.

"Nothing remarkable about that. They were all on the *Eva Aphrodite* when it went missing. Maybe the boat was boarded by pirates, and they removed their jewelry and hid it in a cabin, thinking it would keep them safe."

"The problem with that scenario is the items were found in a box—a box that wasn't that old. A box from Walmart."

"Walmart?"

"It's a store that wasn't around when you were alive. The box still had a price tag from Walmart on it. Plus, the condition of the jewelry was not what one would expect it might be, left all those years in damp salt air. Not to mention, Jack confirmed to me a diver placed the box on the *Eva Aphrodite* just a day before he brought the boat here."

Walt said nothing for a few moments, considering all that Danielle had told him. Finally, he looked at her and said, "We have to find out what happened on that boat. I need to know, was Jack involved?"

SEVENTEEN

Floor-to-ceiling bookshelves lined two of the four walls in the darkly paneled room. The impressive collection of leather-bound books captured Rowland Sterling's full attention, much to his wife's annoyance.

"You can look at the books later," Stella told Rowland. "I want to see the sunken ship."

Danielle wondered if portly Rowland, who was a good head shorter than his wife, had once been the taller spouse. Considering how the woman had been harping at her poor husband since their arrival, Danielle thought it was entirely possible she might have beaten him down over the years.

To Danielle's surprise, he ignored his wife's newest demand and asked, "Did they all belong to Walt Marlow?" By the way his gaze lingered over the collection, Danielle guessed Mr. Sterling was a lover of books.

After checking them into their room downstairs, Danielle had begun to give the older couple a quick tour of the house when the library had stopped Mr. Sterling in his tracks. "Pretty much," Danielle replied. "I added a few, but most of my books—the ones I brought with me from California—I keep in my room or in the parlor. From what I understand, Walt Marlow was a voracious reader."

"Rowland," Stella said impatiently as she tugged on the sleeve of his sweater, "I want to go see it before it gets dark."

Rowland let out a weary sigh, and instead of reminding his wife there was plenty of daylight left, as it was barely 2 p.m., he reluctantly acquiesced to her demand. Turning to Danielle, he asked, "Where did you say we can see this boat?"

"It's just up the street. It's a short walk.

You'll see the police car parked along the side of the road. You can enter the beach there."

"And you say Walt Marlow owned it?" Stella asked Danielle as they walked toward the door leading to the front hallway.

"Yes, it was his yacht."

"Yacht. My, he must have been rich," Stella said. "But you can't really tell by this house."

"Stella," Rowland scolded under his breath.

Danielle glanced at Rowland and smiled, noting the red blush coloring his pale complexion.

"I'm just saying this is a rather ordinary house for someone who owned a yacht. Did he own other homes?" Stella asked.

"Umm…no, just this one. This house was built by his grandfather, Frederick Marlow, who founded the town." Danielle walked the couple to the front door.

"I think it's a beautiful house," Rowland said, flashing Danielle an apologetic smile.

A few minutes later, Danielle chuckled to herself as she closed the front door after Rowland and Stella Sterling went off to see the

Eva Aphrodite. Mrs. Sterling had heard about the wreckage on the radio during their drive to Frederickport. She was thrilled to discover it had washed up on a beach not far from the bed and breakfast.

Danielle was just heading to the kitchen to talk to Joanne when her cellphone rang. Pulling it from her back pocket, she saw the caller was Chris. Stepping into the parlor, she answered the phone.

"Hi there! How's it going?" she asked.

"Everything's going along as planned," Chris told her. "How's it going there? Any new developments?"

Danielle took a seat on the sofa and spent the next ten minutes filling Chris in on what had been going on regarding the *Eva Aphrodite* since their last phone call.

"Never a dull moment in Frederickport. Have your weekend guests arrived?"

"Yes. The couple from Portland, the ones staying in your room—"

"My room?" Chris sounded amused. "You better not let Walt hear you say that. Where is he, by the way?"

Danielle glanced up to the ceiling. "In the

attic. Or at least he was the last time I checked."

"So what were you saying about the couple from Portland?"

"I put them in the downstairs bedroom because of the stairs. Retired couple. When they made the reservation, they mentioned something about his artificial knee and wanted to know if I had a room on the ground floor. I think I told you about the other guest, she's a writer—a mystery writer. Seems very nice and interesting. She's upstairs right now, getting settled in her room. The Portland couple just took off to see the *Eva Aphrodite*."

"The writer? Is that the one who's staying a month?"

"Yes. From what I understand, this is a working vacation. She'll be writing a new book here—wants to do it someplace where she'll be inspired."

Chris laughed. "A haunted house would be the perfect place."

"In all fairness—" Danielle chuckled "—she doesn't know it's haunted."

"Any chance you might be able to get

away for about an hour or so this afternoon?"

"I suppose. Joanne is here. What do you need?"

"Adam called me. Escrow is scheduled to close on the Gusarov place this afternoon, and since I'm not there to do a final walk-through with him, I was wondering if you might go over there and do it for me."

"Sure. But isn't it just a technicality?"

"You never know, maybe some kids got in there within the last couple weeks and vandalized the place. Or the light fixtures decided to fall from the ceilings. And while I basically trust Adam—"

"He is still Adam," Danielle finished for him. She could hear Chris chuckle.

"I'd just feel better if you did it with him."

"No problem. But what if I find a… umm…well, a ghost in residence?"

"You told me Stoddard and Darlene aren't haunting that place."

"Well, I don't think they are, and neither of us noticed anything when Adam took us over there a couple weeks ago, but still. It's always possible."

"I don't want a haunted house."

"Does this mean if I come across a ghost during the walk-through, you want to cancel the deal?"

Chris didn't answer immediately. Finally, he said, "No. I hate seeing a grown man cry. I'm pretty certain if I cancelled now, Adam would start sobbing."

"Considering you're in Chicago and I'm the one in Frederickport, it would be a dirty trick to leave me with a blubbering Adam to soothe."

"Not to mention, the last time I looked, cancelling a real estate deal because of ghosts isn't a valid reason."

"I'll go over there. Do I need to call Adam, or is he going to call me?"

"I told him you'd call him if you can go. Thanks, Danielle, I appreciate it."

FRIDAY'S late afternoon breeze sent the front shrubbery at the Gusarov Estate leaning north while tree branches brushed repeatedly against the front windows. The landscaping had been severely neglected since Darlene

Gusarov's death. Upstairs, all the blinds remained closed, as did all the window cover-
ings on the lower floor except for the large
picture window in the living room.

Danielle sat in her car parked in front of
the property, waiting for Adam's arrival. She
remembered the first time she had seen the
estate, after she had first arrived in Frederickport during the past summer. Back then, she
had assumed it was an industrial building,
considering its massive size and utilitarian
feel. The wrought-iron fence surrounding the
property was its only feature that hinted at
residence instead of business.

The sound of a horn honking interrupted
Danielle's mental wandering. Glancing up in
her rearview mirror, she saw Adam parking
his car behind her. Pulling her key from the
ignition, she grabbed her purse off the passenger's seat and exited the Flex.

Thirty minutes later Adam and Danielle
finished the walk-through. She hadn't noticed
a single lingering spirit. The rooms were all
empty, devoid of both spirits and furniture.
Danielle assumed all the furnishings and personal belongings of the Gusarovs had been

sold. It reminded her of a blank slate, ready for Chris to transform. It wouldn't be his home, but the new headquarters for his non-profit organization.

Danielle stood on the front porch, watching Adam lock up the house.

"Are you still donating that emerald to the museum?" Adam asked as he turned from the front door and slipped the keys into his front pocket.

"Yeah. In fact, I'm supposed to meet with some of the historical society's board members in the morning to discuss it." Danielle and Adam made their way down the front walk toward the street.

"I still find it odd Heather gave it to you. If you think about it, Walt Marlow didn't actually inherit the original gemstones from the necklace, just the second set."

"I've pointed that out to Heather on numerous occasions. I even offered to give it back to her after she had to move out of her house because of the mold. I know the repairs cost her a fortune, and considering she'd just lost the Presley property, she needed the money."

"From what I hear, nothing ever came of that," he said when they reached the sidewalk.

"You mean, did Morris illegally get ahold of the property?" Danielle asked.

"I know she originally thought that."

"From what I understand, it turned out Morris got ahold of it legally. Not much she can do about it now. The last time I discussed it with her, sounded like she'd come to the conclusion it was for the best. Heather is big on karma."

"You mean the sins of the father? Or in this case the sins of the great-grandfather?" Adam walked Danielle to her car.

"Pretty much."

"Then I suppose it's a good thing I don't have any kids," Adam said as he opened her car door for her.

Danielle flashed him a bemused smile as she got into the vehicle. "Why do you say that?"

"Think about it. Would be rather unfair to saddle my kids—or theirs—with karma I generated."

"Ahh, because you're such a bad guy?" Danielle asked with a chuckle as she pulled her car door shut and looked up at Adam through the open window.

"I try," he said with a laugh.

ADAM'S QUESTION about Heather and the emerald prompted Danielle to stop by Heather's before returning to Marlow House. Less than fifteen minutes after leaving Adam, she sat in Heather's kitchen, watching her neighbor prepare them each a cup of green tea. Taking a deep breath, Danielle inhaled a hint of peppermint. She spied a diffuser sitting on the counter in the corner of the kitchen, a stream of steam swirling upward from its lid. Danielle was fairly certain that was the source of the peppermint.

"So what about the emerald?" Heather asked as she handed Danielle a cup of tea and joined her at the table.

"Tomorrow I finalize the plans with the museum, and I just wanted to check with you first. Like I said before, I really don't believe I'm the emerald's rightful owner."

Heather shrugged and took a sip of tea

before responding. "Neither am I. You're the closest thing, in my opinion. Plus, I rather like the idea of donating it to the museum. I think you made a good call there."

"Maybe it should be you who donates the emerald, not me."

Heather shook her head. "No. Absolutely not. I don't want anything to do with all that. I'm glad you're donating it, but I don't want to be involved. I did what I needed to do; I returned the emerald and sent it on its rightful course."

An emerald has a destiny? Danielle asked herself, resisting the urge to giggle.

Heather looked up from her tea, looking Danielle in the eyes, her expression serious. "But now that we're discussing this, there is something I've wanted to talk to you about—without Lily around."

Danielle took a sip of tea and then set the cup back on its saucer. She studied Heather's almost pleading expression. "What's that?"

"Back on Halloween, after we got out of Presley House, we talked about Harvey. You admitted seeing him. And yet, since that time, it's like none of it ever happened. It's like…well, sometimes I wonder…am I crazy?"

With a deep sigh, Danielle glanced down to her tea and then looked back up. Heather, who Danielle often saw as not just quirky, but opinionated and overconfident, now reminded her of an uncertain little girl, a look reinforced by her childish black pigtails.

"No, you aren't crazy." Danielle's voice was almost a whisper.

"So you did see him! I didn't imagine it all!"

"I know you plan to write a book about what happened, but I'll be honest, I don't feel comfortable being included in your book. I don't want to go public with what I personally experienced."

"Why, Danielle? If you aren't willing to verify it happened, no one will believe me!"

"Because I know what it feels like when people start looking at you like you're crazy. I remember how it felt when my parents sent me to a psychologist because they couldn't believe I was really seeing ghosts. I've learned, Heather, some gifts are best kept to yourself—or shared with a select group of people."

"So Harvey wasn't really your first ghost?"

Danielle shook her head. "No, Heather, he wasn't."

EIGHTEEN

Rowland and Stella stood behind the yellow tape and watched the police officers haul equipment from the police van parked on the side of the street to the wreckage. Stella had been shooting questions at the officers, but so far, the only response she had received was a request to stand back from the yellow tape.

"They're busy, Stella. Stop bothering them," Rowland reprimanded her in a hushed voice.

"I want to know what they're doing. Why are they putting all that equipment in the boat?" She craned her neck out in hopes of getting a better look.

Rowland pointed toward the wreckage. "See over there, that's a generator."

"What do they need a generator for? Are they going to start the boat?"

Rowland laughed. "Hardly."

"Don't laugh at me!" Stella snapped, flashing her husband an ugly look.

Rowland's smile quickly faded. "I'm just saying they're probably using the generator to run those lights they just took onto the ship."

"What do they need lights for?"

"I imagine it's dark inside."

"WHO'S the couple gawking and asking questions?" Brian asked when he joined Joe in a cabin on the lower deck. Other members of their team were busy setting up lights to help them do a more thorough, final inspection of the ship's interior.

"From what I gather, they're staying at Marlow House."

"Tourists." Brian let out a grunt. "I'll just be glad when we're done with this one. We should have brought the generator and lights down yesterday. It's creepy in here."

The ship's interior looked less haunting fully illuminated. Instead of flashlight beams exposing isolated sections of corroded walls and furnishings, the interior's ambiance seemed more exposed and abandoned under the floodlights' harsh glare.

After re-exploring the cabin where they had discovered the box of jewelry, Brian and Joe waited for the floodlights to be set up in the adjacent cabin. When they were ready, Brian walked inside and stood by what appeared to be a trunk shoved and forgotten in the corner, covered with barnacles. Reaching out, he lightly touched the trunk's exterior and said, "This ship had to have been under water at one time, and judging by how these feel, it wasn't that long ago."

"When I came in here the last time, I thought that was part of the wall." Joe stood next to Brian.

"Everything looks different under the floodlights." Brian reached down and attempted to open the trunk, but it appeared to be rusted shut. "I really don't want to have to drag this thing out of here."

"Just a second," Joe said. He left the cabin for a minute and returned with a crowbar. Brian stood by and watched as Joe pried open the trunk's lid. Once loose, Brian and Joe lifted it up, revealing its gruesome contents.

"I guess we missed this one," Brian said dully as he stared at the skeleton shoved into the trunk. Unlike most of the skulls they had found on board, this man's skull remained attached to the rest of his skeleton, while remnants of his suit hung limply from the bones: bones folded like a pretzel into the barnacle-encrusted trunk.

Brian leaned closer and examined the remains. "By what's left of his clothing, I'd say it was a man."

"I wonder why they put him in here." Joe reached out and touched the skull, gently turning it from side to side. "I don't see a bullet. Do you think he was shoved in here alive?"

Brian shook his head. "If he was, I don't see any signs that he tried to get out."

After Joe pulled back his hand, Brian

reached out and gently moved what was left of the shirt's fabric to one side, exposing the skeleton's rib cage. "No, he was killed here."

"What is it?" Joe leaned in, his head just inches from Brian's as the two officers hovered over the open trunk.

Brian pointed to the small metal object resting on the bottom of the trunk, below the rib cage. "I'd say that's a bullet. My guess, they shot him in the chest, not in the head like the others."

"I wonder why they bothered putting him in the trunk." Joe stood up straighter, no longer leaning over the remains.

"I don't know," Brian muttered, reaching for the skeleton's right hand. "But this might be able to help us identify him."

"A ring?" Joe asked.

With his gloved hand, Brian slipped the gold ring off the bony finger, examining it. "Not just any ring. It's a Masonic ring." Tilting it from side to side, he looked closer, searching for an inscription.

"Anything?" Joe asked.

"Looks like initials. But I can't tell. I'll need a magnifying glass."

"Old man," Joe teased, taking the ring from Brian. "Let me see." He studied it for a moment, holding it near one of the floodlights. Finally, he said, "J. W."

"J. W.? By the way he's dressed, I don't think he's part of the crew. And I don't remember any of the passengers with those initials."

Joe handed the ring back to Brian and then pulled his cellphone from his pocket. After searching through the notes he had stored, he came to what he was looking for. Shaking his head, he looked up at Brian and said, "No. I don't have a passenger with those initials."

"What about the last name?" Brian asked.

"What do you mean?"

"Maybe it's not his ring. Maybe it was his father's. Same last initial, different first initial."

Joe took a second look, shook his head, and tucked the phone back in his pocket. "No. None of the passengers' last names started with a W."

IT WAS dark by the time Stella and Rowland returned to Marlow House. They had driven their car up the block to see the wreckage instead of walking. Rowland was willing to walk, in spite of his artificial knee; it was Stella who had insisted they drive the short distance.

Instead of returning immediately to Marlow House after their visit to the *Eva Aphrodite*, they headed to town in search of a restaurant for dinner. Rowland enjoyed the Friday night special of fish and chips, Stella not so much. She claimed hers was greasy and returned it to the kitchen—after eating two-thirds of the meal.

At Marlow House, they found Lily and Danielle in the living room, sitting side by side on the sofa. The Sterlings hadn't yet met Lily. Stella's gaze went immediately to Lily's right arm and the dragon tattoo.

"What would ever possess you to get something like that?" Stella gasped.

"Stella, please," Rowland said under his breath.

"Why can't I ask? If a young girl puts something like that on her body for all to see, then she must want people to look at her. So why is it wrong for me to ask a simple question? I'm sure I'm not the first person to ask her about it."

Lily glanced down at her right arm and then back to Stella. "Well, it all started with tequila."

Stella arched her brows. "Tequila?"

Lily nodded solemnly. "And an ill-advised trip to Mexico."

"You got a tattoo in Mexico?" Stella gasped.

Lily shrugged. "I can't really be sure. When I woke up, I was in San Diego."

"You got a tattoo when you were drunk?"

"Isn't that when most people get tattoos?" Lily asked innocently.

"If so, our generation has a serious drinking problem," Danielle muttered under her breath as she rolled her eyes over Lily's impromptu explanation.

Abruptly changing the subject, Rowland said, "It was most interesting down at the beach this afternoon. I was surprised at how large the boat is. Or would it be called a ship?"

"It was a yacht. I suppose some might call it a ship, others a boat," Danielle said.

"They took a dead body off the ship," Stella told them.

"Dead body?" Lily and Danielle asked at the same time.

"We assume that's what was in the trunk," Rowland corrected.

Danielle frowned. "Did they say there was a body inside?"

Stella shook her head. "No. they didn't say anything. In fact, your police aren't very friendly here. They wouldn't answer any of my questions; they kept telling us to stay behind the tape. But I overheard a couple of them talking before they brought the trunk out, and they said something about finding a body."

Rowland shook his head. "I didn't hear them say that. But Stella insists—"

"Are you calling me a liar?" Stella snapped.

"No, dear. I'm just saying I didn't hear them."

"Well, I did!" she said stubbornly.

"Did you notice if they had lights set up on the boat?" Danielle asked.

"That's what it looked like," Rowland said.

"The chief did mention something to me about bringing lights down and doing a more thorough search of the boat. It's possible they found more skulls."

"Skulls?" Rowland asked.

"So far, all they've really found are human skulls on board—and a few random bones. That boat went missing almost a hundred years ago," Lily explained. "After so long, even bones will deteriorate. If you overheard them say they found a body, I wonder if that meant an actual body, which would indicate he or she was put on that boat recently—or that it was just skeletal remains, like the rest."

"I'm sure they said they found a body," Stella insisted.

When Stella and Rowland left for their room fifteen minutes later, Danielle looked at Lily and asked, "Tequila? Seriously?"

"I certainly wasn't going to waste my time telling her the real story. Annoying woman."

"One thing about running a bed and breakfast, you get all kinds."

"I feel a little sorry for her husband," Lily said.

"I know what you mean."

"So tell me about the author. Ian went all fan-boy when I told him who'd be staying here."

Danielle chuckled. "Fan-boy? For some reason, I don't see Ian going fan-boy over anyone."

Lily grinned. "I guess she's one of his favorite authors."

"That's saying something, considering Ian's no slouch in the author department."

"I know, but I guess even famous authors can crush over other authors."

"I suppose it's a good thing she's old enough to be his mother," Danielle teased.

"I think your butt's ringing," Lily chirped.

"Funny." Danielle stood up and pulled her ringing phone from her back pocket. She glanced at it before answering. "It's Chris."

Lily stood up. "Then I'll let you lovebirds have some privacy."

NINETEEN

Before coming to work that morning, Joanne had stopped by Old Salts Bakery to pick up Danielle's favorite cinnamon rolls. Sitting quietly at the head of the dining room table, Danielle reminded herself she needed to give Joanne a raise for picking up the pastries. Not because she wanted to eat them, but because they seemed to be the only thing that could shut up Stella Sterling, who was now stuffing her third roll into an already full mouth.

Sipping her coffee, Danielle looked down the table. To her right, Lily sat next to Hillary Hemingway, the mystery writer who was renting the Red Room for the next month. During check-in, Danielle had asked her new guest if she was related to *that* Hemingway. Hillary only laughed and said, "*I wish.*"

The Sterlings sat on the opposite side of the table. It was obvious to Danielle that Mrs. Sterling was determined to get her money's worth—hence the breakfast binging. Danielle found it hard to believe scrawny Stella Sterling ate copious amounts of food on a regular basis.

"What's everyone have planned for today?" Lily asked.

"I'd like to do some fishing," Rowland announced.

"I didn't come here to fish," Stella snapped. "You can fish anytime."

With a frown, Rowland looked at his wife. "I can?"

"I'd like to visit the local museum sometime while I'm here," Hillary said, looking from Lily to Danielle. "Stepping into the past feeds my muse."

Stella frowned across the table at Hillary, but continued chewing instead of responding.

"It's a nice little museum," Danielle said.

"You can go through it in less than an hour, so it won't really take up much of your day. I think it's worth seeing, and it might inspire some story ideas."

"Aren't you going to the museum today?" Lily asked Danielle.

"Yeah, I am. I have to meet with the board of directors." Danielle took a bite of her cinnamon roll.

"Danielle's donating an emerald from the Missing Thorndike to the museum," Lily announced.

"Missing Thorndike?" Stella frowned. "Isn't that the necklace I read about? The one you found in the attic?"

"Yes. Technically speaking, the emerald is not from the Missing Thorndike. That necklace is sitting in the bank safety deposit box, with all its emeralds and diamonds. The setting originally had another set of stones—that were stolen years ago—and then replaced with what it has now. The emerald I'm donating to the museum is one of the stones that was stolen years ago."

"How did you get it?" Stella asked.

Hillary leaned forward, looking intently at Danielle. "Yes, sounds fascinating."

"A descendant of one of the jewel thieves found one of the emeralds in her grandfather's belongings—along with information proving his father had been involved with the crime. She felt it was her responsibility to return the emerald to its rightful owner, so she gave it to me."

"I don't understand; why are you the rightful owner? Just because you found the necklace here? Didn't Walt Marlow steal the necklace you found? That's what I read," Stella asked.

"It's kind of an involved story." Danielle glanced down the table at Lily, who gave her a guilty shrug. Lily knew what Danielle was thinking at this point. *Did you have to bring up the emerald?*

"I'm listening," Stella said impatiently.

Danielle let out a deep breath and then forced a smile. "The necklace was originally owned by silent screen star Eva Thorndike. It was a family heirloom. She died at a young age from a heart condition. Before she died, she realized her ex-husband had removed the real diamonds and emeralds from the setting and replaced them with fakes. She didn't want her parents to know, so she asked Walt Marlow—who was a close friend and by her side when she died—to steal it. Which he did. He hid the necklace in the attic at Marlow House."

"Oh my, that is so romantic," Hillary said wistfully.

Scrunching up her face, Stella looked across the table to Hillary. "How do you see that as romantic?"

"So the necklace you found had fake gems?" Rowland asked.

Danielle shook her head. "No. What Walt and Eva didn't know, her parents had discovered what their ex-son-in-law had done, so they had new diamonds and emeralds put into the setting. I believe they figured out Walt was the one who took the necklace and why. They didn't say anything to him, but they left the necklace to him in their will. I suspect it was done to protect Walt in case he was ever found with the necklace after they were gone. As it turned out, Walt died first and they never changed their will."

"You inherited his estate, which included the necklace?" Hillary asked.

Danielle nodded. "Pretty much. Walt Marlow left everything to his housekeeper, whose daughter married my grandfather's brother. My great-aunt left everything to me. As for the emerald, I don't believe I'm necessarily its rightful owner; yet I believe the Thorndikes would approve of the emerald going to the museum. They have Eva's portrait there. You'll see it if you visit today."

DANIELLE SAT at the large table in the back office of the museum. Sitting at the table with her were four Frederickport Historical Society board members: Millie Samson, Ben Smith, bank manager Steve Klein—and someone she hadn't met before, Jolene Carmichael.

Steve had introduced Danielle to Jolene when she first entered the back office. Jolene, a slender woman in her late sixties, with dyed platinum blond hair, sat quietly on the other side of the table, studying Danielle. Instead of standing and offering her hand when Steve made the introductions, Jolene remained seated, giving Danielle a stoic nod in greeting.

"Jolene just moved back to town," Millie said excitedly after Danielle had taken her seat. "We're thrilled she agreed to fill the vacancy in the board. She'll bring so much to the historical society."

Danielle smiled across the table at Jolene, who looked as if she had just stepped out of the beauty shop, with her meticulously coiffed short hair. Manicured nails sporting blood red polish absently tapped the tabletop. It wasn't the tapping sound that caught Danielle's attention, it was the sparkling flicker bouncing off Jolene's many diamond rings. The woman had a ring on every finger—even her thumbs, and Danielle was fairly certain it wasn't costume jewelry. Looking up from the fidgety fingers, Danielle noted Jolene's designer silk blouse and diamond earrings. When Danielle's gaze settled on Jolene's face, she was a bit taken aback by the cool, less than friendly expression.

"So you lived in Frederickport before?" Danielle asked with forced cheerfulness.

"Jolene comes from one of the original

Frederickport pioneer families," Steve explained.

"Her family moved here even before Marie's," Millie added.

Jolene reached over to Millie and patted her hand. "True, but Marie is much older than me, so I suppose technically she's been here longer." Jolene smiled, her first smile since her introduction to Danielle.

"You grew up here?" Danielle asked.

"Oh yes. Met my husband here. This is where we raised our family. But after he died, I decided to move closer to our daughter. She lives in New York. She's an attorney, just like her father. But I felt it was time to come home. I missed Frederickport."

"And we're so glad to have you! Seems like most of our members are recent transplants —like Danielle here. It's good to have representation from the founding families," Millie said.

"Carmichael, why does that name sound familiar?" Danielle asked, looking across the table to Jolene.

"My husband, Doug, was Clarence Renton's business partner."

Momentarily speechless, Danielle stared at Jolene. Finally, she asked, "The man in the fishing photographs in Clarence Renton's office?"

Jolene nodded. "Yes, Clarence and Doug loved to fish. They used to joke about giving up their law practice and working on a fishing charter boat."

"I forgot how much those two enjoyed fishing," Steve said.

"It was such a shame, Clarence murdered like that. People thinking he had actually killed himself." Jolene shook her head. "Just horrible. I'm so glad the truth finally came out. It wasn't right for people to think Clarence would do something like that."

Danielle could feel the eyes of the other three board members suddenly on her, waiting for her response. She looked across the table to Jolene, who seemed oblivious to how her words might sound, considering Danielle and Clarence's history.

Unable to keep silent, Danielle spoke up. "I agree, I'm glad the truth came out and we know who killed Clarence Renton. But let's not forget the man murdered my cousin."

Jolene shook her head. "I'm sorry about your poor cousin. But Clarence was a good man. He was my husband's best friend. I knew him for years. Whatever happened with your cousin must have been an accident. After all, didn't I hear your cousin was on the run after stealing the Missing Thorndike, when Clarence happened across her?"

"It was hardly an accident. Clarence Renton also tried to kill me."

Jolene arched her brows. "Kill you? When? I heard you hit the poor man over the head and sent him to the hospital. Didn't they even arrest you?"

"Yes, I hit him. After he tried to kill me. And remember, he was embezzling from my aunt's estate for years."

Jolene let out a bored sigh. "I really don't think it's fair to talk about dear Clarence this way. The poor man is dead now, murdered. He isn't here to defend himself."

Danielle could feel her blood pressure rising. She glanced around the table, noting the dumbfounded expressions on the other board members' faces. It was as if they weren't sure what to say, so they kept quiet.

Finally, Ben spoke up. "I think we'll all agree Clarence made some bad choices, and while we understand he was your old friend, Jolene, you can't expect Danielle to share those feelings."

"That's easy for you to say. You never liked Clarence," Jolene snapped.

Ben let out a weary sigh. "Clarence and I had our disagreements over the years. But he's gone now, and I think we should focus on why we came here today. The emerald that Danielle is graciously donating to the museum."

"Yes, the emerald," Steve agreed.

Danielle glanced around the table. Steve, Millie, and Ben were now smiling, as if relieved the awkward moment had gone by.

"I have something I'd like to discuss before we move onto the emerald," Danielle announced.

"What's that?" Steve asked.

"It's my understanding the historical society's position on Walt Marlow's death is that it might have been a suicide, when I've clearly proven otherwise," Danielle reminded them.

"You don't know that for certain," Jolene

said. "Until my husband died, I had lived in Frederickport for my entire life. I grew up hearing the story of Walt Marlow's death. How he hanged himself in the attic after his wife ran off."

"The story wasn't true," Danielle insisted.

"Does it really matter?" Jolene asked.

"It obviously matters to you that the world knows Clarence didn't kill himself," Danielle countered.

Jolene gasped. "You certainly aren't comparing Clarence's recent death to someone who died almost a hundred years ago!"

Danielle seethed. "At least Walt Marlow never killed anyone!"

"Apparently you don't know as much about the *great* Walt Marlow as the rest of us," Jolene hissed. "He killed my grandfather's brother and wife! Not to mention all those other poor people!"

"What are you talking about?" Danielle asked.

"Jolene's great-uncle, Howard Templeton, and his wife, Thelma, were passengers aboard the *Eva Aphrodite* when it went missing. The museum acquired a diary belonging to a close friend of Thelma's, and from what I've read, it's entirely possible Walt Marlow was responsible for the ship going down," Ben explained.

"I don't imagine you know," Jolene said primly, "since it's not common knowledge, but those people on the boat—they were murdered. Shot in the head, every one of them."

TWENTY

G ripping anger used to make Danielle cry. When debating topics she felt passionate about, tears would swell. It was a trait she loathed—one she had worked years to suppress. Yet now, sitting at the table in the back office of the Frederickport Museum, she battled tears. How could she ever explain her outrage at their slander of her dear friend Walt Marlow? A man who had died before anyone at this table had even been born.

Taking a deep breath, Danielle willed herself to calm down. Her heart continued its rapid beating, but the threat of tears receded.

Once again, she was in control of her emotions.

"I guess I'll have to read that diary myself," Danielle said with supreme calm.

"Then you'll see what I'm saying," Jolene piped up.

Ignoring Jolene, Danielle looked at Ben and said, "I've decided it would be best if I loan the emerald to the museum for their exhibit."

"Loan it? Are you saying you no longer intend to donate it?" Steve asked.

"I may eventually. Just not now." Danielle smiled politely.

Jolene looked from Millie to Ben. "I don't understand. I thought you said she was donating the emerald, not loaning it."

Ben studied Danielle for a moment. When their eyes met, he gave her a smile. "The emerald belongs to Danielle; she's obviously free to do with it whatever she wants. It'll be a wonderful exhibit for the museum, even if it's just on loan. That's not really so unusual."

"Maybe not unusual, but we can hardly purchase land for a new museum with someone else's emerald," Jolene snapped. All eyes flashed to her.

"Excuse me? Who said anything about selling the emerald to buy land?" Danielle asked. "The understanding was the emerald would be on display with the Eva Thorndike portrait."

"And it would. But eventually, if we found a buyer for it, I'm sure even Eva Thorndike would rather see the emerald put to better use. If we're lucky, the buyer might be willing to keep it on display for a while. Displays rotate all the time at museums. Certainly, you didn't expect the historical society to hold onto the emerald indefinitely, did you?" Jolene asked.

"Of course, we were going to talk to you about it first," Steve assured her. "We would never accept such a donation without full disclosure of our intentions. In fact, that's why we're here today. To discuss what we had in mind for your most generous donation."

Millie added, "I know your bed and breakfast is in Walt Marlow's home, and you have a sense of loyalty to his memory. But we can't really rewrite history to fit what we wish it was. That would be going against everything the historical society stands for."

"I agree," Danielle said with a nod. "I would never expect the museum to present fairy tales to its visitors. But the information I've uncovered about Walt Marlow's death does not support suicide. Talk to Joe Morelli. He reviewed the coroner's report. Walt Marlow was murdered. Even Emma Jackson verified the fact that Walt Marlow's brother-in-law was in Frederickport when Walt was murdered."

"That old colored woman?" Jolene said with a snort. "What is she, one hundred and twenty or something?"

"I don't think they call them colored anymore," Millie said with a gentle scold.

"Oh pshaw. Fact is, Emma Jackson had no business living in Oregon back then. Nothing but a lawbreaker. Not someone whose word I'm going to take," Jolene insisted.

Danielle noted the uncomfortable glances exchanged between the other board members as they looked from Jolene to Danielle.

"You aren't seriously condoning a law that made it illegal for black people to live in Oregon, are you?" Danielle asked incredulously.

Jolene shrugged indifferently. "I had nothing to do with that law; I wasn't even born yet. But it was the law at the time, and the fact she was living in Oregon when it was in effect makes her a lawbreaker. It may be unpleasant, but it's true. Just like with Walt Marlow. Just because you'd rather believe he was murdered than did something as sinful as commit suicide doesn't change the facts."

"No, the facts support murder, not suicide," Danielle said with forced calm.

Jolene stood abruptly and looked at Danielle. "I won't belabor our obvious differences in opinion regarding historical fact and conjecture." She turned her attention to the other board members. "If Ms. Boatman won't be donating the emerald to the historical society, I see no reason for me to stay. You certainly don't need me to confer on a simple loan to the museum. Although, I'm not sure why we spent so much money for a display case for something she can remove at any time."

"THAT WAS PLEASANT," Ben said dryly after Jolene left the office a few minutes later.

Millie let out a weary sigh. "I forgot how Jolene can be a little difficult sometimes."

"I really did not expect it to go this way today," Steve added. "I don't know Jolene that well. She moved from Frederickport not long after I moved here. I really thought she'd be an asset to the historical society, considering her ancestors were Frederickport pioneers. But I really was surprised at her defense of Clarence Renton. I'm sorry, Danielle. I had no idea she'd carry on like that."

"I have to admit, that surprised me too," Millie conceded.

"I wish I could say I was surprised," Ben confessed. "Fact is, I was a little concerned about what she might say if Clarence was brought up."

"Why didn't you say anything?" Millie asked.

Ben shrugged in response.

"I'm not trying to be difficult about the Thorndike emerald." Danielle spoke up. "I hope you can understand, but I do feel a loyalty toward Walt Marlow, and if the museum portrays him unfairly—then I have to reevaluate my support of the historical society."

"Are you saying you won't support the historical society if you don't get your way?" Millie asked.

"Absolutely not. But, Millie, you know the facts are there. Walt Marlow did not commit suicide. To tweak the story because you imagine it might increase traffic to the museum is just as wrong as me expecting the museum to alter history because I prefer another version."

"To be honest, I think Danielle's version is more interesting," Steve said.

"And what is Danielle's version?" Millie asked impatiently.

"That for years everyone believed Marlow killed himself, and then Danielle uncovered new information that suggested Marlow's wife and brother-in-law conspired to kill him," Steve explained.

"But isn't that what we're saying?" Millie asked.

"Not exactly," Ben admitted. "We have been leaning a bit back to the suicide story—suggesting to our visitors it's still an unsolved mystery."

"It is," Millie said stubbornly.

Danielle shook her head. "No, it's not, Millie."

Steve let out a sigh and glanced at his watch. "I really need to get going. I promised my wife I'd finish painting the den."

"I need to go too. What did you decide about the emerald?" Millie asked.

Danielle glanced from Millie to Steve, considering the question.

Ben stood up. "Why don't you two go? I'll stay here and discuss the emerald with Danielle. I think for now it would be best if it was simply on loan with the museum until Danielle feels more comfortable."

"I also have some questions for you about that diary," Danielle told him.

———

"SO WHAT DO you want to know about the

diary?" Ben asked Danielle after Millie and Steve left. The two sat alone in the museum office.

"Why do you think Walt Marlow killed those people?" Danielle asked. "I can't believe he would do something like that. You mentioned you read something in the diary that supports that theory. What?"

"The diary belonged to Ethel Pearson, a close friend of Thelma Templeton," Ben began. "One of the women who was killed on the *Eva Aphrodite*."

"I guess the chief has talked to you about what they found."

"Yes. Those people had been shot. Murdered."

"Thelma is related to Jolene?"

"Yes, by marriage. Jolene's paternal grandfather was Ralph Templeton. Ralph's brother was Howard Templeton. Howard was married to Thelma. Howard and Thelma were on the *Eva Aphrodite* when it went down."

"What does Ethel's diary have to do with any of this?"

"There was an estate sale a few months back. Someone came across the diary, realized its author had lived in Frederickport during the year she wrote in it, so they donated it to the museum."

"Certainly Ethel didn't know Thelma had been murdered."

"No. And I didn't either when I first read the diary. But after Chief MacDonald came into the museum, asking about the *Eva Aphrodite*, I told him about what I'd read in the diary."

"Which was?"

"Ethel suspected Thelma was having an affair. She confronted her several times, and finally Thelma confessed, telling her she was secretly seeing Walt Marlow."

"How does that make Walt a killer?"

"According to Ethel, Thelma's lover had gotten violent. Apparently, Ethel walked in on her when she was dressing, and she was covered with bruises. At first, she thought Howard was responsible. This was before Ethel knew of Thelma's affair."

"Are you saying Walt Marlow was physically abusive to his lover?"

"It does happen."

Danielle shook her head. "I don't believe that. Walt would never hit a woman."

Ben laughed. Noting Danielle's lack of shared amusement, Ben stopped laughing. "I'm sorry, Danielle, but you have to admit, your defense of a man who died almost a hundred years ago is a little amusing. Perhaps even a little disturbing."

"Disturbing, how?"

"For one thing, you're living in his house. Perhaps you're a little too wrapped in the past. Whatever Walt Marlow may have done is ancient history. While I'm a lover of history, I find it best to look back with a critical, objective eye. If not, then those sins of our fathers will do nothing but weigh us down."

"Fine." Danielle let out a deep breath. "Let's say Walt Marlow was having an affair with Thelma Templeton, and he liked to smack her around. How does that lead to him ordering the hit—assuming he didn't do the job himself—of his yacht's crew and all its passengers?"

"For one thing, according to Ethel, Thelma was upset because Walt was trying to break it off. She told Ethel he didn't know who he was dealing with."

"So? Walt wanted to end the affair. Why kill Thelma?"

"According to her diary, Ethel couldn't understand why her friend was so upset about losing a lover who beat her. She also wrote about how Thelma had the upper hand, considering Ralph's involvement with Walt Marlow."

"Ralph? Jolene's grandfather? What do you mean his involvement with Walt?"

"Ralph and his brother Howard had inherited their family's business. That's where Jolene inherited her money. When Jolene said her husband loved to fish, she wasn't kidding. He was never much of an attorney. But considering Jolene's family money, he didn't need to be."

"You're losing me here; what does this have to do with Walt?"

"It was common knowledge, according to the diary, that Walt and Ralph—Jolene's grandfather—were working on some business deal, and Howard wasn't sold on it. Had Thelma gone to her brother-in-law, confessed the affair, and convinced Ralph that Walt had seduced her, he would have probably ended the business association with Walt and possibly done more to hurt him. Jolene's grandfather was known for being rather ruthless."

"So you think Walt killed all those people so Ralph wouldn't discover his affair with his sister-in-law?"

"It also got Howard out of the way. He was not in favor of the business alliance between his family and Walt. He may have been an occasional customer on Walt's party boat; they weren't friends. And after the *Eva Aphrodite* went missing and everyone on board was declared dead, Walt and Ralph formed a brief business alliance."

"Brief?" Danielle asked.

"I'm not sure what happened; I can't find anything on it aside from what was in the diary. And Jolene didn't even know her grandfather and Walt had ever been partners."

"I still don't see how any of this proves—or even suggests—Walt would do something like this."

Ben shrugged. "Maybe he didn't. But he did have a motive. And according to Ethel, when they eventually had a memorial service for Thelma, Walt didn't even bother to attend. He was out of town at the time. She was appalled at how little Thelma's death affected a man who she had been having an affair with for over two years."

TWENTY-ONE

D anielle hadn't expected to be gone that long. After pulling into the side drive at Marlow House and parking, she checked the time. It was almost 4:00 p.m. Joanne's car was still out front, so Danielle knew she hadn't left. Wearily getting from the vehicle, she slammed its door shut and headed to the house.

"How did everything go at the museum?" Joanne asked when Danielle entered the kitchen from the side yard.

"Not quite as I thought it would." Danielle tossed her purse on the kitchen counter and opened the refrigerator.

"Did you have some lunch?" Joanne

asked, looking up from the vegetables she was dicing for Sunday's breakfast.

"No. I was at the museum longer than I anticipated, and by the time I got the rest of my errands done, I just wanted to come home." Danielle grabbed some lunch meat and a jar of mayonnaise and then used her hip to close the refrigerator door.

"You are going to wash your hands before you make yourself a sandwich, aren't you?" Joanne asked in a scolding tone.

Danielle chuckled. "Yes, *Mom*." Setting the lunch meat and mayonnaise on the counter, she quickly washed her hands in the kitchen sink before grabbing a loaf of bread from the bread box.

"When does the museum take official ownership of the emerald?"

"The display case is supposed to be finished by this coming Wednesday, maybe sooner. I may take it down then. It officially goes on display Friday. But for now, the emerald is just on loan to the historical society."

Joanne looked up from the chopping

block and glanced over at Danielle. "You decided not to give it to them?"

"Not right now. Probably eventually. Long story." Danielle sat down at the kitchen table with her freshly made sandwich. Before taking a bite, she asked, "Where is everyone?"

"Your guests are all out. The nice mystery writer said something about stopping at the museum. Did you see her?"

"No." Danielle grinned. "If she's the *nice* mystery writer, what are you calling the couple?"

Joanne set her knife down and chuckled. While moving the freshly diced vegetables into a small Tupperware container, she said, "I'll be generous and just call them your downstairs couple. But she doesn't seem like a particularly happy woman."

"No, no, she doesn't." Danielle took another bite of her sandwich.

IT WAS ALMOST 5:00 p.m. when Joanne finally left for the day. Instead of going to the attic in search of Walt, Danielle went to the living room, where she found Max curled up on the sofa, sleeping. When she sat down on the sofa next to him, he opened his eyes and yawned.

"Hey, Max. You have a rough life." Smiling, Danielle reached out and stroked the cat's neck.

Standing up, Max strolled over to Danielle, walking onto her lap. After making himself comfortable, ignoring her grunts due to his excess weight, Max settled down and began to purr. Looking down at the black cat curled up on her lap, Danielle smiled while gently rubbing the white fur along the tips of his otherwise black ears.

"I thought you'd come upstairs," Walt said when he appeared in front of the sofa a moment later. Both Max and Danielle looked up at Walt.

"Hi, Walt," Danielle greeted him in a subdued voice. Max yawned and then settled his face back on his front paws, closing his eyes. He began to purr again.

Walt took a seat across from Danielle. "I saw Joanne drive off. How did it go at the museum?"

Danielle shrugged indifferently while still stroking Max's neck. "I met the new board member. Jolene Carmichael. She grew up in Frederickport, just moved back. Her husband was Doug Carmichael."

"Doug Carmichael? Should I know who that is?"

"Probably not. He was Clarence Renton's partner in the law practice. Jolene moved to New York to be with their daughter after her husband died a number of years ago."

Waving his hand, Walt summoned a lit cigar. Before taking a puff, he narrowed his eyes and asked, "Was he also embezzling from clients?"

Danielle shrugged. "I wondered that myself when she told me who she was. She's also the granddaughter of one of your old business partners."

Prepared to take another puff of the cigar, Walt paused, flashing Danielle a brief frown. "Business partner? Jack was my only business partner, and as far as I know, he never had any children."

Studying Walt's expression, Danielle

licked her lips and then said, "Ralph Templeton."

"Ralph Templeton?" Walt stood up. "I haven't heard that name in years." He began pacing the room.

"From what she told me, her grandfather's brother—Howard—and Howard's wife were on the *Eva Aphrodite* when it went missing."

Walt sat back down and looked at Danielle. "So why did you call Ralph my business partner?"

"According to Ben, you and Ralph went into some business venture together."

Walt shook his head. "That's not true. Ralph Templeton would be the last man I'd do business with."

"According to Ben, you and Ralph were negotiating some business deal, his brother was against it, and after the *Eva Aphrodite* went missing, you two moved ahead with it—whatever it was."

Leaning back in the chair, Walt smiled at Danielle. "Where is Ben getting all this information?"

Licking her lips again, her gaze meeting

Walt's, Danielle said, "From Ethel Pearson's diary."

If Danielle expected a reaction, she didn't get one. Leaning forward, Walt continued to stare at her, a frown on his face, as if he was attempting to place Ethel Pearson. Finally, he said, "I'm afraid you lost me. Who is Ethel Pearson?"

"A close friend of Thelma Templeton. Don't you remember her?"

Walt shrugged and leaned back in the chair. "I'm sorry. I barely remember Thelma aside from the fact she was married to Howard Templeton."

"You don't remember Thelma?" Danielle asked incredulously.

Again, Walt shrugged. "I'm sorry. That was a long time ago, and we weren't exactly friends."

"What exactly were you?" Danielle asked in a humorless voice.

"Social acquaintances?" Walt suggested.

"Is that what they used to call mistresses in your day?"

Walt scowled. "Mistresses? What are you talking about?"

"According to Ethel, you and Thelma were lovers."

Walt sat there a moment, staring at Danielle, momentarily dumbfounded. Then he did something Danielle didn't expect; he began to laugh. Bending over from uncontained laughter, his cigar disappeared. "Me… me and Thelma Templeton?" Walt choked out between fits of laughter.

"Would you please tell me what is so funny!" Danielle demanded.

She didn't get her answer because in the next moment Ian and Lily came through the front door with Sadie. Walt was still laughing when Sadie ran into the living room, jumping onto the chair with him. Walt disappeared and Sadie jumped down to the floor.

"We saw your car out front," Lily said when she walked into the room a moment later.

Danielle looked from the chair Walt had been occupying to the doorway, where Lily stood with Ian, their expressions solemn.

"Is something wrong?" Danielle asked.

"It's Emma Jackson," Lily said when she walked into the room. As she approached the sofa, Danielle noticed Lily's red-rimmed eyes. She had been crying.

"Oh…you don't mean…" Danielle said sadly.

"Mathew called," Ian explained. He took a seat on one of the chairs across from Danielle, pulling Lily to him. She sat on his knee, leaning against his shoulder.

"She went peacefully," Lily said. "The neighbors found her. She was sitting in her rocker on the front porch and just went to sleep."

"Wow. She would have been one hundred and seven in just a couple months," Danielle murmured. "She had a good, long life."

"Most of it was good," Ian corrected.

"You have a point." Danielle sighed. "I'm glad she was able to read her biography before she passed away."

Ian wrapped his arm around Lily and gave her a quick hug. "Something I might not have written had this one not put that idea in my head."

"How often do you come across a one-hundred-and-six-year-old black woman—one who is still sharp—willing to tell you what her life was like back when it was still illegal for blacks to even live in Oregon?"

"That didn't stop her." Ian chuckled.

"True." Lily smiled.

"So when is the funeral?" Danielle asked.

"They aren't having one," Lily said.

"What do you mean? They have to have a funeral," Danielle insisted.

Ian shook his head. "No, Emma was pretty emphatic about that. She didn't want a funeral. Instead, she told her family she wanted them to visit her when she was still alive, not spend money on airplane tickets after she was dead. Which is one reason they all showed up at her one-hundred-and-sixth birthday party."

Danielle smiled. "I remember now. Mathew once told me she called all her kids, grandkids, nieces, and nephews on the phone and told them if they weren't coming to her birthday party because they were saving their money to pay travel expenses for her funeral, then they didn't have to worry about coming to either one, because she wasn't having a fu-neral. Told them that if they loved her, they would prove it by showing up at her birthday."

Lily laughed. "I remember hearing that."

They spent the next thirty minutes reminiscing about Emma Jackson and discussing the biography Ian had written about her. Finally, Lily asked Danielle about her visit to the museum.

"For the time being I'm loaning the emerald to the museum; I won't be donating it. At least, not yet." She then went on to explain her afternoon at the museum.

"I can't believe that woman would say those things to you," Ian said incredulously. "I wonder if her husband was as corrupt as his law partner. Was he also embezzling from his clients?"

"That's what Walt wondered," Danielle said without thinking.

Ian frowned. "Walt?"

Danielle froze, her eyes widened. "Did I say Walt?"

"Yes, you did," Lily said, suppressing her giggle.

Danielle shrugged. "I meant that's what I wondered."

"YOU GOT OUT OF THAT ONE," Lily teased after Ian went home with Sadie. She and Danielle remained sitting in the living room.

Danielle glanced briefly to the ceiling. "I guess I should go tell Walt about Emma's passing."

"Do you think you'll see her before she moves on?" Lily asked.

"I doubt it. If she's not having a funeral, she'll probably move on to see her husband. Maybe she'll hang around and watch her kids go through her house."

"You know, I cried when I heard she died. I really liked Emma. But I'm not really sad that she's moved on," Lily said. "She was pretty lucky that she managed to live in her house all this time and never had to go into a home. What a peaceful way to go, sitting in your rocking chair."

"You're right. But I do wish I could talk to Emma again. There are some things I'd like to ask her. I'm almost tempted to drive over to her house and see if her spirit is still sticking around."

"Why?"

"How about we take a drive, Lily? Go grab some dinner."

Lily soon discovered Danielle wasn't all that hungry, since she had eaten a sandwich two hours earlier. Yet leaving the house gave Danielle the opportunity to speak candidly with Lily, without Walt listening in. She needed to tell Lily what she hadn't shared when Ian was at Marlow House.

TWENTY-TWO

It had been a long day. Danielle hadn't seen Max since all her guests had returned to Marlow House. She had intended to slip up to the attic and talk to Walt after everyone went to bed, but Hillary Hemingway had left the door to her room wide open.

When Danielle had passed by the open doorway a moment earlier, she noticed Hillary sitting in the easy chair, reading. If Danielle went up to the attic now, Hillary might get curious and follow her upstairs. The last thing Danielle wanted was for her curious mystery writer to catch her in the middle of a conversation with Marlow House's resident ghost. That would be extremely awkward, especially since Hillary couldn't see him.

Danielle climbed into bed, pulling the blankets up to her chest. She sat up, leaned against the headboard, and waited for Walt. Since she hadn't gone up to the attic, she expected Walt to pop into her room and say goodnight. She wanted to finish their conversation Lily and Ian had interrupted earlier. Danielle patiently waited, her hands folded neatly on her lap. Glancing up to the ceiling, she whispered, "Walt, hello? Where are you?"

After thirty minutes, Danielle could no longer keep her eyes open. Reluctantly, she leaned over and turned off the side lamp, sending her room into darkness. Scooting down in the covers, she pulled the blankets up to her chin and curled into a fetal position, closing her eyes. Within minutes, she was fast asleep.

A WOMAN LAUGHED. Danielle opened her eyes. She looked around and found herself sitting inside what appeared to be a rustic, old-fashioned saloon—yet she wasn't sitting on a chair. Where was she?

Jazz music hammered its tune on a keyboard. Danielle looked down. She sat on an upright piano, her feet dangling in front of the piano player, who seemed oblivious to her presence. Letting out a surprised yelp, she pulled up her knees and wiggled to the end of the piano. From where she perched, she had a clear view of the entire room.

A man laughed. Danielle looked to her left. Walt sat on the other end of the piano, dressed in a dark blue pin-striped suit, a lit cigar in his hand.

The sound of the piano dimmed—it was barely audible. In the background, voices and laughter blended into a faint hum.

"What do you think?" Walt asked.

Ignoring her surroundings, Danielle focused on Walt. "I was going to come upstairs to talk to you, but I couldn't. I was hoping you'd come to my room to say goodnight."

"I'm here now." He smiled.

"I wanted to tell you Emma Jackson passed away this afternoon."

Walt grinned. "Good for her."

Danielle's face broke into a smile. "Not a reaction I expected."

Walt cocked his head and shrugged. "The woman had a long, full life. She lived almost four times longer than I did, and now she can see all the people from her life who've already moved on."

"You think she'll see them?"

"That's what you're always telling me." Walt grinned. "So what do you think?"

"Where are we?" Danielle glanced around. "Is this what they call a speakeasy?"

"Yes."

She guessed there were at least thirty people—some sitting at tables or at the bar, others lingering along the wall, a few standing nearby watching the piano player, and a couple danced at the back of the room. She couldn't hear what they were saying, but they seemed to be enjoying themselves. By their dress, she knew the era was the 1920s. While she expected all the women to be dressed as flappers, with short-fringed dresses, that wasn't the case. A few were, but others were dressed in more stylish clothing of the era. One woman wore a stone marten fox stole, with the heads and feet of the poor dead foxes dangling from her shoulders.

Danielle cringed. "That's disgusting."

"What?" Walt looked in the direction of Danielle's stare.

"Those poor dead animals. Why would anyone want to drape dead foxes around their shoulders? Did they really think that was attractive?"

"That's Thelma Templeton."

Danielle wrinkled her nose. "Oh yuck. You actually had a thing with her?" If Danielle were honest with herself, she would have to admit Thelma was an attractive woman, with short coal black hair, alabaster skin, and delicate features. Tall and slender, she held a long-stemmed cigarette holder in one hand and she punctuated the air with its lit cigarette while she chatted with those around her. Yet it was Thelma's gruesome stole Danielle couldn't see past.

"I told you there was never anything between me and Thelma Templeton. I just thought it would be easier for me to prove my point if I let you see her."

Screwing up her face into a lopsided

frown, Danielle studied the woman. "Okay, I admit she is attractive. At least she would be if she got rid of that horrid fox stole."

Walt let out a sigh, his gaze still on Thelma. "I suppose you need to listen to her to understand."

Danielle shook her head. "No, no, I don't want to listen to her. I've no desire to listen to anyone who would wear something like that."

Walt chuckled. "Danielle, not to sound—as Lily calls it—sexist—but Thelma Templeton is dumb as a stump."

Danielle turned to Walt. "I suppose that explains her fashion accessory. But since when did men care about a mistress's intelligence?"

Walt glared at Danielle. "That is insulting. I expected better of you."

Danielle let out a sigh. "I'm sorry. I guess you're right. So tell me about Thelma."

"For one thing, she flirts entirely too much for a married woman. See those two men she's talking with?"

"Yes. They don't seem to have a problem with her intelligence, considering the way they're drooling all over her."

"She isn't married to either of them."

Walt pointed to a man sitting at the bar. "That's Howard Templeton."

Danielle looked to the bar. The man Walt pointed to was busy talking to the bartender, while he sipped his drink. If he was concerned over his wife's flirtatious behavior, he didn't show it.

"Explain something to me," Danielle asked.

"What's that?"

"Obviously this is a dream hop. I'm not coming up with all this myself; you're doing it. So is this place like a speakeasy you used to go to back when you were alive? Did Thelma really wear that disgusting stole, or was that something you added?"

Walt leaned back against the wall and smiled at Danielle. "I would have thought you already knew. Remember what you told me about Harvey's dream hop when you were trapped at Presley House?"

With a shudder Danielle said, "I don't want to talk about snakes."

"I'm not talking about that dream hop— or dream nightmare—Harvey put you through. I'm talking about when Harvey showed you, in a dream, how he was killed. And later, he took you to the beach to show you how they got rid of his body, and then you went to the cemetery."

"What are you saying?" Danielle asked.

"Some dream hops are nothing more than visits with a spirit that create an environment from the imagination—either mine or yours."

"Like when we go sailing or when you took me to Hawaii?"

"Exactly. Other dream hops, such as this one or the ones I just mentioned that Harvey took you on, are a little like a movie replaying what occurred in the past."

"So you're saying this speakeasy really existed, and all these people were once here, just as they are now? With Thelma flirting with those men and her husband drinking at the bar?"

"Yes. And if I'm not mistaken, in a couple of minutes I'll be walking through that door." Walt pointed to the door on the other side of the room.

"What?" Danielle looked quickly from Walt to the door.

He reached over and offered Danielle a

hand. "Let's get off this thing. This piano player keeps hammering away on my feet, and I'd like to turn the sound up so you can hear what's being said."

Danielle flashed Walt a grin as they jumped off the piano. Just as Walt said, the door opened and he walked in. He wasn't alone. Danielle recognized the other man. It was Jack. They walked together to the bar.

"This was just a week before the *Eva Aphrodite* went missing," Walt explained.

"If you can do this, couldn't you take us to the boat on the night it went down so we could see what happened?"

Walt laughed. "That would be a good trick, but no. I was actually here, which is why I'm able to recreate what happened."

"You weren't here before you walked in that door just now," Danielle reminded him.

"That's true, but if you notice, until I walked in the door with Jack, no one really moved from where they were standing or sitting. I simply created the scene as I remembered it looked when I walked in with Jack."

"Drat, I'd love to eavesdrop on Thelma, but I guess that isn't possible."

"I assume whatever we hear will be what I heard back then—not what was said out of earshot."

"Too bad. We might be able to figure out why her friend thought you two were having an affair."

"You believe me now?"

Danielle shrugged. "Well, the way you are with Sadie, I just don't see you cozying up with some woman wearing dead dogs around her neck. Maybe not dogs exactly, but close enough."

Walt chuckled. "You really do hate that stole, don't you?"

"I really do."

"Let's go over and see what Jack and I are talking about," Walt suggested.

Danielle started walking toward the bar when she paused and looked at Walt. "Wait a minute; you've never taken me on one of these types of dreams before. How did you know how to do it? That it would work?"

"After you told me about those dream hops with Harvey, I began wondering if there was more I could do with a dream hop than I imagined. Would it be possible to recreate a scene from my past, and once there, would everyone do and say what happened back then, at least what I observed when it originally occurred? So I tested it out."

"Tested it how? On who?" When Walt didn't answer, Danielle repeated the question.

"Marie. I tried it on Marie."

"You took Marie on a dream hop?"

"I figured she would just assume she was dreaming about her childhood. I slipped into her dream and took her back to when she lived across the street with her parents, when she was just a baby."

"And it worked?"

"Yes. We didn't stay long because she recognized me and began asking me all sorts of questions. It worked—but I cut it short."

"So I'm assuming she was there in the dream with you like she is today, a ninety-year-old woman, with you by her side, and in the room was her other self, her as a baby—and her parents?"

"Yes."

"Interesting. Surprising she never mentioned it."

They were about to continue on to the

bar when Thelma was suddenly by her side with one of the men she had been talking with. They paused, looking to the bar.

"Is that Walt Marlow?" Thelma asked.

The man by her side looked over. "Yeah."

"Howard and I are going out this weekend in his boat."

"Wish I could afford that," the man grumbled.

Thelma laughed. "We've gone out a number of times. Walt Marlow's never been out on the boat with us; I suppose he's too busy making moonshine in his basement." She laughed again and made her way to her husband while the man she had been talking to walked in the opposite direction.

Danielle glanced at Walt, who stared at Thelma with an odd expression.

"Improvising, Walt?" Danielle asked.

With a frown, he glanced from Thelma to Danielle. "I don't understand. I didn't hear that conversation when I was here before—I had no idea what she said back then. Look where I'm sitting at the bar. There's no way I overheard her."

"Do you think that's really what Thelma

said back then, or did you subconsciously improvise her conversation?" Danielle asked.

Confused, he stared at Thelma, who leaned against her husband, sipping her drink. "I have no idea."

TWENTY-THREE

Jack from the dream stood up, said something to the Walt sitting next to him, and then walked to the piano player.

Spirit Walt grabbed hold of Danielle's wrist and said, "This is what I wanted you to hear." He pulled her to the bar and stood next to his former self, who sat quietly, sipping a drink.

Danielle looked from the Walt sitting at the bar to the Walt at her side. "You know, you really haven't changed much."

"This was only a few years before I died."

A few seats down, Howard stood up and walked away, leaving Thelma alone. Danielle watched as Thelma's gaze followed her husband, who a moment later left the speakeasy from a door on the opposite side of the room from where Walt and Jack had entered. Once the door closed behind Howard, Thelma picked up her glass and scooted down the bar to Walt, standing by his side.

Spirit Walt and Danielle silently listened to the exchange.

"Hello, Walt Marlow?" Thelma asked in a flirtatious tone.

Walt turned to her, a bored expression on his face. "Yes?"

"I'm Thelma Templeton. We met at Sissy Bancoff's party."

Walt nodded. "Yes, I know who you are. You're Howard's wife."

Sipping her drink, she let out an exaggerated sigh. "Howard had to leave. He had some silly appointment."

When Walt didn't respond, she leaned toward him and asked, "Howard and I are going out on your boat this weekend, and I was wondering, will you be on board?"

Walt studied her a moment and then took

a sip of his drink before saying, "No. I've a prior appointment."

Thelma's gaze darted to her right. She spied Jack walking back in their direction. In a rush, she reached out and touched Walt's right hand, which rested on the bar top, still holding his drink. Expressionless, his gaze looked down at her hand on his.

"Maybe sometime you could take me out on it, a private cruise. Just the two of us. We could go now."

Walt jerked his hand from her touch and took a swig of his drink. He then looked Thelma in the eyes. "The *Eva Aphrodite* always has a full crew. It will never be just the two of us."

Thelma looked as if she had been slapped. The next moment, Jack reached the bar as Thelma abruptly turned from Walt. Not saying a word to either man, she rushed away, abandoning her drink on the bar top. She retreated to a friendlier section of the speakeasy.

"Wow, you were cold," Danielle said with a chuckle. "I don't think I've ever seen you look at anyone with that expression of contempt before."

"What was that all about?" Jack asked. Leaning an elbow against the bar top, he glanced across the room to where Thelma had landed. She stood alone by the piano player, watching him play.

"Dumb Dora at it again." Walt chuckled.

"It was only a matter of time before she got around to you." Jack snickered.

"No thanks." Walt downed the rest of his drink.

Jack glanced over to Thelma. He picked up Thelma's forgotten drink. The glass was half-full. "I think she forgot something."

Walt turned to Jack and frowned. "You aren't serious?"

Jack shrugged and then said with a laugh, "Unlike you, I like them dumb."

Danielle watched Walt's reaction—the Walt sitting at the bar, not the spirit Walt at her side. He didn't seem overly concerned with his friend's intentions and ordered another drink.

"So you really didn't know each other very well?" Danielle asked.

"I knew who she was. Her reputation wasn't a secret in our circles. Sissy Bancoff's party wasn't the first time we'd run into each other. Just the first time we'd exchanged more than ten words."

Danielle looked across the room to where Jack now stood with Thelma. He had just handed her the drink.

"So did they get together?" Danielle asked.

"Watch," Walt said with a brief chuckle.

Danielle watched, and a moment later Thelma and Jack walked through the same doorway her husband had gone through not that long ago.

"Shouldn't we follow them? See what they're saying? Maybe we'll find a clue to what happened on the *Eva Aphrodite*. There must be some reason Jack's spirit went to the wreckage."

"And you're the one who's always telling me I can't snoop on the guests when they're in their bedrooms." Walt laughed.

Ignoring Walt's comment, Danielle grabbed him by the hand and started dragging him toward the doorway Thelma and

Jack had just gone through. Walt went along without protest. When they reached the door, Danielle tried opening it, but her hand went through the doorknob, as when ghosts try, without success, to grab hold of an object.

"Just walk through the door, I think that will work," Walt suggested.

Danielle glanced back at Walt, her hand still holding his. "Really?"

Walt gave her a nod. With a shrug, Danielle took Walt's suggestion. Together, she and Walt moved effortlessly through the wooden door.

Once on the other side, nothing was as Danielle had expected. They were no longer inside, and any sign of the speakeasy had vanished. Instead, they stood in open space, as if walking on clouds.

"What happened?" Danielle looked around. "Where did they go? Where's the door we just walked through?"

"That speakeasy has several entrances. I know the door we just went through leads to another room and then to the outside. Jack usually enters that way, I never did."

Danielle looked around again. "So they're just gone?"

Walt shrugged. "I'm sorry, Danielle. Like you, I don't know how all this works. This rather proves my original assumption; I can't recreate what once happened unless I was present at the time."

"But we heard what Thelma said about you to that man. It was a conversation you'd never heard before."

"True. But my former self was sitting just a few feet away. Perhaps that makes a difference."

"Did Jack ever tell you what happened between him and Thelma?'"

Walt shook his head. "I never asked. Frankly, I didn't really care."

"I thought Jack was seeing someone? Some woman who lived at a local motel with her aunt and uncle."

Walt shrugged. "He was."

Danielle rolled her eyes. "That dog."

AFTER BREAKFAST ON SUNDAY

MORNING, Danielle walked her guests out the front door. Hillary Hemingway planned to do some sightseeing. The couple from Portland was staying another night, and they were on their way to the pier. Danielle told them it was an easy walk, but Mrs. Sterling didn't seem inclined to walking. Danielle stood by her front swing and watched them drive off—the Sterlings in their car, and Hillary in hers. She was just about to go back into the house when another vehicle pulled up in front of Marlow House and parked. It was Chief MacDonald.

"Morning, Chief!" Danielle greeted him. She noted he wore street clothes, not his uniform, and the car he had been driving was his own, not a squad car.

"Morning, Danielle. I'm glad to catch you outside," the chief said when he reached her.

"Outside, what do you mean?"

He glanced up to the attic window. "I wanted to talk to you without Walt listening in."

"About Walt, you were wrong," she insisted.

"Can we talk?" he asked.

"Sure, but we can go in the house."

He shook his head. "No. I don't want him listening in."

Danielle let out a sigh and then motioned to the porch swing. Together she and the chief sat down.

"You were wrong about Walt. He wasn't having an affair with Thelma. They barely knew each other." Danielle's toe of her right foot lightly pushed against the ground, keeping the swing in gentle motion.

"Danielle, you need to read the diary. I know Walt is your friend, but—"

"Would you hear me out, Chief?"

"Okay, what do you have?"

Danielle went on to tell the chief about her dream hop the previous night. When she was finished, the chief looked at her a moment before commenting.

"That's it? That's why you don't think he was Thelma's lover?"

"They barely knew each other. This all happened just days before the *Eva Aphrodite* went missing. You weren't there; there's no way those two were having an affair."

"Maybe you weren't there either."

Danielle frowned. "What do you mean?"

"It was a dream, Danielle. What makes you think it was any less make-believe than the other dream hops he's taken you on. It was fantasy."

"My Christmas dream was not just make-believe," she insisted, her expression somber.

"Maybe that one wasn't. But you have to admit, this really proves nothing. I can believe it possible for spirits to visit you, like in your Christmas dream. But for Walt to conjure up something that happened in his past, and then it plays back like a recording, even playing back something Walt never heard in his life, no. I don't believe that. He created that dream and everyone that was in it. He wrote the script. It proves nothing."

Danielle pushed her right foot on the ground, stopping the swing. "You're wrong. And I'll prove it."

"I didn't come here to argue with you."

Danielle looked at him, her expression hostile. "Why did you come?"

"We found more skeletons on the ship. But one was different. It was in a trunk."

"Yeah, Stella mentioned that."

"Stella?" He frowned.

"One of our guests. She and her husband were down at the beach, watching when your guys were taking a trunk off the boat. They overheard one of your people saying something about finding another body."

"Unlike the others, his skeleton was still intact. He wasn't shot in the head. Looks like they got him in the chest. We found a bullet under his rib cage."

"You're sure it was a man?"

"That was our initial feeling based on the clothing remnants we found in the trunk. But the coroner confirmed it." The chief reached into his pocket and pulled out a small plastic bag. "We're hoping this might help us identify him." He handed the small transparent bag to Danielle. It contained a man's ring. Holding the baggie in her hand, she stared, speechless.

"It's a Masonic ring," he explained. "We've contacted the local lodge, hoping they might be able to help us. No one with those initials was listed on the passenger list."

Still staring at the ring in the bag, she asked, "You mentioned there was some fabric

—from his clothes. Can you tell me what kind of fabric? Color, anything?"

"Pin-striped fabric. Looked gray, but it might have been blue at one time. There are initials inside the ring; that should help."

Clutching the bag in her hand, Danielle said, "J.W."

"Excuse me?"

"The initials are J.W."

The chief frowned. "How did you know that? There's no way you saw the initials."

"Because I've already met the spirit attached to the body you found. It's Jack Winters, Walt's business partner who disappeared with their money at the same time the *Eva Aphrodite* went missing. He's the one I saw on the boat, the one I talked to. This is his ring. I saw it on him—the spirit him." Danielle handed the small bag back to the chief.

"Did Walt murder his business partner?"

Danielle let out a groan. "Don't go there, Chief."

"Obviously, there is nothing I can do about Walt. I just worry about you and Lily."

Danielle stood up. "I'm going to figure this out and you can stop worrying."

TWENTY-FOUR

Danielle pulled up in front of Marie's house and parked her car. After the chief had left that morning, Danielle had asked herself how she could prove to the chief that he was wrong about last night's dream hop—that Walt hadn't written Thelma's script. Unfortunately, the chief was right. The dream hop could have been entirely of Walt's making. It was impossible to prove otherwise.

The only thing she might be able to prove was the possibility of that type of dream hop —one where a spirit replays an unedited version of the past. There was only one way

Danielle could prove the possibility; Marie needed to confirm Walt's claim that he had visited her in a dream to test his theory. If Marie recalled the dream he had described, Danielle would use that information to try to convince the chief to see it her way.

Danielle knew Walt was telling the truth. Never for a moment did she ever consider the possibility Walt was involved with those people's deaths. As for having an affair with Thelma—she understood that was possible. When married to Lucas, Danielle never imagined for a moment he would have an affair. She had been wrong.

However, the visit to the speakeasy convinced her Walt was telling the truth. Perhaps the chief didn't trust Walt; she did.

"I'm glad you stopped by," Marie told Danielle when she led her into the living room a few minutes later. Danielle had called Marie before coming over, which explained the hot pot of tea sitting on the coffee table along with two empty teacups and a platter of cookies.

Danielle took a seat on the sofa. "I wanted to tell you about Emma Jackson."

"I already heard." Marie picked up the teapot.

"You did?"

Marie filled the two cups with tea. She then picked up one with its saucer and handed it to Danielle. "Yes. Mathew called me this morning right after you called."

"I guess there won't be a funeral." Danielle sipped her tea.

Marie sat on a chair facing the sofa, holding her cup of tea, its saucer sitting on her lap. "You know, after your open house, Emma and I became rather good friends. We would talk on the phone every day."

"I guess she went peacefully."

"Yes. That's how I want to go. Of course, after Adam gets married."

Danielle laughed. "Then you're going to live forever!"

"You may be right." Marie picked up the platter of cookies and offered one to Danielle.

"By the way, I met Jolene Carmichael yesterday at the museum."

"Really? I knew she was back in town. Millie mentioned they were going to try to get her to fill a board vacancy."

"Well, we didn't exactly hit it off." Danielle nibbled on the cookie.

"Jolene could be a little opinionated, from what I recall."

Danielle went on to tell Marie about yesterday's visit to the museum. When she was finished, Marie set her teacup and saucer on the coffee table while spouting a few tsk, tsk, tsks. "I don't blame you for not donating the emerald right now. Ungrateful bunch, if you ask me."

"To be honest, the rest of them were pretty nice, and I did feel bad about it. But I'm just not sure how I feel about them selling the emerald. Maybe they could have made their case, but I'm not really sure they intended to be up front with me. If Jolene hadn't said something, would they have?"

"I thought you just said they were nice?"

"Well, they were. Just not sure how forthright they were."

Marie leaned forward and patted Danielle's hand. "Now perhaps you understand why I avoid getting too involved with that group."

"You know, they talked with Lily about

having her do some educational programs for the museum with the area schools. But when Lily went down there to talk to them about it, nothing really came of it aside from the fact they hit her up for a donation."

Marie gave Danielle a knowing nod. "It's that settlement Lily got from Stoddard's estate. Impossible to keep things like that secret in this little town."

"Then I suppose I did the right thing. I'll loan the emerald to the museum for the exhibit. At least for the time being."

"That's probably for the best, dear."

Danielle shifted in her seat, uncrossing and recrossing her legs. Licking her lips, she looked over at Marie. "After yesterday's visit to the museum, and the way they're so cavalier with the truth regarding Walt Marlow's death—well—I dreamt about him last night."

"You dreamt about Walt Marlow?" Marie's face broke out into a grin. "What was the dream about?"

"Oh, I don't know. We were sitting in the library together—reading. Yes, we were reading," she lied.

"Now that you mention it, I dreamt about Walt Marlow not that long ago."

"You did?"

Marie nodded. "Not sure why I dreamt about him. He looked just like he did in his portrait, yet perhaps better looking. I remember mother telling me he was a handsome man. Such a shame he died at such a young age. It was really an odd dream."

"Odd how?"

"We were in my parents' house—the one Ian lives in, across from you. I was just a baby."

"You were a baby in the dream?" Danielle asked.

Marie smiled. "Yes and no. I was as I am now. But there was also a baby in the dream, and the baby was me. Walt was there. Actually, two Walt Marlows."

"Two?"

Marie laughed. "Are you sure you want to hear about an old woman's dream?"

Danielle leaned forward and set her teacup and saucer on the coffee table. "Oh yes! I really do."

Marie laughed again and then continued.

"It reminded me a little of Dickens' *Christmas Carol*, where the ghost takes Scrooge back to see his past. In this case, I was Scrooge and Walt was the ghost. My father was there, sitting on the sofa, holding a baby—me—in his arms. I knew it was me. The way they were talking, I could tell it was the first time Walt had seen me. My mother walked into the room and asked Father if he was going to let Walt hold me. Walt's expression was priceless. For a moment, I imagined he was going to leap from the sofa. He told Father, 'Babies scare me.'" Marie laughed.

"Then what happened?"

"I wanted to know why I was there, watching this. I started asking Walt, the Walt by my side not the Walt sitting on the sofa with my father, why we were there. And then, well, then I woke up."

"Interesting," Danielle murmured.

"I suppose I understand the dream; I'd heard that story from both of my parents a dozen times."

"What story?"

"After I was born and Walt Marlow saw me for the first time, my mother asked him if he wanted to hold me, and he looked appalled at the idea." Marie laughed again. "He told my parents babies scared him. My mother often wondered how he would have been as a father had he ever had children of his own."

"I think he would have been a good father," Danielle murmured.

"You know what's peculiar?" Marie asked.

"What?"

"I normally forget my dreams right after I wake up. But I can still remember this one clearly, every detail."

"Some dreams are like that."

"Perhaps. Silly dream, though. Not sure what it meant, if anything. Was there some significance to Walt and me making a Dickens-like appearance, showing up in an old story my parents used to tell me? Or had I simply eaten ice cream too late that night?"

IT WAS lunchtime when Danielle returned to Marlow House. She found Joanne vacuuming in the parlor. The moment Danielle walked in the room, Joanne turned off the vacuum.

"I thought I'd clean up in here while everyone is out," Joanne explained.

"So you're alone?" *Except of course for Walt —and Max.*

"Yes, and enjoying the solitude. That Mrs. Sterling certainly has a lot to say."

Danielle chuckled. "She does. I'll leave you to your solitude; I need to look for something in the attic."

"I imagine you'll find Max up there," Joanne said right before she turned the vacuum back on and returned to her work.

"I'VE BEEN WONDERING why the chief was here and where you took off to," Walt said when Danielle entered the attic a few minutes later.

"Stella mentioned that when she and her husband were down at the beach, looking at the *Eva Aphrodite*, the police pulled a trunk from the ship, and for some reason she thought there was a body inside. Or at least the remains of one."

"Yes. So?"

"She was right. And I think I know who it was." Danielle took a seat on the sofa and looked at Walt, who remained standing by the spotting scope at the window.

"Who?"

"Jack."

"Jack? How would his body get on board?"

"Apparently you were wrong. Jack didn't run off; he was on that boat when all those people were killed. And he was killed too."

Shaking his head in disbelief, Walt walked from the window and took a seat next to Danielle on the sofa.

"From what Jack said, he wasn't on the boat when he died. For some reason his spirit went there. Maybe he can't remember how he died, but wouldn't he remember getting on the boat before he was murdered?" Walt asked.

"Perhaps he was killed somewhere else. Brought to the boat in the trunk. The chief speculates he was shot in the chest, since they found a bullet on the bottom of the trunk, right below his rib cage."

"Why are you so sure it's Jack? I'd have to

assume that after all this time, all that's left of him are his skeletal remains."

"There was fabric left from his clothes—blue pinstripe."

"Not so uncommon," Walt noted.

"True. But he was also wearing a ring. A Masonic ring with the initials J.W."

Walt let out a low whistle and sat back in the sofa, absorbing all that Danielle was telling him. "He was killed on the boat."

"Why do you say that?" Danielle asked.

"I just don't see how someone could get a trunk on board—or why they would. It doesn't make sense. We're talking about a cruise where our passengers returned within twenty-four hours."

"Was there a trunk on board?"

Walt considered the question a moment. "Yes."

"Which probably means Jack was killed on board, like the rest of them. But why was he there?" Danielle asked.

Walt stood up and waved his hand, summoning a lit cigar. "Perhaps he was meeting Thelma there, which would explain why he didn't tell me he was going out on the boat."

"Why would he meet Thelma there? Her husband was on the boat."

Walt turned to Danielle and arched his brow. "If you'll recall, Thelma made it perfectly clear what her intentions were should I join them on the *Eva Aphrodite*."

"But she asked you about going on a private cruise at a later date."

Walt shook his head. "That was after she asked—in her coy way—if I would be on the *Eva Aphrodite* when they were. It was pretty clear to me she was more than willing for us to slip away for an illicit rendezvous while her husband was on board. The yacht had plenty of rooms for someone to find a quiet place away from the rest of the crew and passengers for an illicit meeting. And when I turned her down, she focused her attention on Jack."

"Why wouldn't he have told you about going out on the boat that day? Why keep it a secret? After all, you were with him when they took off together."

"True. But Jack also knew I didn't approve of mixing that type of pleasure with business. We didn't need that kind of grief should Howard happen upon Jack and his wife, especially on board my boat, where Jack's a partner in the business venture. No. If Jack did something that reckless, he wouldn't have told me."

"I suppose I should go down and talk to him."

With a wave of his hand, the cigar vanished. Walt looked at Danielle with a solemn expression. "Please tell Jack to come see me. This changes everything. Tell him I want to apologize."

"Apologize?"

"For thinking he took off with that money. I'll be honest, I feel awful about that. All these years, imagining he had betrayed our friendship that way. I should have looked into it more."

"So what happened to the money? You said it wasn't where he normally kept it hidden."

"I don't know. But if he went out on that boat, then he must have moved it like he said. It may still be out there somewhere. Maybe even across the street."

TWENTY-FIVE

Sadie's wet nose persistently nudged Lily's left arm. Sitting in the passenger seat of Ian's car, Lily glanced back at the dog. "No, Sadie. This isn't for you."

The golden retriever stood on the floorboard, squeezed into the narrow space behind Ian's and Lily's seats. Her butt moved with her tail, repetitively bumping the back of Ian's car seat. Sadie wanted what Lily had on her lap: a sack of hamburgers they were bringing home from the local drive-through.

"Sadie, on the backseat," Ian snapped.

Letting out a defeated whimper, Sadie climbed onto the backseat and lay down, her chin resting on her front paws. She continued to stare forward, looking into the opening between the front seats, her attention focused on what she knew was on Lily's lap.

Glancing over at Marlow House as Ian pulled into his driveway, Lily said, "Looks like Dani's home. I wonder if I should have asked her if she wanted us to pick her up something."

"She probably ate while she was out," Ian said as he parked the car and turned off the ignition.

When they walked into Ian's house a few moments later, Sadie lost interest in what was in the paper sacks. Instead, she rushed inside, headed for the living room, and started barking.

Ian followed his dog into the house and stood by the entrance to the living room. He watched as Sadie stared at the back wall, barking and wagging her tail. "Sometimes that dog does the craziest things. What does she think she's barking at?"

Lily walked into the living room and set the sacks of food on the coffee table. She watched Sadie, who was now sitting down, her tail wagging as she continued to stare at the blank wall. "Has she been doing that a lot lately?"

"Just the last couple of days. I wonder, do you think we have mice in the walls or something?"

Still staring at Sadie, Lily shrugged and muttered under her breath, "Or something."

"I'll be right back." Ian turned and headed for the bathroom, shaking his head while muttering, "Crazy dog."

Lily walked to Sadie and stood by her side. Staring at the spot holding the dog's attention, Lily reached down and patted Sadie's neck. "Whatcha see, girl? Hmm…" Lily smiled. "Is that you, Jack? Have you been hanging out over here?"

WHEN DANIELLE ARRIVED at the site of the *Eva Aphrodite*, she was surprised to discover there was no longer a police car parked by the street, nor did there seem to be anyone guarding the area. The wreckage remained taped off, yet one section had come unfastened and flapped flag-like along the sand. Notices to keep off the boat were posted along the lower section of the hull. Those were new; she hadn't seen them the last time she had been to the wreckage site.

Standing some twenty feet from the bow, she looked up, searching for Jack along the upper deck. Raising her right hand to her brow, she used it to shade her eyes from the sunshine as she looked for him.

A flash of light along a section of remaining railing on the upper deck caught her attention. Focusing on the area, she watched as a faint image of a person began to materialize. To her surprise, the transparent image was not Jack. It was Thelma Templeton staring down at her.

Startled, Danielle gasped and took a step back, her eyes never leaving the ghostly image. In the next moment Howard Templeton appeared. He stood next to his wife, and then another one appeared and another. Lined up along the top deck were transparent images of what Danielle imagined were once the passengers and crew of the *Eva Aphrodite*'s last voyage. Motionless, they stared down at her.

Just as suddenly as they appeared—they vanished.

"Rather unnerving, isn't it?" a voice from behind her asked.

Danielle swung around abruptly, coming face-to-face with Jack. She could feel her heart racing. Taking a deep breath, she asked, "How long have they been here?"

Jack shrugged. "They showed up right after the last time I talked to Walt. Is it possible for a ghost to be haunted?" Now standing by Danielle's side, he looked up at the boat; there was no sign of the spirits.

"What do you mean?" she asked.

"I'm a ghost, right?"

"Umm…yeah. I don't get your question."

Casually tucking his hands into his pants' pockets, he stared up at the wreckage as he talked. "Reminded me a little of a picture show. I can remember going to the theater; sometimes the film would just flicker, and sometimes too much light would come through. Not sure if the film was damaged or the guy in the projection room did something wrong. But that's what they rather remind me of. They just appear like that, all lined up.

And then, they're gone. They don't say anything. Don't even acknowledge me in any way. I have to wonder, can they even see me? Are they really there—in the same way I am?"

"So they just sort of appear and then go away?"

Jack nodded. "I don't even want to come down here anymore. I know I need to move on, but I'm not really sure how. And…I don't think I can."

"Where were you when I first got here?" she asked. "I didn't see you on the beach."

Jack shrugged. "I've been hanging out over at George's house. It's familiar. Plus, over there I have someone I can talk to."

Danielle smiled. "Sadie?"

"Strange how that works. I never had a dog. Figured keeping one as a pet was for old people who wanted company. I understood work dogs, like ones that herd sheep, but as pets? Why?" Jack shook his head. "I think I was wrong. Dogs are a hell of a lot smarter than I ever imagined. And better than most people I know."

Danielle laughed. "Well, I would have to

agree with you there. Walt's rather fond of Sadie too."

"Yeah, she told me."

"Walt wants to see you."

"Why? So he can tell me what a disappointment I am as a friend? No thanks."

"I think he wants to apologize."

Jack looked at Danielle with a frown. "Apologize, for what?"

"For thinking the worse of you. For not realizing you'd never steal from him."

"Are you saying Walt now believes me?"

"Jack, were you down here when the police took a trunk off the ship?"

Jack shook his head. "No. As I said, I don't like coming down here. Not since they showed up."

"Have you been able to remember anything about how you died or where you were at the time?"

"No. I remember going to pick up Sally. But that's all I can really remember. It gets all hazy after that."

"Sally was your girlfriend, right?"

"She was a doll I was seeing."

"Like you were seeing Thelma Templeton?"

Jack turned to Danielle. "What about Thelma?"

"I know how she tried to pick up Walt at a speakeasy, and when he declined, you decided to step in."

Jack let out a snort. "I can't believe he told you about that."

"In a manner of speaking," Danielle mumbled.

"Nothing happened between me and Thelma."

"But you left with her."

Jack shrugged. "Yeah, we walked out together, but when we stepped outside, her husband, Howard, was standing there, waiting. She looked surprised to see him. I made some excuse, like I just happened to walk out at the same time, and then I went home. That was the last time I saw her."

"So you didn't go on the *Eva Aphrodite* to see her again?"

Jack laughed. "With her husband on board? I don't think so. Risky enough seeing a married woman, no reason to be stupid about it. A cuckolded husband won't spend any time behind bars for killing his wife's lover."

"So you don't remember anything about getting on the boat that night?"

"Why do you keep asking me that? I think I'd remember getting on the *Eva Aphrodite* that night. So it probably wasn't when I was still alive. Not sure why my spirit was sent to that boat. Hell if I know. Maybe God supported prohibition and wanted to teach me a lesson."

"I think you were killed on board the *Eva Aphrodite*."

"Why do you say that?"

"Because the other day the police found your body—what was left of it. Your skeletal remains were found in a trunk on board the wreckage. It still had your ring." Danielle pointed to his right hand. "Your ring was in the trunk with the body. And according to Walt, that trunk was already on board. You were shot. They think in the chest, maybe the stomach. Somewhere lethal. The bullet was also in the trunk."

"I was shot? Who would shoot me?"

"I don't know. That's what I'd like to find out."

Taking his hands out of his pockets, he combed his fingers through his hair. "I don't know why anyone would want to kill me."

"Jack, everyone on board the *Eva Aphrodite* was murdered, each shot in the head. Their skulls were found scattered around the ship. You were the only one hidden, stuffed in a trunk."

TWENTY-SIX

"Have you always been able to see people like me?" Jack asked Danielle as they walked back to Marlow House.

"Probably. But the first time I was aware of it was when I saw my grandmother at her funeral. I was just a little girl at the time."

"How did you end up at Marlow House?" he asked.

"When Walt died, his estate went to Katherine O'Malley."

Jack stopped walking. He looked at Danielle, who stopped after he did. "Who's Katherine O'Malley?"

"She was his housekeeper at the time."

"Must have been one good housekeeper." Jack snorted.

"I think Walt may have felt a little sorry for her. She was an unwed mother and had a young daughter. That daughter married my grandfather's brother. She was my great-aunt by marriage. She left me her estate, which included Marlow House."

"Don't tell me the little girl was Walt's!" Jack asked in surprise.

"Are you talking about my aunt?"

"What other little girl was there?"

"Are you suggesting Walt hired his mistress after she had his illegitimate child, and then made her be his housekeeper?" Danielle asked incredulously.

"It certainly doesn't sound like the Walt I knew. But he did leave his estate to her, and he did jump to the conclusion I stole that money, so maybe he was never the Walt I thought he was."

Danielle started walking. "No, Katherine was not his mistress. Walt changed his will after he got married so—"

"Walt married? I suppose that shouldn't surprise me, but it does. How many children did he have? I always imagined I'd have children someday."

"No children. Walt died just a few years after you, in 1925. He met his wife, and within a year he was married and murdered."

Jack stopped again. "Walt was murdered too?"

Danielle paused and glanced up at Marlow House. It was only one door down. "Yes, by his brother-in-law, at Marlow House. Made it look like a suicide."

"Why did he do it? What happened to the wife?"

IAN STOOD at his front window and watched Danielle as she walked up the other side of the street. She had just paused in front of the house next door to Marlow House.

"Lily, I'm not sure that Bluetooth headphone was such a terrific idea for Danielle."

Lily walked over to the window, stood

next to Ian, and looked outside. "What do you mean?"

"It looks like she's walking up the street, talking to herself."

Lily peeked behind her and spied Sadie, who was busy attacking the dog bone Ian had given her five minutes earlier. Glancing around the room before turning back to the window, Lily smiled to herself. *I've a feeling I know who Dani's talking to, and it's no one on the phone.*

WHEN DANIELLE REACHED her front door, Hillary pulled up in front of Marlow House and parked her car. As Danielle and Jack stepped inside, Walt was waiting for them in the entry.

Danielle wanted to go with Walt and Jack and see what they had to say. She was naturally curious. Yet Joanne stepped into the entry as soon as she closed the front door, making it impossible for her to continue her conversation with Jack or to engage in one with Walt. The two spirits disappeared, and a moment later Hillary walked through the front door.

Slipping off to the attic to see what the two ghosts were saying proved to be more challenging than Danielle had imagined. She spent the next hour talking to Hillary, who wanted to know everything about Marlow House's history. By her questions, it was obvious she had already read every online article mentioning Marlow House, including what Ian had written. Yet that didn't stop her from seeking more details.

When Hillary finally excused herself and went up to her room, Chris called. Danielle spent the next hour alone in the parlor, talking to Chris on the phone and updating him on all that had happened since their last phone call.

Finally off the phone, Danielle stepped out of the parlor and came face-to-face with Stella, who informed her Rowland wasn't feeling well and had gone to their room to lie down. Stella was sure it was food poisoning.

"I told him not to eat those fish and chips. Too greasy."

Danielle chose not to remind Stella she

had also eaten the fish and chips and wasn't sick; she didn't want her surly guest to start pointing her finger at Marlow House's kitchen. Danielle suspected Rowland had feigned illness to get a break from his harpy wife.

IT WAS after 9 p.m. on Sunday. Lily had gone up to bed, Rowland was asleep in the downstairs bedroom, and Danielle managed to slip away from Stella, who was now watching television alone in the living room. Since Stella had no reason to come upstairs, Danielle decided to take this opportunity to slip up to the attic and see how Jack and Walt's reunion was going. Fortunately, the door to Hillary's room was closed.

"I'm surprised you stayed away so long," Walt greeted Danielle when she came into the attic. He sat with Jack on the sofa; each had a thin lit cigar.

Danielle's eyes went immediately to the cigar in Jack's hand. "You figured out how to do it?"

Jack took a puff and said, "These really aren't bad. I always preferred cigarettes, but this will do."

"If you weren't already dead, I'd be tempted to lecture you on the dangers of smoking," Danielle said as she perched herself on one arm of the sofa while waving away the influx of cigar smoke.

"Finally an advantage to being dead!" Jack said cheerfully before taking another puff.

"Have you two figured out what happened to Jack?" Danielle asked.

"The last thing he remembers is going to the motel; everything else is basically a blur until he remembers being on board the *Eva Aphrodite*."

"What about the money?" Danielle asked.

"If you're talking about the money Walt thought I stole—"

"I apologized for that," Walt reminded Jack.

"Fair enough," Jack said with a shrug. He then addressed his answer to Danielle. "It has to be where I left it. Unless of course, someone found it."

"And where would that be?" Danielle asked. "According to Walt, he looked for it at the Hemmings house when you went missing, and it wasn't there."

"Yes, but I moved it. Walt was concerned someone would break into George's place, and they'd find my hiding place. I didn't understand why bringing it over here would make any difference."

Walt stood up. "You always had to argue over everything."

Jack frowned up at Walt. "It's true. What difference would it have made, here or across the street? As long as it was well hidden."

"Where you put it was the first place a crook would look," Walt said.

"Which is why I moved it, to show you I could find an excellent hiding space."

"Which was where?" Danielle asked.

"That's the problem. He can't remember." Walt laughed.

"You can't remember?" Danielle asked.

"That's not entirely true. I'm sure it's somewhere at George's."

"Are you saying there's over a million dollars' worth of gold hidden across the street at Ian's?" Danielle asked.

Jack frowned. "Who said anything about a million dollars? It was only a couple thousand dollars."

"Wasn't it in gold coin?" Danielle asked.

Jack shrugged. "Sure, so what?"

Danielle laughed. "Because about ten years after you were killed, the United States government made it illegal to hold gold coins or bullion. It was all recalled and melted down. It's legal to own gold coins today, and that money you hid is now worth a fortune. That's assuming it's still hidden and wasn't melted down."

Jack shrugged and puffed his cigar. "Over a million, you say?"

"I think so."

Jack watched the smoke from his cigar swirl upwards. "If I knew it was worth so much, I would've looked for it when I was at George's. Although, not sure what good it'll do me now."

"Do you think it's possible George found the treasure?" Danielle asked.

"If he did, it wasn't before I was killed. George knew about the missing money, and he would have given it back to me if he had found it."

"Marie has never mentioned anything about finding a hidden treasure at her parents' house. As for Adam…" Danielle began to laugh. "Oh my, Adam would be so busy buying crazy things with that money; I can't imagine him keeping something like that to himself. Unless, of course, he was afraid he might lose it."

"You think Adam found the money?" Walt asked.

Danielle considered the question a moment. "I find that rather hard to believe."

"You find what hard to believe? And why are you up here alone talking to yourself?" Stella asked as she walked into the attic and looked around.

Danielle's heart lurched at the unexpected visitor. She abruptly stood. "Stella, what are you doing up here?"

"I was wondering the same thing about you." Stella glanced around the room. "Who were you talking to?"

"I...I was just talking to myself," Danielle stammered.

"I thought you said you were going to bed?"

"I just came up here to see if I turned off the lights."

Stella started walking around the room, curiously peeking into each corner and nook. "And you decided to stay and talk to yourself?"

Danielle started walking toward the door. "Did you need me for something?"

"No, I was just bored down there alone. Rowland is snoring away. Thought I'd check out the attic. This is the room where you found that necklace, isn't it?"

Danielle looked helplessly at Walt and Jack, who responded with shrugs. She spent the next twenty minutes answering Stella's questions and showing her where she had found the necklace. Finally, she convinced Stella she needed to close up the attic and go to bed; it was getting late.

Begrudgingly, Stella made her way down from the attic with Danielle. When she wanted to continue talking, Danielle reminded her that Lily and Hillary were asleep in their rooms, and if they talked, they might wake them up.

As Stella made her way down the stairs from the second floor to the first, Danielle went to her bedroom. Her plan was to return to the attic after she was convinced Stella had gone to bed for the night. There was also the possibility Jack and Walt would simply come to her room to resume the conversation. In the meantime, she decided to lie down on her bed and close her eyes. Just for a couple of minutes.

BACK AND FORTH—BACK and forth. She was in a swing. Danielle opened her eyes. No, she wasn't in a swing; she was sitting in a rocking chair.

"It's nice out here, don't you think?" A soft accented voice came from Danielle's right —it was Emma Jackson. The centenarian sat in a rocking chair on the front porch of what appeared to be her Astoria home. Emma's chair was just a few feet from Danielle's.

Smiling contently, Emma leaned back in the rocker. The lines once creasing her chocolate complexion blurred into a soft haze, the skin appearing younger as the moments lingered on.

"Emma?" Danielle said in surprise. She stopped rocking and leaned out to touch Emma's arm.

Emma stilled her chair for a moment to give Danielle's hand a pat and then resumed rocking. "Good to see you, child. They said you wouldn't be surprised by my visit. You know this isn't a regular dream, don't you?"

"It's a dream hop," Danielle said in a quiet voice.

Emma laughed. "Is that what you call it? I used to call it my Emmett dreams."

"Emmett? Your husband?"

Emma nodded. "After Emmett died, he'd visit me in my dreams. I always knew they weren't regular dreams. My Emmett was there to comfort me. He was a good man. I'll be joining him soon. But first, we've work to do."

"Work? Why are you here?"

"I always knew there was something special about you. You've the gift. My mama had the gift, yes, she did. I never did, aside from Emmett's visits."

"You know I can see…and talk to…spirits?"

Emma nodded. "Yes. They're all in an uproar. Now that the *Eva Aphrodite* has resurfaced, they want the truth to come out."

"They? Are you talking about the people who died on the boat?"

Emma shrugged. "That's who I figure they are. All yelling and shouting, wanting to be heard."

"I saw them on the boat, down at the beach. They were standing on the top deck. I assumed that's who they were; I recognized several of them from photographs in the old newspaper articles. Why didn't they talk to me then?"

Emma shook her head. "They can't. They've all moved over to the other side and can barely make themselves known to someone like you. Instead, they have to work through someone like me—a newly arrived spirit. And I can't move on until they've settled down."

"So what do we have to do?"

"I was hoping you'd know that. It's nice to see you, Danielle, but I want to move on and be with my Emmett; he's been waiting for me for such a long time."

TWENTY-SEVEN

"Are they giving you a message to pass on to me?" Danielle asked Emma's spirit.

"No, child. They're telling me to show you. But show you what? I don't know what they want."

Danielle considered the possibilities and then asked, "This may seem obvious, but have you asked them what they want you to show me?"

Emma laughed. "Oh, dear, if it were just that easy! No, they're not answering my questions. I just know they want me to show you something, and until I do, I'll be stuck here."

Danielle stopped rocking and focused her

attention on Emma. "If they're telling you to show me something, maybe it's something you saw back then. Something they want me to see."

Emma shook her head. "I don't know what that would be. I really didn't know any of those people."

"But you knew about the *Eva Aphrodite* going down in the storm."

"Sure, everyone knew about it. There were stories back then. How Walt Marlow would take those rich folks out to party or meet the big ship that came down from Canada. I can't remember none of those folks, the ones that died that night, ever coming into the Bluebell Diner. Aside from my work at the diner, I kept away from the white folks back then."

"Maybe it was something you saw happen with Walt Marlow. I know you ran into him from time to time."

Emma considered the question. Finally, she shook her head. "No, girl. I can't think of a single thing I ever saw Mr. Marlow do that'd shed light on any of this. From what I remember, he'd just come into the diner from time to time, was always polite." Emma smiled softly. "I wonder if I'll get to see Mr. Marlow when I pass over. I'd like to tell him thank you."

"Thank you? For what?"

"He was always very respectful when I waited on him. Treated me just like he treated the white waitresses. But I'll tell you, girl, some of those customers back then didn't treat the white girls much better. Plenty of the men who came into the Bluebell didn't think twice about giving one of the girls a smack on her backside. Felt it was their right. Mr. Marlow wasn't like that. No siree, he was a gentleman, that one."

Danielle smiled. "I can see Walt being a gentleman."

Emma arched her brows. "Walt?"

Danielle shrugged. "Walt is sorta haunting Marlow House. Has been since he was killed there. By the way, he always appreciated your help in proving that his brother-in-law could've been responsible for his death instead of it being a suicide."

Tossing back her head, Emma let out a hoot of laughter. "Oh goodness, child, he's haunting your house? I remember he was a fine-looking man."

Danielle blushed. "Well, he still is."

"Goodness gracious. I had no idea! I wonder if Emmett knows Mr. Marlow is haunting Marlow House."

"I suppose you can ask him," Danielle suggested.

"I will, once I move on."

"If it wasn't something you saw Walt do— and if you don't recall meeting any of the people who died on the boat—"

"There is always that business partner of Walt Marlow's," Emma suddenly re-membered.

"Jack?" Danielle asked.

Emma nodded. "I think that was his name. He disappeared right after the *Eva Aphrodite* went down. Heard he stole a bunch of money from Walt Marlow, which really never surprised me."

"Why do you say that?"

"Because those people were after him, threatened to kill him."

"Umm, Emma, I think maybe I know what you're supposed to show me."

"What's that?"

"Whatever it is you know about Walt's partner, Jack. Because you see, Jack didn't run off with Walt's money. He was murdered. They found his remains on the *Eva Aphrodite*."

DANIELLE WAS NO LONGER SITTING on a front porch. Instead of a rocking chair, she sat with Emma at a table in what Danielle assumed was the Bluebell Diner. One clue was the menu on the adjacent table that said Bluebell Diner.

Half of the tables were occupied, and by the dress and hairstyles of the customers sitting at those tables, Danielle was fairly confident the time frame was the 1920s.

"If I did this right, they don't see us," Emma said as an attractive black waitress approached their table and began wiping down the tabletop before straightening the condiments.

Leaning toward the server, Danielle read her name tag. "Oh my gosh, it's you!"

Emma smiled. "I forgot how young I was back then. Where did the time go?"

"You were gorgeous," Danielle said in awe. "You look like a movie star."

Emma laughed. "I have to say, no one has ever compared me to a movie star."

"I'm serious," Danielle said with a convincing nod. "You were quite stunning…oh…not that I mean you don't look nice now."

Emma laughed again as her former self turned from the table and went on with her work. "Since I'm no longer attached to either flesh and blood body, I suppose those earthly tethers no longer apply."

In the next moment, the Emma sitting next to Danielle transformed herself into the younger version of herself.

"Very nice," Danielle said with a smile.

Emma shrugged. "I'm hoping that when all this is resolved, I'll be able to move on to Emmett, and when I do, I'd rather come to him like this so he'll recognize me."

"When your husband used to visit you, how did you look in your dreams?"

Emma smiled at Danielle. "Like this. My mama always said I was vain."

Danielle was about to respond when Emma quickly hushed her and said, "This is what I wanted you to hear. Listen up."

Turning in the direction of Emma's focused stare, Danielle watched as Jack entered the diner alone and headed for the table she and Emma sat at. He wore a gray suit, with a flap hat perched cockily on his head. She silently watched as he sat down with them, a folded newspaper under his arm. He unfurled the newspaper and began reading. Emma pointed to two men sitting across the room in a booth. One of them nodded in their direction. They stood up and approached their table.

When the two men suddenly appeared at his side and began to sit down, Jack startled, looking up from his paper. One of the men took Danielle's seat, forcing her to stand abruptly and move out of his way.

"I'm sorry. I should have had you sit in the other chair, I forgot," Emma apologized.

Now standing by the table, Danielle couldn't help but think of all the times something like that had happened to Walt. Someone who couldn't see him—which was everyone but her and Chris—would decide to sit down on the chair he was using. Just like Walt, she couldn't actually feel the person claiming the chair, and theoretically, they could both use it simultaneously; but the thought of doing so was not only distracting, but also, to her, somewhat creepy.

Emma the waitress appeared by their table as the two men sat down. She glanced back to the booth they'd previously occupied, just as she started to hand Jack a menu. "Did you want to change tables?"

One of the men roughly pushed back the menu she was handing to Jack, shoving it into the front of her apron. "Go away, girl, we have something to discuss with this boy."

Visibly nervous, Emma gave a nod and stepped back and, when doing so, tripped, dropping the menu to the floor behind Jack's chair. Emma bent down to pick the menu up off the floor when the second man told Jack, "You've a week to pay us, or we're going to cut you up and sell you for bait. Understood?"

The room froze. Danielle glanced around. It reminded her of a movie stopping on a single frame. Across the room, a server had been in the process of filling a customer's cup with coffee. The stream of coffee hung in midair, arching from the spout of the coffee pot to the mug sitting on the table.

"What just happened?" Danielle asked.

"That's all I heard of the conversation," Emma explained. "Back then, I didn't want to hear more, so I hustled myself away from that table. Never a good idea to know too much."

"Do you know who those men were?" Danielle studied the two men sitting at the table with Jack. She guessed they were in their forties. Yet she could be wrong. One thing she had noticed in the past was, when looking at photographs of people from Walt's era, they always seemed older than their modern-day counterparts did.

One of the two men sported a pencil mustache and a fedora hat atop his head. Proper etiquette dictated men remove hats when indoors, yet neither Jack nor this man had done that, Danielle noted. The third man was clean-shaven, and she could see his hat still sitting on the booth bench across the room, where he had recently been sitting. What style of hat he wore, she couldn't tell from this distance.

"Oh, I knew who they were all right. Local muscle. I never knew who they worked for exactly. Emmett always said it was best that way. The one with the hat, I heard him called Ballot Bob. Emmett said that was because he had a way of persuading people how to vote. The other one was called Reggie something. Never knew their last names that I recall."

"So Jack owed them money?"

"I think he had a gambling problem. At least that's what Emmett said after I told him what I overheard. When Jack disappeared the next week, I figured he either ran off with Walt Marlow's money to get away from those men, or they made good on their promise."

"Did you ever say anything to anyone about what you heard, after Jack disappeared?" Before Emma could answer, Danielle said, "I guess that was a stupid question. I don't imagine you told anyone."

"Just Emmett. He told me to keep my mouth shut."

"Can you unfreeze this so I can hear the rest of their conversation?"

"I told you that's all I heard," Emma reminded her.

"Let's just try." Danielle remembered the recent dream hop Walt had taken her on, where she was able to listen in on conversations, even ones Walt hadn't overheard at the time they actually took place—providing his former self had been in the same room.

"Okay," Emma said with a shrug. In the next moment, everyone around them came back to life.

Licking his lips nervously, Jack leaned forward and said under his breath, "I told you guys I'll have your money. I just need a little time. Give me another week and I'll have it for you."

"Time's run out, Jack-o," Ballot Bob said.

"But you're in luck," Reggie added. "We have a little favor to ask you. You do this for us, and you'll be square."

Jack frowned. "What do you want me to do?"

"Once we tell you what we need, you understand you can't say nuthin' to anyone. Got that?" Ballot Bob said.

Jack shook his head. "Don't ask me to kill anyone. I'm not going to do it, so don't ask. I don't want to know who you want to get rid of. I don't want to be involved."

Ballot Bob laughed. "Don't worry, Jack-o. It's nothing like that. We just need you to help us board the *Eva Aphrodite*."

"What do you mean board her?" Jack frowned.

"No one's going to get hurt," Reggie assured him. "We just need you to help us get on and off without any problem."

"And afterwards, you'll be square with us," Ballot Bob promised.

Once again the room froze. Danielle glanced around. "What happened?"

Emma frowned. "I don't know."

"Where are you, Emma?" Danielle asked.

"What do you mean? I'm right here."

"No, you from back then, the waitress. I don't see you anywhere," Danielle told her.

Emma glanced around the room. "I think it was the end of my shift, so I went home."

TWENTY-EIGHT

Danielle opened her eyes. She was back in her bedroom, still in her clothes. Groggy, she sat up and looked around. She picked up her iPhone off the nightstand and looked at the time. It was 3:12 a.m.

Glancing up to the ceiling, she decided not to go see Walt and Jack right now, even though she was fairly certain Stella was asleep downstairs. She wanted time to process what she had learned from Emma. Had Jack been responsible for pirates boarding the *Eva Aphrodite*? Had it all been a home invasion at sea? Did they double-cross Jack, killing all the witnesses, including the person who helped them board the ship?

Getting up, Danielle changed into her sleepwear and climbed back into bed. *I'll shower in the morning*, she told herself.

"DOES it really matter after all this time?" Lily asked Danielle the next morning. The two sat in the side yard, drinking their morning coffee. Danielle had just told Lily about last night's dream hop.

"That's sort of what I asked myself when I woke up this morning. It's pretty obvious to me what happened. Why else would they want to get on board that boat? To steal from the wealthy passengers. Maybe something went wrong, and they were forced to kill everyone."

"It would explain why Jack was on the boat. It might also explain why he doesn't re-member. It was probably all too traumatic." Lily paused mid-sip and looked to Danielle. "You're certain he doesn't remember what happened, right?"

Danielle shrugged. "Unless he's a really good actor. But no, I don't think he remembers. While it may not matter after all this time, I'm curious about that old jewelry they found on board."

"Oh, I almost forgot about that. You're certain it wasn't there when the ship went down?"

"No way. For one thing, if the motive was robbery, I can't imagine they'd leave those behind. But even if they were somehow overlooked, how do we explain the box they were in? Not to mention, Jack claims to have seen a diver leave the box not long before he ended up here."

"Okay, let me restate—maybe it doesn't really matter after all this time who killed those poor people, because you're probably right about what happened. But I'm curious about that old jewelry. Who put it there? Why? And where did they get it?" Lily asked.

"Plus, we can't forget about Emma. Something kept her here. The spirits wanted her to show me something. If it was Jack's encounter in the Bluebell, what now? Sometimes, spirits simply want someone from the living to know the truth. Me knowing may be enough, and Emma can move on. But if not, what then? What am I supposed to do with the information?"

"Maybe tell Walt?" Lily suggested.

"Walt…yeah, I'm sort of not looking forward to that. All these years he thought Jack stole from him, and now, well, now it's actually worse. His actions contributed to the deaths of all those people. Which will definitely put a damper on their reunion."

"True. But they killed him too. And the poor guy has spent close to a hundred years stuck on the bottom of the ocean, all alone."

"Aren't you cold out there?" Stella called out from the kitchen door. Danielle and Lily looked to the now open door leading from the side yard to the kitchen, where Stella stood.

"It's a little chilly, but nice," Lily answered.

"Breakfast is on. You two are going to join us, aren't you?" Stella asked. "We'll be leaving this afternoon."

"Certainly," Danielle said with a forced smile as she stood up with her now empty cup of coffee. She glanced down at Lily, who hadn't yet budged from her chair. "Lily? Breakfast?"

Lily looked up at Danielle and let out a sigh before standing up. They went into the house with Stella.

JOLENE CARMICHAEL STOOD at the front desk of the Frederickport Police Department. She had just demanded to see Chief MacDonald. The woman working at the front desk was newly hired to the department and had only lived in Frederickport a few months. She had no idea who Jolene Carmichael was, but she politely phoned the chief's office, telling him a Ms. Jolene Carmichael was at the front desk, requesting to see him. She fully expected the chief to have her ask the woman what this was in regards to and then direct her to one of the other officers. Yet the chief didn't do that. Instead, he told her he would be right out.

"Jolene, this is an unexpected visit. If it's about what the historical society wants to do with the *Eva Aphrodite*—"

"Edward, can we talk alone, please?" Jolene asked stiffly.

The chief paused a moment, then shrugged and gave a little nod. "Let's go to my office."

———

AFTER THE CHIEF led Jolene into his office, he gestured toward an empty chair facing his desk and closed the door behind them.

"What's this about?" the chief asked as he took a seat behind his desk and faced Jolene.

"I understand you've recovered jewelry from the *Eva Aphrodite*."

Picking up a pen from his desk, he leaned back in his office chair and began absently tapping the pen's end against the tabletop. "I guess you read this morning's newspaper."

"Actually I haven't. But this is a small town, and I know you spoke with Ben."

He smiled. "I see you haven't missed a beat. You've been gone all these years, you've been back just a couple months, and already you know what's going on without having to read the local paper."

"One thing I know: I don't care for how my hometown's changed since I've been gone."

Dropping the pen, Edward MacDonald leaned forward, resting his elbows on the desktop. He studied Jolene. "How's that?"

"All this attention on Marlow House, for example. Glorifying Walt Marlow. Someone who was nothing more than a bootlegger and murderer."

"I'm not sure I'm following you. How is anyone glorifying Walt Marlow?"

"For one thing, Danielle Boatman is trying to rewrite history with all that murder nonsense. I understand she's just trying to promote her bed and breakfast, but I don't appreciate her doing it at the expense of the historical society's integrity."

"I'm a little curious, Jolene. The historical society was organized, what, five, six years ago? After you left town."

"What's your point?"

"No point, I guess. Just that technically speaking, you're a relatively new member of the group and Danielle's probably been a member longer than you."

"Don't be ridiculous," Jolene snapped. "I'm a Frederickport pioneer, and she's nothing more than a California interloper."

With a shrug he said, "Either way, this issue you have with her is really a matter to address with the historical society, not with me."

"I'm not here to discuss the historical society. As I stated a moment ago, I'm here to discuss the jewelry your men discovered on board that boat. I'm here to reclaim my property."

"Your property?"

"Of course. My great-uncle and his wife were on board the *Eva Aphrodite*. They were among those who were slaughtered by Walt Marlow's henchmen—"

"We really have nothing to prove he was responsible for the murders."

"I know about the diary written by my great-aunt's dear friend. After all, I'm on the board of the historical society. Anything that belonged to my great-aunt rightfully belongs to me."

"Why do you say that?"

"Because in my great-uncle's will, he left

everything to his brother—my grandfather. Which would include his wife's jewelry. And since I'm my grandfather's sole heir, it belongs to me."

"We're not even sure where that jewelry came from. Some might argue since the boat belonged to Walt Marlow, then his heir, which would indirectly be Danielle Boatman, would be the rightful owner of whatever was on the boat."

Jolene laughed. "You know very well treasure trove laws don't work that way in Oregon."

"Always the attorney's wife," Edward said with a smile.

"However, treasure trove laws would not apply in this case, since I'm the rightful owner of my great-aunt's jewelry," she reminded him.

"Perhaps you need to read this morning's newspaper, because you obviously don't have all the information. The jewelry we found on board wasn't left there when the boat went down."

"Don't be ridiculous. I've already spoken to Aaron and seen the photographs."

"Aaron?" The chief frowned.

"Aaron Michaels, he's the jeweler you had look at the pieces you found, isn't he?"

"I thought you didn't read this morning's newspaper."

"Aaron is an old family friend. I happened to have dinner with him and his wife last night, and he showed me the pictures he took of the jewelry recovered off the *Eva Aphrodite*. I recognized several of the pieces. They match pictures I have of my great-aunt wearing them."

"That may be true, but we're still investigating how they got on board."

Jolene stood up. "This is ridiculous. For whatever reason, that jewelry was overlooked by whoever murdered those poor people, and it was left on board."

"No, Jolene. The box we found on board —the one with the jewelry in it—it wasn't left on the *Eva Aphrodite* when the boat went down over ninety years ago. The box was purchased at Walmart; it still had a price tag on the bottom. I'm fairly certain Walmart wasn't around back then."

With a frown, Jolene sat back down. "That doesn't make any sense."

The chief shrugged. "None of this does."

Jolene sat quietly for a moment, her elbows resting on the chair's arms, hands folded together, as her knuckles lightly rapped the point of her chin. After a moment, she froze and looked up to the chief. "Danielle Boatman, she put that box on the boat."

"That's impossible. We had security down there; no one but authorized personnel had access to the boat."

"It could have been placed there before you posted security down at the beach. Perhaps even before the boat was brought up on shore."

Curiously eyeing Jolene, the chief leaned back in his chair. "What are you suggesting?"

Abruptly, Jolene stood. "This all makes sense! It's been nothing more than a publicity stunt. Why did Brianna Boatman have to leave her estate to that woman? She has brought nothing but trouble to Frederickport!"

"Jolene, if you're suggesting Danielle is in some way responsible for bringing the wreckage of the *Eva Aphrodite* to our shore, that's ridiculous."

"Is it? There wasn't a storm that night. Someone had to have hauled that monstrosity here. Everyone says the boat looks like it's been under water. Chances are, she knew where it went down. For all we know, she found Walt Marlow's diary when she found the Missing Thorndike."

"I never heard about Walt Marlow having a diary."

"Don't be obtuse, Edward. There was some way she knew where the *Eva Aphrodite* went down, and the only explanation is Walt Marlow's diary, since he was obviously the one responsible for murdering those people and sinking his own yacht. The jewelry you found on board was probably hidden all these years with the Missing Thorndike. Her big mistake was not being more careful in selecting a box to store the stolen pieces in when placing them back on board, obviously for you to find."

"And how exactly did Danielle manage to bring up a sunken ship and haul it here?"

"She has the financial resources. And obviously, she managed to do it. The proof is sitting on that beach, down the street from Marlow House!"

The chief stood. "That's an imaginative tale you've cooked up, Jolene. But seriously, something like that would cost a fortune to pull off, and I don't see how she'd ever recoup her expenses from the bed and breakfast. How many rooms would she have to rent out to even cover something like that?"

Wagging her right index finger, Jolene ranted, "Danielle Boatman isn't doing this for the money. She already has all the money she needs. She's doing it for the attention. That woman is nothing but trouble! She destroyed poor Clarence. He was a good man. I don't believe for a moment he meant to hurt anyone, but Danielle drove him to it with all her publicity shenanigans, beginning with conspiring with her cousin to run off with the Missing Thorndike. If it wasn't for her, he wouldn't have been sent to prison, and he wouldn't have been murdered. She's the one to blame!"

TWENTY-NINE

"Why didn't your guests take their suitcases with them?" Walt asked Danielle when he appeared in the parlor, Jack by his side.

Danielle, who sat at the small desk, jotting a quick note in her ledger, looked up. Setting her pen atop the open page, she said, "Because they aren't checking out until noon. They went to do some more sightseeing."

"We expected to see you before now," Walt said as he took a seat on the sofa. Jack remained standing, his attention on the flat-screen television on the wall. It was turned on, but there was no sound.

"I'm afraid Stella Sterling is a little demanding. I swear, every time I headed for the attic, she seemed to appear out of nowhere and needed something. I was going to go up to the attic when I finished here, but since you're both here now..." Danielle closed the ledger and looked from Walt to Jack and back to Walt.

"Jack and I had a long talk, and while he can't remember how he was killed, we know he didn't steal from our business. I was wrong all these years."

No longer studying the television, Jack wandered over toward Walt, taking a seat on the chair facing him. "I understand how it must have looked to you."

"I saw Emma Jackson last night," Danielle blurted out.

"She was here?" Walt asked.

"Who's Emma Jackson?" Jack asked.

"In a manner of speaking." Crossing her arms over her chest, Danielle leaned back in her chair. She looked at Walt. "It was a dream hop. She took me to see something— like you did when you took me to the speakeasy."

"Who's Emma Jackson?" Jack repeated his question.

"She's a woman who recently passed away just shy of her hundred and seventh birthday. Back when you were alive, she worked at the Bluebell Diner," Danielle explained.

Jack frowned. "I don't remember an Emma who worked there."

"She was a colored girl," Walt explained.

"We don't say colored anymore," Danielle reminded him.

Walt shrugged. "Sorry. I didn't mean anything by it."

"I know." Danielle sighed. "I hate to bring all this up now, since you two seem to have resolved some issues. And considering all this happened almost ninety years ago, does it really matter anymore?"

"Does what matter anymore?" Walt asked.

"Emma showed me an encounter Jack had at the Bluebell Diner just a week before the *Eva Aphrodite* went missing."

"What are you talking about?" Jack asked.

"Jack, maybe you didn't take that money, but it looks like you helped—well, for a lack of a better word—pirates board the *Eva Aphrodite*."

"Pirates? What are you talking about, pirates?" Jack said angrily.

"What did you see, Danielle?" Walt asked.

Danielle let out another sigh and then proceeded to tell Jack and Walt about her dream hop the night before.

When she was done, Jack shook his head in denial. "No, Danielle. I didn't help those men board the *Eva Aphrodite*. For one thing, the next day I paid them off and told them to stay away from the yacht. She was off-limits. I told them they were crazy if they thought I'd sit by and let them steal from our passengers. I'd repaid my debt, so they had to keep their hands off."

"Who did you owe money to?" Walt demanded.

"I don't want to talk about it. It doesn't matter now."

"Gambling. Right? You were gambling again?" Walt accused.

"I said I don't want to talk about it. And I paid them off."

"Where did you get the money?" Danielle asked.

"I sold my car," Jack explained.

"Who did you sell it to?" Walt asked.

"Some guy in Portland."

"So that's where your car went. When you disappeared and we couldn't find your car, it was because it had been sold?" Walt asked.

"It that's true, then why were you on board the *Eva Aphrodite*? Why were you killed?" Danielle asked.

"I told you, Danielle, I don't remember," Jack snapped. "My last memory is walking to the motel. Walking because I no longer had a car. The guy I'd sold it to had just picked it up. My next memory was on board the *Eva Aphrodite*. But I was dead by then."

"I thought you said you'd paid off the debt the day after they approached you in the Bluebell. But now you say you sold your car a week later, before you disappeared," she asked.

Jack shook his head. "No. The guy I sold it to, he couldn't pick the car up until the following week, but I told him I had to have the money right away. I was giving him a good deal, so he paid me up front."

BILL JONES STROLLED into Adam Nichols's office, clipboard in hand. He didn't knock on the door or wait for an invitation to enter. Instead, the handyman walked straight to Adam, tossing the clipboard onto the desk before plopping down on a chair.

Stretching out in a yawn, Bill crossed his work boots at the ankle before nodding to the clipboard on the desk. "Finished. There's the invoices."

Snatching the clipboard off the desk, Adam flipped through its pages. "Did you have lunch already?"

"Yeah, I grabbed something at the drive-through. I wanted to finish listening to Paul's radio show."

"Anything interesting today?"

"You didn't listen?" Bill asked.

Adam shook his head. "No, what was it about?"

Bill sat up straighter. "Paul was interviewing Ben Smith from the museum. It was about that guy they found in a trunk on the *Eva Aphrodite*."

"I read about that in the newspaper this morning. Looks like it was Walt Marlow's business partner. Jack something. Grandma told me everyone assumed the guy had taken off with Marlow's money. Although I guess it belonged to both of them, they were business partners."

"Did you know that money he supposedly ran off with would be worth millions today?"

Adam tossed the clipboard back down on the desk. "Yeah, Grandma told me that. It's because it was mostly gold coins."

Bill leaned forward. "And it was never recovered."

"Just because we don't know what the guy did with the money doesn't mean it's still out there."

"Ben was talking about the missing money on Paul's radio show. He speculated Marlow's business partner probably had it with him when he went on board the boat, and whoever killed him and the others took the money."

Adam shrugged. "Likely scenario."

Bill grinned. "But what if he didn't?"

"What are you talking about?"

"Why would he take all that money with him on the boat? According to Ben, back then it was estimated to be a couple thousand dollars. According to the stories, he kept the money stashed somewhere."

"I know. Grandma's father told her the reason Marlow knew his partner had ripped him off was because both the partner and the money went missing at the same time."

"Or had it?" Bill grinned.

Adam frowned. "What are you getting at?"

"Ben mentioned the dead guy was reportedly renting a room from your great-grandfather at the time he went missing."

"So?"

"So if he didn't have the money with him, then it means he left it somewhere. If he was living with your great-grandfather, then maybe that money is stashed somewhere in your grandmother's house!"

Adam chuckled and shook his head. "Nahh, there's no way. Like I said, Marlow already checked the place where his partner usually kept the money. And yes, it was at the house across the street from Marlow House. But it wasn't there then, so I don't see why it would be now."

Bill stood up. "Come on, Adam. This isn't like you. Just because Marlow didn't find it in the place his partner normally stashed the loot doesn't mean it wasn't somewhere else in that house."

Adam shook his head. "No, I've been through the house."

"Bull. You haven't looked under all the floorboards and in walls."

"So what do you suggest, I give Ian the required twenty-four-hour notice that we need to get into the house and then start ripping out walls?"

"It sure beats breaking into the place like we did at Marlow House. Hell, the house is yours. You have every right to go through it. Who can stop you?"

Adam stood up. "I know it's not there. Trust me, Bill, if there was any chance the money was there, I'd be personally knocking down walls."

When Bill finally left the office fifteen minutes later, Adam stood by the window and watched his old high school buddy and handyman drive off in the truck.

A slow smile played on Adam's face. "No, Bill old pal, this time I'm going on my own. If that money's still there, it's mine."

KURT JEFFERSON PULLED his vehicle over to the side of the road and parked his car. A moment later, he held his cellphone by his ear, waiting for his party to answer.

Instead of a friendly greeting, she said, "I thought I told you not to call me anymore."

"Did you listen to the radio show this morning?" he asked. "They were talking about the dead guy they found in the trunk?"

"Yeah, so what?"

"You have that gold, don't you?"

"What are you talking about?"

"Come on, I also read the article in this morning's newspaper. If you got that jewelry off the boat, then it means you got the gold too."

"You know I was never on the *Eva Aphrodite*. I don't know how to dive."

"Okay, so whoever you hired before me. Or did they keep it for themselves?"

"You were the only one I ever hired. I don't know anything about any gold," she insisted.

"That means you had what was in that box all the time. According to the article, those pieces match what some of the passengers were wearing. The big mystery they're trying to figure out is why they were found in a box that didn't exist back when the boat went down. But we know the answer to that, don't we?"

"What do you want?" she snapped.

"I've been doing a little research on you. I think I know how you happened to have what was in that box. I think I might also know why you had me put the box back on the boat. And I'm pretty sure you have the missing gold coins."

"I don't care what you think you know. I don't have any gold coins."

"I hope for your sake you do."

"What do you mean?" she asked.

"I told you, I've been doing my own research. Amazing what one can uncover by asking the right questions, looking under the right rocks."

"You don't make any sense. I'm done now."

"Don't hang up, you'll regret it. Not unless you want everyone to know your secret."

She didn't respond.

"You still there?" he asked.

"Yes."

"Good. I'm not going to be greedy. I want to see them first, and then we'll divide them up. Don't worry, I'll leave you plenty. Considering you were willing to dump those jewels on the bottom of the ocean, I don't see why you care."

"I told you I don't have any gold coins!"

"Why should I believe you?" he asked.

"Because if I had them, I would have had you put a second box on that boat."

THIRTY

B en from the museum called Danielle just minutes after Stella and Rowland Strickland checked out that Monday afternoon. He told her the display case for the emerald had been installed earlier than they had expected, and she was welcome to come down and have a look.

"Should I bring the emerald with me?" she asked.

"That would be wonderful, if you'd be willing to do that. I have to admit I can't wait to see how it's going to look. Of course, Friday's the official opening of the display."

"Would it hurt to bring it down early and leave it?"

"I don't think so." He then added with a laugh, "We could drape a curtain over the display case and not let anyone see it until Friday; it would add a dramatic flare, something of a visual drumroll."

"I was also wondering, do you think I could have a look at that diary?"

"Diary?"

"Yes, the one that claimed Walt Marlow was having an affair with Thelma Templeton."

"Sure, but I can't really let you take it out of the museum."

"That's okay; I could read it down there."

"It's going to take a while to read it," Ben said. "And I'm only free for about an hour this afternoon."

"That's okay. I have some things I have to do this afternoon too. Any chance I could come back to the museum this evening and read it?"

"I'm afraid I already have plans tonight."

"Ben, you really don't need to be there. I understand you not wanting me to remove anything from the museum, but why can't I read it there by myself? If I was a docent, you wouldn't have a problem with me being down there alone, letting myself in, and locking up. I'm a member of the historical society, and considering everything, I don't really think you have to worry about me stealing anything."

"Oh, I didn't mean to imply I don't trust you!" Ben said in a rush. "Certainly you can come back later and read the diary here. I tell you what, when you come down to the museum with the emerald, I'll give you a key, show you where you can find the diary, and how to lock up. Okay?"

"Sounds great, Ben." Danielle glanced at the time. "How about I meet you down there in about an hour. Would that work?"

"Perfect. See you then."

DANIELLE ARRIVED at the museum an hour later, emerald in hand. Before going inside, she checked the time on her cellphone and turned off its ringer. When she entered the museum, she was surprised to find not just Ben waiting for her, but also the other board members she had met with earlier: Steve Klein, Millie Samson, and even Jolene Carmichael.

"We're so excited to see how the emerald looks in the display case!" Millie said enthusiastically when Danielle walked through the front doorway of the museum.

"Yes, especially considering how much the museum paid to have it made—a case to display something we don't even own," Jolene said sharply.

"I'm sure Danielle doesn't plan to remove the emerald any time soon," Steve quickly countered, flashing Danielle an apologetic smile.

"You're right, Steve. I've no other plans for the emerald. I think it should be on display with the Eva Thorndike portrait." Danielle handed the box with the emerald to Ben.

Ben thanked her and then rushed off toward the new display case, Millie and Steve in tow. Jolene lingered a moment with Danielle, who had paused to slip her car keys into her purse.

"This is just one of your publicity stunts," Jolene told Danielle when the others were out of earshot.

"Excuse me?" Danielle frowned.

"I can't prove it yet, but I know you're responsible for bringing the *Eva Aphrodite* back to Frederickport."

"What in the world are you talking about?"

"It's all about the publicity to you, isn't it? I know you were some big-shot marketing person before you moved here."

"My late husband and I owned a marketing agency, yes. But I wouldn't really call myself a big shot." Danielle couldn't help but laugh at Jolene's words.

"This isn't funny. None of it is."

Cocking her head to one side, Danielle studied Jolene a moment. The woman was practically hyperventilating, she was so agitated. Considering her age, Danielle didn't imagine it was particularly healthy for her.

"I guess we got off on the wrong foot somehow. I'm not really sure why you dislike me so much. Or how you can even imagine I had anything to do with bringing the *Eva Aphrodite* back to Frederickport. I'm not even sure how that would be possible."

"It's pretty obvious; it's all about promoting your bed and breakfast, beginning with that foolish stunt at your grand opening."

"I do regret wearing the Missing Thorndike that day," Danielle conceded.

Jolene let out a harsh laugh. "I wasn't talking about wearing it. It was having your cousin pretend to steal it. Nothing like milking it for all it's worth. You practically wrote the next morning's headlines. What was it, *The Missing Thorndike Goes Missing Again*?"

"I had nothing to do with that."

"Maybe you've fooled everyone else, but you aren't fooling me. You wanted to keep everyone talking about Marlow House. Just doing what you do. All about publicity. But poor Clarence got caught up in it and ended up dead because of you."

Danielle bristled. "Clarence Renton killed my cousin. He'd been embezzling from my aunt's estate for years. He killed Cheryl because when she contested our aunt's will; he knew the courts would take a closer look, and when they did, he'd be exposed for the crook he was."

"I don't believe that for a moment! Clarence was a good man. If any mistakes were made, they were honest clerical errors. And considering your aunt had Alzheimer's, how do you even know what she wanted?"

"What is this really about?" Danielle asked. "Does this have something to do with your husband? He was Clarence's partner for all those years. Was he complicit? Did he know what was going on? Was he part of it?"

Jolene gasped. "How dare you!"

Neither Jolene nor Danielle noticed Millie Samson had just returned to the front of the museum, curious to see what was taking the two so long. Millie failed to notice the two women were not engaged in an amicable discussion, and she called out, "Come see, it looks beautiful!"

Flashing Jolene a hostile look, Danielle turned toward Millie and made her way to the display.

"WELL, WHAT DO YOU THINK?" Ben asked proudly.

Eva Thorndike's portrait no longer perched atop its easel. The new glass cabinet displaying Danielle's emerald—one of the original gems from the famed Thorndike necklace—provided a new resting place for the portrait. Eva, who Danielle always felt bore an uncanny resemblance to Charles Dana Gibson's Gibson Girl from the late 1800s, now looked down at the emerald. Or at least the woman in the portrait did.

Danielle found it ironic Jolene had made a snide remark about the museum spending so much money on a cabinet to display something they didn't own when just two days earlier, Jolene and the other board members had expressed the desire to eventually sell the emerald. *What did they intend to do with the cabinet then?* she wondered.

Stepping up to the display, Danielle studied the woman in the painting for a moment, noting her aloof, somewhat haunting expression. Danielle wondered if Eva realized she was dying when she sat for the portrait. From what she understood, the artist completed the painting not long before Eva's death.

Turning her attention to the necklace worn by the woman in the portrait—the necklace that came to be known as the Missing Thorndike when Walt stole it at Eva's request—Danielle wondered if the necklace Eva wore at the time of the sitting contained the fake stones or the second set of real gems, which Danielle now kept in her bank safety deposit box.

"Well? What do you think?" Ben repeated his question.

"I think they did a wonderful job. I love the way the emerald display ties in with the portrait."

"They did, didn't they?" Steve gushed.

Millie stepped up to the display, silk cloth in hand. "If you're done, let's get this covered before someone else walks in here. I think I just heard the front bell."

Danielle stepped back from the display and watched as Steve helped Millie cover the new display case with the cloth. "I didn't realize Ben was serious when he mentioned covering the display until Friday."

"Oh yes," Millie said as she tucked one end of the cloth around the base of the portrait. It rested against the lower portion of the frame, not the canvas. "We can't let anyone see it yet; it would make Friday's display party anticlimactic, wouldn't it?"

"I suppose it would," Danielle murmured.

"Oh yes, we don't want to do anything to diminish the full impact of this publicity stunt," Jolene sniped.

Ben frowned at Jolene. "I'm not sure what you mean?"

Jolene rolled her eyes, and without another word, she abruptly turned from the small group and walked away, heading to the restroom.

"I don't know what's gotten into her. I don't remember her being like this," Millie said after Jolene was out of earshot.

Ben shook his head. "She's been acting strange ever since the chief started asking me questions about the history behind the *Eva Aphrodite*. I almost wish I hadn't mentioned anything at our last board meeting."

"Well, that's just silly," Millie said.

While tempted to mention Jolene's accusation regarding the mysterious return of the *Eva Aphrodite*, Danielle resisted. Instead, she stood quietly by the display, listening to the three remaining board members discuss Jolene's peculiar and somewhat hostile behavior. They concluded Jolene was simply disappointed that Danielle had decided to lend the historical society the Thorndike emerald instead of donating it.

When Jolene returned, the conversation had already shifted to the plans for Friday's event. Danielle only half listened, telling herself she would simply show up whenever they told her to. With Jolene as a board member, Danielle decided she would limit her involvement with the historical society.

Her mind wandered as she absently studied Eva Thorndike's portrait. The undiscernible, chattering voices of the four board members provided background sound. Her gaze drifted down to the now covered display case and then back to the portrait, a pool of silk fabric at its base. Her eyes wandered up the painting, pausing a moment on the necklace and then moving up to the face.

Something about the facial features gave Danielle pause, her own eyes widening in surprise. Eva—the woman in the portrait—her eyes sparkled. Danielle blinked several times, certain she was imagining things. Yet then the lips of the woman in the portrait curled, no longer somber but smiling—smiling at Danielle.

Without thought, Danielle stepped back from the display, her attention riveted on the portrait. The board members, so engrossed in their own discussion, failed to notice Danielle's peculiar change of demeanor.

Mesmerized, Danielle watched as Eva Thorndike's spirit calmly stepped out from the portrait—a transparent vision, her edges blending into soft haze while reflecting random beams of sparkling light.

The apparition embodied calm as she stood before Danielle. The two women stared at each other—one made of flesh and blood and the other from the spirit world.

"You're Danielle Boatman. I heard you were coming," Eva said in a soft voice.

In response, Danielle glanced to the board members and then back to Eva.

Smiling, Eva reached out to Danielle, the tips of her fingers, transparent and glowing, just a few inches from Danielle's right cheek. "We need to talk. We need to talk about Walt." Lowering her hand to her side, Eva took a step back and then vanished.

THIRTY-ONE

anielle finished running her errands
sooner than expected. Before leaving the
museum earlier that afternoon, Ben had given
her a key, explained the alarm system, and
shown her where to find Ethel Pearson's diary.
It was possible for Danielle to return to the
museum before it closed without having to use
the key, since the museum was open until 5:00
p.m. But Danielle wanted to wait until it
closed for the evening. When meeting Eva
Thorndike again, she didn't want an audience.

Instead of going back to Marlow House,
Danielle decided to stop by and visit with

Marie. Danielle knew she would tell Walt about seeing Eva, but considering their initial meeting was so brief, she preferred to postpone telling him until she could have a real conversation with the spirit.

When Danielle pulled up to Marie's house, she found Adam's car parked in the driveway. Marie hadn't mentioned her grandson was there when Danielle had called a few minutes earlier to see if Marie was up to a visit.

"Adam brought brownies; help yourself," Marie explained when she led Danielle into her living room a few minutes later; a platter of chocolate brownies sat prominently displayed on the coffee table. Adam, who lounged on the easy chair, gave Danielle a lazy hello wave.

"Adam, where are your manners?" Marie reprimanded.

Letting out a weary sigh, he started to stand up but stopped when Danielle walked by his chair and gave him a little nudge, pushing him back into the recliner. "He doesn't need to be a gentleman,"

Danielle said as she reached for a brownie. "He brought chocolate."

Marie chuckled as she shook her head and sat down on the sofa. Patting the cushion next to her, she nodded for Danielle to join her.

Holding a napkin under the brownie, Danielle took a bite. Closing her eyes a moment, she savored the decadent treat. "These are from Old Salts, aren't they?" Danielle asked after she swallowed the bite.

"Yep," Adam answered, his feet propped upon the recliner's footrest.

"I love that bakery," Danielle said, taking a second bite. "Their pastries all taste like something your grandma would bake."

"Not like what my grandma would bake," Adam said with a snort.

"Oh hush, you!" Marie scolded, suppressing a laugh.

Danielle scowled at Adam. "That's not very nice, Adam."

Marie laughed and patted Danielle's knee. "Adam's right, dear. I grow a mean garden, but I've never been one for baking. Which is why I do appreciate Adam's regular treats from the bakery."

"I suppose I'm just the opposite. I love to bake, and if it wasn't for Lily and our gardener, I imagine the yards surrounding Marlow House would look like a blight."

Marie patted Danielle's knee again and looked at her grandson. "Adam, go get Danielle a glass of milk."

Sighing, Adam lifted his head and looked at Danielle; their eyes met. Danielle smiled. "No, I don't need any milk. Thanks."

Adam smiled. Just as he rested his head against the back of the chair again, Danielle said, "But a glass of iced water would be terrific."

Rolling his eyes, Adam begrudgingly got up from the chair and made his way into his grandmother's kitchen. When he returned with the ice water, Danielle and Marie were discussing that morning's radio show.

"I met with Ben this afternoon after he was interviewed by Paul," Danielle explained. "I took the Thorndike emerald over to the museum for the exhibit. I missed the interview, but from what I understand, most of it was about Walt Marlow's business partner, Jack."

"I guess that mystery is solved," Adam said, snatching up another brownie from the plate.

"We know where he went. Why he was there, that's another question," Danielle said.

"That's why Adam's here. Trying to soften me up with brownies," Marie teased.

Licking frosting from her fingers, Danielle glanced from Marie to Adam. Her gaze met Adam's. Curious, she arched her brows.

Looking away from Danielle, Adam said, "Gee, Grandma, you're always so suspicious. Can't a grandson do something nice for his grandmother?"

Marie laughed.

Danielle looked back to Marie, still curious.

Giving Danielle a quick wink, Marie said, "Adam has all kinds of questions. I guess he figures chocolate will trigger my memory."

"Memory about what?" Danielle asked.

"Grandma—"

"About Walt's partner, Jack. He lived at my parents' house. Adam wanted to know if I knew what room he stayed in."

"Grandma, I just—"

"Oh posh, Adam. I listened to that radio interview too! You want to know if those missing gold coins are still in my house."

Danielle quickly wiped the edge of her mouth with the napkin before crumpling it in her hand. She looked from Adam to Marie. "Jack's missing gold. It could be. A treasure hunt!"

Dejected, Adam slumped back in the chair. "Seriously, Grandma, did you have to say something to Danielle?"

"Don't be silly. Why not tell Danielle?"

Adam groaned. "Because if the coins are there, I'll have to give them to her now. Now that you said something."

Danielle laughed. "Why would you have to give them to me?"

"Because, dear, they would belong to you since the money belonged to Walt Marlow. That is, if they're still there. Of course, Adam would have given them to you even if I hadn't mentioned it." Marie looked at Adam. "Wouldn't you, dear?"

"Don't worry, Adam; I wouldn't try to claim the money. For one thing, I doubt it would be legally mine. You could argue it was

Marlow's ill-gotten gain. Not sure if they broke any laws transporting people out to the booze ship, but considering he hosted a few of his own parties and was running moonshine, I suspect whatever money Jack and Walt shared might be considered a little like drug money is today. You'd probably be smart to keep it a secret if you do find it."

"You can't mean that!" Marie gasped.

With a shrug, Danielle said, "Actually, yeah. I don't need the money, Marie. And it doesn't belong to me anyway. The house is yours. As far as I'm concerned, if that money's still there after all these years, it belongs to you."

"You're sweet, dear, but I'm sure that money is long gone. It's probably what got Walt's partner killed."

"Perhaps."

"Now tell us all about the new exhibit," Marie said.

"Actually, I was hoping you could help me understand Jolene Carmichael."

"What about her?" Marie asked.

"She really does not like me."

"I bet it's because of Renton," Adam said.

Danielle and Marie looked over at Adam.

"You're probably right," Marie agreed. "Ever since Clarence went to prison, there's been talk around town, speculating on how long he'd been bilking his clients. More than a few wondered about Doug's involvement in all those shenanigans. And now with Jolene back in town and Clarence getting killed, there's plenty of whispering going on. I imagine Jolene knows, and she's just defensive. Has to blame someone, and unfortunately, you're her target."

"Not just me. She blames Walt Marlow for her great-uncle's death."

"Did she even know him?" Adam asked.

"No, dear. But she was close to her grandfather." Marie looked from Adam to Danielle. "I suppose she blames Walt because it was his boat?"

Danielle shook her head. "No. Something more ominous. She insists Walt was having an affair with her great-uncle's wife and that Walt ordered the murder of all those people to cover up the affair or some such convoluted reason. I don't know exactly. But I'm going back to the museum later and reading the diary of the woman who wrote about it, to see if I can figure it all out."

Marie shook her head. "Ridiculous story. And I'll tell Jolene that to her face."

"And here I thought those were more innocent times," Adam mused from the recliner.

"Her great-aunt was Thelma Templeton, wasn't it?" Marie asked. "The one she claims was having an affair with Walt?"

"Yes."

"You sure love to get wrapped up in these old soap operas," Adam said with a chuckle. "Who really cares after all these years?"

"You seem to, dear," Marie reminded him. "When gold's involved."

Adam conceded with a shrug and continued to listen.

"I remember my mother talking about Thelma Templeton, one of the women who went missing on the *Eva Aphrodite*. Of course, back then we all thought they died in the storm. After Paul's radio show today, I suppose everyone in town knows that wasn't true. According to mother, Thelma got romantically involved with an actor."

"An actor?"

"Quite scandalous." Marie smiled. "Mother told me the story. She and Father happened to run into the Templetons at the theater in Portland. Mother stepped away from Father for some reason, turned down the wrong corridor, and witnessed Thelma in a rather passionate kiss. The man wasn't Mr. Templeton, and later, Mother recognized him in the cast."

"This really is a soap opera," Adam mumbled.

"Rather bold of her," Danielle said. "Fooling around when her husband was nearby."

"That's what my mother thought too. She told Father about it, but he insisted it must have been a woman who just looked like Thelma Templeton."

"What did your mother say?" Danielle asked.

"I don't believe she argued the point with him. Yet she told me—of course, years later when I was an adult—that it was either Thelma or Thelma's twin wearing the same dress as her sister. Of course, Thelma didn't have a sister. I believe the first time Mother told me that story was when we went to that same theater in Portland."

They chatted for another twenty minutes, and when Danielle glanced at her phone, she saw she had missed several calls from the chief. She had forgotten to turn the cell-phone's ringer back on. He had also sent her a text message, asking her to call or stop in the station if she was downtown. Curious, Danielle ended her visit with Marie and Adam and headed to the police station.

"I THOUGHT YOU WERE IGNORING ME," the chief said when Danielle entered his office late Monday afternoon. Sitting at his desk, he leaned back in the office chair.

"I've had a busy day," Danielle said as she flopped down in a chair facing him. "And it's not over yet."

"I wanted to talk to you privately about Jolene Carmichael."

"Jolene?" Danielle groaned.

"She really does not like you."

"Umm, yeah, I sort of noticed that."

The chief then went on to tell Danielle about his visit with Jolene. In turn, she told him about her afternoon, excluding the encounter with Eva Thorndike. Telling the chief she had seen Eva before telling Walt did not seem right.

Finally, Danielle asked, "Well, are you going to give them to her?"

"The jewelry?"

"Those pieces do match what her aunt was wearing in those photographs. Of course, who's had them all these years and why they returned the pieces to the boat—assuming that's where they came from—is the million-dollar question."

The chief stood up and walked around the desk. Sitting along the edge of the desk front, he faced Danielle, his arms folded across his chest. "That's what I've been trying to figure out. When you told me a diver—according to your ghost friend—left that box on the boat, I decided to call someone I know in Seaside."

"You do know I hate it when you say ghost friend. His name is Jack."

"Why?"

"Why is his name Jack?"

The chief rolled his eyes. "Why does it bug you when I say ghost friend?"

Danielle shrugged. "I don't know. Just feels like you're mocking me, I guess."

"Sorry. I'm not mocking you. I promise. But this still all feels very strange to me."

"Fair enough. So what about this friend of yours?"

"You and I know that boat's been under the water all this time—it wasn't a ghost ship like some people claim. The guy I called in Seaside, he's a diver I know. I told him we were trying to figure out where the *Eva Aphrodite* had been all this time, if it was possible she was under the water for all these years, and then maybe some earthquake unsettled her. No one's ever claimed to have come across the wreckage before."

"What were you really asking him?"

"I wondered if some of the local divers had come across the wreckage and we just didn't know about it."

"And?"

"He told me an interesting story. About a

month ago, he was contacted by a woman who was looking for someone to do salvage work. The conversation didn't go far, because she asked if he would be willing to sign a nondisclosure agreement."

"Nondisclosure agreement?"

"Yes. She claimed to know the location of a sunken ship, and before she hired him— or disclosed the location of the ship—he would need to sign a nondisclosure agreement."

"Sounds like maybe she thought there was treasure on board and didn't want someone else getting to it before her," Danielle suggested.

"He started asking her some questions, and she got a little weird, and then she just hung up."

Danielle frowned. "Weird?"

"Didn't want to answer any of his questions."

"Did she call him on his cellphone? Did he try calling her back?" Danielle asked.

"Yes. And this is where it gets interesting. He got the museum."

"The museum?"

"The line the woman called him on—it was from the Frederickport Museum."

"Who was it?"

The chief shook his head. "I don't know. The museum message machine picked up when he called. He has no idea who the woman was. And he never followed up on it. All he knows is whoever made that phone call made it from the museum."

THIRTY-TWO

It wasn't dark yet. There was still a good hour and a half left of daylight. But Danielle knew the sun would be down when she closed up the museum, so she parked as close to the entrance as possible. While Frederickport was generally a safe little town, if you didn't consider the dead bodies Danielle had tripped over during the last eight months —like her cousin Cheryl, Bart Haston, or Peter Morris—she still didn't like wandering around downtown alone after nightfall.

Letting herself into the museum with the key Ben had given her, she quickly relocked the door behind her and punched the security code into the alarm system. The lights were turned off, but there was enough sunlight streaming in the front window to illuminate the museum entrance without turning on the overhead lighting. Setting the keys and her purse on the front counter adjacent to the gift shop entrance, Danielle looked down the darkened hallway leading to the exhibit area of the museum.

Nightlights, plugged into random electrical sockets throughout the building, broke up the darkness, providing a soft glow. Walking down the dimly lit hallway en route to the exhibits, a scene from Ben Stiller's *Night at the Museum* flashed through her mind. For most people, that movie was nothing more than a fanciful comedy. *Museum exhibits don't come to life.* She knew differently. Taking a deep breath, Danielle decided to see what Eva Thorndike had to say before she tackled the diary.

Since Eva had died a few years before the yacht went missing, Danielle doubted Eva's spirit would have any pertinent information regarding the true fate of the passengers and crew, especially if she had spent almost a century hanging out with her portrait. Yet, according to Eva's words earlier, she had something to say about Walt.

Stepping into the exhibit area, Danielle glanced around. To her right was the natural history exhibit, the once-live wildlife creatures frozen in time by the taxidermist. On the other side of the room was the Marlow Shipping Line exhibit with its intricate models, identical replicas of the ships once built by Frederick Marlow's company. Beyond that was an exhibit on the local fishing industry, while other exhibits highlighted points of local and state history.

Taking another deep breath, Danielle steeled her nerves and focused on the center of the room, the location of the Thorndike exhibit. A nightlight's glow bounced off a glass case, landing on the portrait's face, eerily illuminating its eyes.

Stepping up to the portrait, Danielle paused when she was about three feet away. Staring at the illuminated eyes, she said, "Hello, Eva, I'm back."

Nothing.

Another deep breath and sigh. "It's me.

Danielle Boatman. You said you knew I was coming. How did you know?"

Nothing.

"I'm alone. We can talk now if you show yourself."

Still nothing.

Danielle stood in front of the portrait for another ten minutes, yet there wasn't a glimmer or sign to indicate the presence of Eva's spirit in the room. Tired of waiting, Danielle stepped away from the portrait and made her way to the office at the back of the building.

It hadn't been necessary to turn on any lights as she walked through the museum. The nightlights provided sufficient illumination. But once in the office, she flipped the switch for the overhead fixture, flooding the room with flickering fluorescent light.

She found the diary in Ben's side desk drawer, just where he told her it would be. Sitting down at the desk, she opened the weathered leather-bound book and began thumbing through its pages.

Ethel Pearson's elegant cursive penmanship flowed from page to page. The style of writing appeared fairly consistent throughout the diary, yet there were periodic changes of letter size and ink density. Danielle was grateful to find the handwriting legible. She had read vintage handwritten documents in the past, often finding them nearly impossible to decipher. Not so with Ethel Pearson's diary.

Settling back comfortably in the swivel chair, Danielle skimmed the pages, moving over such tedious entries as Ethel's detailed account of her visit to the dressmaker. When Danielle came to the next entry mentioning the same dressmaker, she almost skipped forward without reading the pages, when a reference to Thelma jumped out at her. Pausing, Danielle read the page, and then realized she had missed something. Curious, she turned back one page and read the entire day's entry.

I stopped at the dressmaker today for my final fitting. Thelma Templeton went with me to pick up a gown she had altered. Thelma has lost so much weight; I have been so worried about her. But I had no idea how bad it truly was. She insisted on trying on the dress alone and wouldn't allow anyone to help her. I have never known her to be so shy. Thinking her silly, I entered the dressing room, intending to help her.

She was furious with me. And then I saw the reason for her inhibition. The length of her back was blackened with bruises. I wanted to weep. She swore me to silence. When I asked if Howard had done this, she only laughed.

Danielle flipped through more pages until she came to another entry discussing Thelma.

Thelma has admitted she has taken a lover and he was responsible for the bruises. She told me I didn't understand, that he simply loves her so much and often gets frustrated that she can't leave her husband.

Danielle looked up from the diary, taking a moment to reflect. Why a woman would choose to stay with a man who abused her, she didn't understand. Shaking her head, she began to read again. The next entry of interest mentioned Walt.

I was mortified this evening at the Templetons when I was caught lingering outside the door of Howard's study. It really wasn't my fault. The heated exchange between Howard and Ralph over a business endeavor Ralph wishes to enter into with Walt Marlow was simply too delicious to ignore. I'm hoping Thelma can tell me more when we are able to talk.

Danielle paused a moment. *Howard, that must be Thelma's husband. Jolene's grandfather—*

Howard's brother—was named Ralph. Is this the same Ralph? Danielle continued reading.

Thelma has finally confessed the name of her lover. It is Walt Marlow. I was surprised she finally revealed his name; I have asked her so many times only to be met with resolute silence. She told me after I asked her about the argument in the study. She explained Howard suspects the affair, which is why he opposes his brother's business proposition with Walt Marlow.

Danielle looked up from the page for a moment. "Why did Thelma lie?" Danielle asked aloud. After rereading the passage, she mumbled, "I guess that answers my other question; it was the same Ralph." With a sigh, she continued reading.

Another cuckolded husband might be tempted to divorce his wife and endure the scandal or have her put away discreetly, but I don't see that happening with Thelma, considering her inheritance. Howard will endure what he must to keep his golden goose.

"Oh really?" Danielle smirked. "So Thelma had her own money?"

Danielle continued to skim through the diary, paying special attention to any passages mentioning Thelma. She began to wonder why Ben entertained the idea that Walt was behind the murders. It wasn't until she came to an entry posted just two weeks prior to the *Eva Aphrodite*'s fateful voyage that she had her answer.

Thelma cancelled our luncheon date, claiming to be ill. I knew Howard is still away on business and won't be home until the weekend, so I decided to check in on her. I was shocked at what I found! She was all alone, not even her personal maid was there. She had sent them all away. I suspect so they wouldn't see her drunk.

Yes, drunk. I have never seen her like this. I am glad I stopped by because, frankly, I believe the poor girl intended to do herself more harm than what just comes from the bottom of a bottle.

She ranted, "He left me! Me, who is he to leave me?" I asked her if she meant Howard, wondering if perhaps he could no longer endure the knowledge his wife was having an affair. She laughed and told me, that to her grief, Howard would never leave her. I then asked her if she meant Walt Marlow. She just looked at me for a moment and began to sob. She is heartbroken.

When she finally stopped sobbing, she confessed she had threatened him. At first, I assumed she meant physically harm him, but then she told me she intended to ruin him. Foolishly, she also expressed this intent to Walt Marlow, who countered with his own threat, yet his was more deadly. He threatened to kill her. And yet, she still loves him.

Danielle shook her head and said aloud, "Thelma obviously told Ethel her lover threatened her life, and Ethel assumes that's Walt."

An entry the following week again mentioned Thelma.

I can't stand by and do nothing. I must help my friend even if she doesn't want it. She may never forgive me, but I have no choice. I went to Howard Templeton's office this morning. I explained Walt Marlow had seduced Thelma, that it wasn't her fault. She is just a vulnerable woman. I explained Marlow does not want the affair revealed, I assume because he does not want to jeopardize whatever business arrangement he is attempting to put together with Howard's brother. Marlow obviously understands Ralph will walk away if he discovers Walt is having an affair with his sister-in-law.

I was so nervous, but I managed to have my say. When I was done, Howard sat there stoically, saying nothing. I began to regret going to him, but then he

stood up, took my hands in his and told me he appreci-
ated me coming to him, that I was a true friend to
Thelma. He promised he would take care of every-
thing and he would keep Thelma safe. That dear man
really does love his wife.

Danielle looked up from the pages and considered Ethel's words. "That might explain Howard's parting comments about Walt before he moved on. He obviously believed Walt was his wife's lover—and that he had threatened to kill her."

"Walt would never hurt anyone," a female voice said from the hallway.

Danielle looked toward the voice. It was Eva Thorndike, her transparent vision almost glowing as she stood in the office doorway.

THIRTY-THREE

Closing the diary, Danielle set it on Ben's desk and stood up, facing the apparition. "I didn't think you were here."

Eva smiled. "I wasn't. But I am now." Her vision floated into the room, ethereal and glowing, nothing like Walt's presence or even Jack's. Should Danielle happen upon either Jack or Walt and not already know they were spirits, she would initially believe them to be flesh and blood men. Not so with Eva. This Eva Thorndike was the epitome of the haunting spirit—the classical feminine specter cast in countless ghost stories.

"Why haven't I ever seen you at the museum before—before this afternoon?"

"I rarely come here. Although I do occasionally. After all, they do have my portrait."

"I just assumed you were in some way attached to your portrait."

"Haunting the museum?" Eva asked, sounding highly amused.

Danielle smiled. "Yes."

Eva laughed and waved one hand in a dramatic flourish. "This would be a rather tedious venue to spend one's eternity, don't you think?"

"I suppose," Danielle muttered lamely, suddenly feeling immensely inadequate next to Eva Thorndike. She was even more beautiful than her portrait. *No wonder Walt fell madly in love with her. What man wouldn't be captivated by her looks alone?* "Why are you here at all? Why haven't you moved on?"

"It's much too bright in this room; come with me," Eva said, floating back into the hallway.

Danielle followed Eva to the Thorndike exhibit. Once there, Eva perched atop the glass display cabinet housing the emerald. She sat in front of her portrait, striking a flattering pose, and smiled down at Danielle.

"Why haven't you moved on?" Danielle asked again.

"Move on? I was far too young to die. I wasn't ready; I had things I still wanted to do. Maybe I couldn't prevent my death, but I refuse to be rushed along in my journey."

"So you've been here all this time?" Danielle asked. "You've never tried to move on?"

"I'm not ready, and they can't force me," she said stubbornly.

"If you haven't spent the last hundred years with your portrait, where have you been?"

Eva sighed. "For a while, I stayed with Walt. He had been so good to me—taken care of me when I needed him most, asking nothing in return. I loved him like a brother. I wish I would have loved him—differently. Loved him like I know he loved me. But then, I was always a fool."

"A fool?"

"The men I chose." Eva shook her head.

"Horrible choices. But staying with Walt proved most frustrating."

"How so?" Danielle glanced around. She spied a chair sitting not far from the exhibit. Still listening to Eva, she quickly grabbed the chair, pulled it up to the Thorndike exhibit, and sat down. Fascinated with what Eva had to say, she continued to listen.

"He got involved with that horrid Angela. He had spent all those years pining over me—drifting from one meaningless relationship to another. When she dug her greedy claws into him, the foolish man thought he was in love! I tried to stop him, but of course, he wasn't like you. He had no idea I had been with him all those years."

"Were you there when her brother killed him?"

Eva sighed. "I knew it was going to happen, and I knew I couldn't prevent it. Having the freedom of movement comes with a price."

"You can't harness your energy?" Danielle asked.

Eva frowned. "Harness my energy?"

"You can't move objects, right?"

Eva shook her head. "No. Sometimes I can make the lights flicker. Once I managed to bust a lightbulb, but that's about it. I suppose if I settled somewhere, stayed in one place, I would accumulate the necessary energy to make my presence known. But why? I don't want to be tied to one place. I want to move freely, explore the world."

"Were you there when Walt was killed?"

Eva shook her head. "I couldn't stop it, and I didn't want to watch it. And I didn't want to be there when Walt's spirit self-awakened. Our souls are not destined to be together for eternity, and I didn't want to confuse him. I'd hurt him enough when we were both alive. I felt it best to move on."

"If you were with Walt until his brother-in-law plotted to kill him, then you must have been there when the *Eva Aphrodite* went missing."

Eva smiled softly. "He named his yacht after me. I always thought that so sweet of him."

"Do you know why Thelma Templeton told her friend Ethel that Walt was her lover?"

"I have no idea what was in that woman's

mind. But I'll tell you, Walt never had anything to do with Thelma. I remember once Walt was having drinks with a friend when he ran into her and her husband. The husband left, and she approached Walt, making it clear to him she would be interested in something —more intimate."

Danielle remembered Walt's dream hop and the speakeasy. She suspected that was the incident Eva was referring to.

"Of course, Thelma Templeton was on the rebound."

"Rebound?"

Eva sighed. "I didn't spend all my time by Walt's side. I'm afraid I'd get a little bored doing that. Sometimes, I would check in on my ex-husband."

"The one who switched the diamonds and emeralds in your necklace?"

"Like I said, I had horrible taste in men. Although, in fairness to myself, I was not the only woman to fall under his spell. Thelma was quite besotted with the rogue."

"Are you suggesting Thelma Templeton's lover was your ex-husband?"

"He was handsome—I can't really blame

her. And he did have a way with the ladies. Of course, when he was ready to move on, he moved on."

"Marie said something about Thelma having an affair with an actor. Your husband was an actor, wasn't he?"

"Not a very good one. But he didn't need to be as long as the wealthy ladies paid his bills. Unfortunately, Anthony bored easily."

"Anthony, that was your husband's name?"

"Yes."

"According to Ethel's diary, she walked in on Thelma dressing and discovered her back covered with bruises. Thelma claimed it was the work of her lover, which at the time she led Ethel to believe was Walt."

"Walt would never hit a woman. Never. Anthony, on the other hand, had a violent temper. If provoked—he wouldn't hesitate using his fist on a woman. That's why I finally left him."

"He hit you? Did Walt know?"

Eva laughed. "Tell Walt that Anthony hit me? Are you insane? It was bad enough when he discovered Anthony had stolen from me.

No, I never told him. I think my mother may have suspected. My father knew, which was how I managed to get my marriage annulled so quickly. I put up with a lot from Anthony, but I wasn't going to be his punching bag."

"According to Ethel's diary, Thelma's lover broke it off with her—I'm assuming that was Anthony?"

"Probably. I'll be honest; I stopped checking on Anthony around that time. He had just taken up with a new woman, one with even more money than Thelma. Plus, she was a widow. I saw what he was doing. He intended to marry her, as he had married me. The difference with this new woman was that she had already come into her full inheritance and was a rich widow. I didn't want to watch, so I never saw Anthony again."

"I imagine this new woman wouldn't have been thrilled to discover she wasn't the only one he was seeing."

Eva laughed. "No she wouldn't. From what I recall, she was a rather demanding woman. Attractive, but a few years older than Anthony. She had never had children, so there was nothing in his way—aside from his relationship with Thelma."

"Do you have any idea who killed those people on the *Eva Aphrodite*?" Danielle asked.

Eva moved from the display case and stood before Danielle. She shook her head solemnly. "No, but their spirits have been interestingly active recently."

"You're talking about the people who were murdered on the ship?"

"Yes. I had no idea back then anyone had been murdered. Just because some of us reside in the spirit realm does not necessarily mean we are aware of all that's going on around us."

"Just like in real life," Danielle muttered.

"Yes. But for me, this is my real life…or perhaps, my real death."

"So what did you mean when you said they have been interestingly active recently?"

"I periodically stop in at the museum, which is how I happened to hear about the ship washing up on shore. And then I heard the people had been murdered. I went down to the beach to see for myself. There were flashes of those souls calling out to me, demanding the truth finally be told. But they were behind a wall. So there was only so much they could do."

Danielle frowned. "Behind a wall?"

"Yes. Not a wall as you might know it, but a wall nevertheless. Once one passes over, there are very limited ways one can return or communicate with the living—or with the souls like me, who have refused to move on."

"Walt's still at Marlow House," Danielle blurted out.

Eva smiled softly. "Yes, I know."

"He can't leave. He's confined there. When he wants to move on, he can, but until he does, he can't venture beyond Marlow House's walls."

"Yes, I know."

Danielle cocked her head slightly and studied Eva. "If you know he's been there all these years, why haven't you ever tried to make contact with him? Visit your old friend. He can't leave Marlow House, but I imagine you could go there."

Eva shook her head. "No, Danielle. I told you, it would only confuse things. Someday, when we both move on, we can meet again as friends. But while we're here, it's better this way."

"Don't you want to move on?"

"I told you! I'm much too young! I still have so much to do!" Eva laughed gaily and then vanished.

"Eva?" Danielle glanced around. "Eva?"

The room felt different somehow. It felt as it had when she had first arrived at the museum and had approached the portrait. Eva Thorndike's spirit was no longer in the building.

"Wow. There was so much more I wanted to ask her."

Danielle returned to the office and picked up the diary. Sitting back down in the office chair, she opened the book and began reading where she had left off.

It was dark when Danielle finished reading. When she was done, she placed the book back in the drawer and pulled out her cellphone. She called Chief MacDonald. Initially she intended to tell Walt about Eva before mentioning anything to the chief, but considering the chief's obsession with Walt's possible guilt, she didn't want to wait.

"You can stop worrying about Walt," Danielle announced when the chief answered the phone.

"Danielle? Where are you?"

"I'm at the museum."

"At this time at night? Isn't it closed? Are they having a meeting or something?"

"I came down to read the diary, remember?"

"Not sure how you arrived at the conclusion that Walt is not a danger. I read that diary too."

"Yes, but you didn't talk to Eva Thorndike."

"Eva Thorndike? Are you talking about that woman in the portrait?"

"Yes, and she's even more beautiful in person. Well...not in person exactly...in spirit?"

"Are you telling me Eva Thorndike haunts the Frederickport Museum?"

"Don't be silly, Chief. The museum would be a rather tedious venue to spend one's eternity, don't you think?"

THIRTY-FOUR

W alt and Jack were waiting for Danielle when she walked in the kitchen door Monday evening. They weren't alone. Lily was there gathering a stack of napkins and paper plates.

"You're just in time for pizza!" Lily announced. "Everyone's in the dining room. Want some?"

"Thanks, Lily, but I grabbed a burrito at the drive-through on the way home."

Lily closed the pantry door and faced Danielle, her hands occupied with the paper plates and napkins. "Did you find out anything interesting?"

"Yes, what did you find out?" Walt asked.

Jack eyed Lily appreciatively. She wore a snugly fitting T-shirt and lounging pants, her red hair pulled up casually in a high ponytail. "I think I'm falling in love with this little doll. I could have showed her a good time back in the day."

"That day is long gone, Jack," Walt said impatiently. He looked back to Danielle, waiting for her reply.

Danielle flashed Jack a smile and then looked from Lily to Walt. "I read the diary, but it was basically all hearsay. Thelma was having an affair with some guy that was abusive, he broke it off, and when she threatened him, he supposedly threatened her life. Thelma claimed Walt was her lover, but Ethel never saw them together. I stopped at Marie's, and according to her, Thelma was having an affair with some actor. Marie's mother saw them together. I think Thelma told her friend it was Walt because she didn't want to admit who it really was."

"Back then, actors were considered to be from the wrong side of the tracks," Lily suggested.

"I agree. But it's kind of ironic; she was having an affair, so why does it really matter at that point who it was with?" Danielle asked.

"It just did." Walt spoke up. "Cheating on her husband was one thing, but slumming was another."

"Walt agrees with you," Danielle told Lily. Danielle failed to mention that the actor in question had already hooked a woman of greater stature who wasn't afraid of what people thought; that was, of course, had she been willing to marry the actor, as Eva suggested. But Danielle wasn't ready to tell Walt about her encounter with Eva. She needed to figure out just how she would tell him.

"Walt's here?" Lily glanced around.

"Yes. And Jack too. Who, by the way, thinks you're a hot little thing."

Blushing, Lily looked to where she imagined Jack might be standing. "Really?"

With a cheeky grin, Lily tossed her head back, sending her ponytail swishing as she sashayed out of the kitchen, a slight more wiggle to her walk. "You're welcome to join us, Dani!" Lily called back as she stepped from the room.

Chuckling under her breath, Danielle shook her head. "I'm going to go take a shower, guys. I'm wiped out. It's been a long day. I think I'm going to go to bed early."

"Is that it?" Walt asked as she headed for the door.

Pausing, she looked back at Walt. "Yeah, for now."

DANIELLE HAD JUST CLIMBED into bed and pulled the covers up over her when Walt appeared by her side.

"Where's your friend?" she asked.

"He's in the attic with Max. I told him I wanted to talk to you alone."

Danielle snuggled down in the bed, her hands clutching the top of her blanket. "What about?"

"What aren't you telling me?"

Danielle licked her lips nervously. "What do you mean?"

Walt pointed to Danielle. "That."

"That what?"

"You always lick your lips when you're keeping something from me."

"I do not!" Danielle scooted down in the bed, pulling the blankets to her chin.

"What aren't you telling me?" he demanded.

After a moment, Danielle released hold of her blanket; she dropped her hands and arms on top of it with a flop and looked up at Walt. "I saw Eva tonight."

Walt's eyes widened. "Eva?"

Danielle nodded. "Yes, at the museum." She couldn't decide if Walt's expression was that of confusion or simply shock.

Silently, he sat down on the bed beside her. "Why didn't you tell me before?"

Danielle shrugged. "I was trying to figure out how to. I know what she meant to you."

"Just tell me, Danielle."

Danielle scooted back up in the bed. Leaning against the headboard, she looked at Walt and proceeded to tell him about her encounter with the famous silent screen star Eva Thorndike.

When she was done recounting the meeting, she said, "I have to say, she's even more beautiful in person—well, you know what I mean. When I first saw the portrait, I thought she looked like the Gibson Girl, but she's actually more…umm, for lack of a better word…sexier. I always thought there was something a little virginal looking about the Gibson Girl."

Walt laughed. "I always thought the Gibson Girl inspired the portrait artist's portrayal of Eva. He imagined her on a pedestal —untouchable."

"I can also see how she was an actress. She's still very—dramatic."

Walt laughed again. "Yes, Eva had a flair for the dramatic, even when we were children. But why hasn't she moved on?"

"I think it's her way of protesting her early death."

Walt stood up. "I'll let you go to sleep now."

Cocking her head, she studied Walt curiously. "You're okay with this, aren't you?"

"Why wouldn't I be?"

Danielle shrugged. "I just know how in

love you were with her. To find out she's still here—that she hasn't moved on."

"I told you, Danielle, I've moved beyond all that. I loved Eva once. I still love her, but now as a dear friend. We'll see each other again when we're both finished with what we have to do here."

"I suppose I understand. It's kinda how I feel about Lucas."

Walt nodded.

"Can I ask you one thing?" she asked.

"Anything."

"Do I really lick my lips when you think I'm keeping something from you?"

Walt smiled. "Not really sure. But it does seem to be one of your nervous tics—and you did tell me about Eva when I called you on it."

Danielle scrunched up her nose. "One of my tics? You mean I have others?"

Walt smiled, whispered, "Sweet dreams," and then vanished.

SHE WAS ROCKING AGAIN. Back and

forth. Back and forth. Danielle opened her eyes. Once again she was in a rocking chair on Emma's front porch, with Emma in the chair next to her—the older Emma, as she was the last time Danielle had seen her alive.

"I didn't expect to see you again!" Danielle said brightly. "How's Emmett?"

"I haven't moved on yet. I can't. I must have shown you the wrong thing. That's not what they wanted you to see."

"Did they tell you what they wanted exactly?"

Emma shook her head. "That would be too easy. Haven't you figured that out yet? Nothing in life—or death—is easy."

"Okay…" Danielle considered the puzzle. "I assume it has to be something you witnessed—or maybe you were just there. After all, you worked in the Bluebell Diner; people were coming and going all the time. Maybe it's a conversation between some customers—something you didn't actually overhear, but something we can listen to now if we go back."

"Child, do you really expect to go back and listen to every conversation of every person who was ever in the diner at the same time I was? And maybe it wasn't when I was at the diner. Maybe it was when I was at the beach, in the store, at the—"

"Okay, okay, you're right. That would be insane. We should isolate it to, let's say, the week or two leading up to the storm and focus on anyone connected to the people who were killed."

"I told you, I don't remember seeing any of those people."

After a moment of silence, Danielle said, "Well, I just found out Thelma Templeton, one of the women killed on the boat, was having an affair with an actor, and they broke it off a couple weeks before the murders. He did threaten her life. Although, I can't imagine he would kill everyone on board that yacht just to keep their affair a secret."

"An actor?"

"Anthony…I didn't get his last name. But he was once married to Eva Thorndike."

"I know who that was."

"You knew him?"

"I knew who he was. He used to come

into the diner from time to time. The girls would fall all over him."

"We could try him. Focus on any dates he came into the diner right before the *Eva Aphrodite* went missing."

In the next moment, Danielle found herself sitting back in the Bluebell Diner, with Emma by her side. They occupied the same table they had been at during their last dream hop visit. They weren't alone. A handsome man sat across from Danielle, reading his menu.

"That's Anthony," Emma explained.

"Oh, I see what you mean. Eye candy, but a little sleazy." Danielle noted the heavily oiled slicked-back, coal-black hair and pencil mustache. "He could use a good shampoo… and a razor to get rid of that thing on his lip."

"That's how they wore it back then."

"I suppose," Danielle said with a shrug.

"The other one will be here in a moment," Emma explained.

"Other one?"

"The man he had breakfast with."

Danielle glanced at the remaining empty

chair. "Please tell me his friend will be taking that chair and not mine."

Emma laughed. "Yes, I was more careful about that. Sorry."

As Emma promised, a man walked through the diner's door a moment later. Emma nudged Danielle and pointed to the man. Looking up, Danielle watched as he glanced around the room, spied Anthony, and then proceeded to walk in their direction.

Danielle's eyes widened. "I know that man!"

"You know him? How do you know him?"

"It's Ephraim Presley, the man who murdered Harvey Crump—the boy who haunted Presley House!"

Emma shook her head. "I have no idea what you're talking about."

Ephraim Presley had worked for Eva Thorndike's parents as a caretaker when she was still alive. He was also her ex-husband's accomplice in the original Thorndike jewel heist back when the first set of diamonds and emeralds were removed from Eva's necklace and replaced with fake stones.

Harvey Crump, a friend of Ephraim Presley's twin sons, had stumbled upon Ephraim's share of the jewel heist. That discovery led to Harvey's premature death. Danielle had witnessed Harvey's murder in a previous dream hop.

Ephraim Presley was also Heather Donovan's great-grandfather. She had stumbled upon the sins of her ancestor along with one of the emeralds he had taken. That emerald she had given to Danielle in her attempt to set things right. It was the same emerald now on display at the Frederickport Museum.

"What did you want to see me about?" Ephraim asked when he reached their table and sat down on the only empty chair.

"I have a job for us. This is a big one." Anthony stopped talking when Emma the waitress approached the table and poured them coffee. The men hastily gave her their orders for breakfast, and when she left the table, they resumed their conversation.

"How big?"

"This one's all cash. You won't have to worry about finding a buyer for any stones. But you can't be squeamish about putting some bullets through a few heads."

Ephraim laughed. "For enough money, I'd plug my own mother."

"I don't think he had a mother," Danielle muttered, remembering what she had once read about Heather's great-grandfather.

"When, where, who?" Ephraim asked.

"Saturday night, on the *Eva Aphrodite*."

"Marlow's yacht?"

Anthony nodded. "We can't leave any witnesses, so you have to be willing to finish the job. We have to kill everyone on that boat."

"That's a lot of people. How do you expect just the two of us to pull that off?"

"I don't."

"Good lord," Danielle gasped. "He doesn't even flinch at the idea of slaughtering all those innocent people, just wants to know how they're going to pull it off."

"How much money?" Ephraim asked.

When Anthony told him, Danielle let out a low whistle.

"And the perk is, we can keep any of the booty from the ship. Divide up any cash, jewelry, anything of value."

"Who's paying for this and why?" Ephraim asked.

"I can't say."

Ephraim started to stand up. "Forget it, then."

Anthony reached up and grabbed Ephraim's arm. "Wait, hear me out. I need you on this one."

Begrudgingly, Ephraim sat back down.

Nervous, Anthony glanced around the diner and lowered his voice. "If I tell you, you can't let anyone know. I'm being blackmailed."

THIRTY-FIVE

J ogging down the beach from where he had parked his car, Kurt Jefferson glanced out to sea. For a moment, he imagined his boat anchored out beyond the surf and that he was diving into the ocean and swimming to shore. He could just see himself in his diving gear glistening as he emerged from the water, the moon lighting his way. A covert op with a pot of gold as his reward. Kurt wondered if he had been watching too much television.

It was a long shot, he knew. But if he managed to pull it off, he would be rich beyond his wildest dreams. What was the worst that could happen? He could get arrested for breaking and entering—his first offense. Chances were, he would get a slap on the wrist and probation. It was worth the risk.

This morning was just simply a reconnaissance mission. He wanted to get the lay of the land, check out the target. When he did return, he doubted it would be by boat or that he would be wearing his diving gear. It just seemed more dramatic to imagine it under that scenario.

He was certain this was the right house. According to the stories, it was the oldest house along this stretch of the beach and was located directly across the street from Marlow House. It was owned by the Hemmings family. According to the stories, Marlow's partner had been renting a room from Hemming when he went missing—along with their money. Of course, now everyone knew the partner hadn't run away with the money; he had been murdered on board the Marlow yacht along with all those other people.

Kurt wondered if it was possible that after all these years, that money—those gold coins —was still hidden in the Hemming house.

From what he had heard on the radio when they interviewed that guy from the museum, Marlow was on record saying his partner had kept their money with him at Hemming's, and when he disappeared, so did the money. Perhaps the partner had simply left the money hidden somewhere in the Hemming house when he decided to go out on the yacht and never got around to telling his partner he decided to go party. *Some party. Everyone ended up dead.*

Walking along the beach, Kurt reached the point between the Hemming house and its neighbor to the north. From there, he had a clear view of Marlow House. To his surprise, he spied a man and golden retriever walking through the gates of Marlow House. When checking on the status of the Hemming property, he had learned some author had rented the place—and this renter had a golden retriever. He had also learned the man dated one of the women who lived across the street at Marlow House. Could this be the same man?

Kurt smiled to himself. He could simply knock on the back door of the Hemming house. If no dog came barking to the back door, he would know the coast was clear. But if a dog did come barking and the renter answered the door, he could pretend to be lost and ask some inane question, without raising any suspicions.

HEATHER DONOVAN no longer jogged with her eyes closed. She had learned that lesson after she almost ran straight into the wreckage of the *Eva Aphrodite*. She listened to the music pulsating through the headphones as she pounded her way down the beach, her heart beating rapidly and her breathing labored. She had decided to push herself this morning. Exercise alleviated stress, and recently she had been experiencing too much stress. Even her essential oils weren't helping.

Just as Ian's house came into view, she spied someone lurking around the back of the property. It wasn't Ian. Instinctively dropping to the sand to make herself less obvious, Heather narrowed her eyes and watched the trespasser casing the property.

He was now at the back door. She could see him looking up and down the beach. He turned in her direction. She could see his face. Holding her breath, she hugged the sand, grateful she hadn't worn her purple jogging suit that morning. The tan sweat suit melted into her surroundings, camouflaging her from view. She watched as he went into the house.

———

THE SMELL of bacon woke her. Danielle opened her eyes. She yawned.

"I wondered If you were going to sleep all morning," Walt said from where he sat on the sofa.

Danielle bolted up to a seated position and rubbed her eyes. "How long have you been sitting there?"

"For a while." Walt shrugged. "Ian's here, helping Lily fix breakfast. I guess Joanne called in sick."

Danielle glanced at her iPhone. "She didn't call me."

"I heard Lily say something about a text message."

Danielle picked up her phone from the nightstand and looked at it. "You're right. Looks like Joanne sent us a group text message. I must have slept right through it. I wonder why Lily didn't wake me up."

"Maybe she was just being nice. She and Ian have everything under control. I get the feeling that Ian is enjoying your guest."

"The mystery writer?"

Walt nodded.

Sitting up in bed, Danielle leaned against her headboard and looked at Walt. "Emma visited me last night."

"Again?"

"I'm pretty sure Jack was being honest with you about paying off those loan sharks. It was just a coincidence. I don't even think that's what Emma was supposed to show me."

"Then what was it?"

"What she showed me last night." Danielle then went on to tell Walt about her most recent dream hop. Walt sat quietly, listening to Danielle tell him about seeing Anthony and Ephraim and how Anthony claimed he was being blackmailed.

"The reason Jack doesn't remember that

night is that they drugged him. Or at least that was the plan they discussed at the Bluebell. They were going to pay Sally to slip something in Jack's drink when he came over to see her that night. And then they'd use him to get on the boat, pretend he was drunk, not drugged, like they were all drinking buddies just out for some fun."

"And since Jack was my partner, no one would question it," Walt said.

"Their plan all along was to kill Jack once they got him to that cabin, and hide the body. There was a second boat—they were going to board the *Eva Aphrodite* like pirates once it was out to sea."

"And easier if they kill the crew before they board the ship," Walt said, sounding a little ill.

"Pretty much."

"Who was behind this? You said Anthony claimed he was being blackmailed."

"He never told Presley who was behind it, but he kept saying he would; he just had to make sure Presley was totally in. But whoever it was, he didn't want anyone on the job knowing who was behind it."

"This explains what probably happened to Anthony," Walt said.

"What do you mean?"

"From what I recall, he sort of disappeared after the *Eva Aphrodite* went missing. I never put the two together before."

"He went missing that night?"

Walt shook his head. "No, he wasn't killed that night. The reason I remember, he was going to be in a play that was scheduled to open the following week, but because of the storm—"

"You're talking about the storm the night the boat went missing?"

Walt nodded. "Yes. It caused some damage to the theater, delaying the opening. He was in the play the first night, and then I remember hearing he'd taken off—the stand-in had to take his place. I never really thought much about it. Anthony was famous for just taking off."

"You think whoever was behind the murders killed him?"

"If he really was the only one who knew the identity of the person or persons behind the murders, yes. Probably."

"I can understand someone arranging a hit and then getting rid of the hit man—but why would someone go to an actor to arrange something like this?"

"Anthony knew some pretty shady people. And I always suspected stealing the diamonds and emeralds from Eva's necklace wasn't his first, last, or even worst crime."

Danielle cringed. "It certainly wasn't his worst."

"I'd like to know, who was really the target?" Walt wondered.

"Eva's ex was pretty damn cold. While it's monstrous to murder innocent strangers in cold blood, he killed a woman he'd been having an affair with. Someone he had been intimate with."

Walt chuckled. "Now you know how I felt."

JOLENE CARMICHAEL SAT in the office of Steve Klein.

"I'm sorry, Jolene, I just don't see how I can do it," he apologized. "Like I explained last week, there simply isn't enough equity left in your house."

"I have to get out from under that second, the interest is killing me. Can't I just refinance?" she pleaded.

"I'm sorry, Jolene. Really. I wish there was something I could do to help you. This deal with Clarence, it gutted the company, and aside from what you're getting from Social Security, I don't see how you could ever qualify for another loan."

"That was supposed to be my retirement! I loaned them the money to start the law firm; this isn't fair. I should at least get the property."

"I'm sorry. That's a matter for an attorney."

Ten minutes later, Jolene Carmichael drove away from the bank. She told herself to calm down. This wasn't good for her blood pressure. Yet she couldn't calm down. What was she going to do? It was all gone—and all because of Danielle Boatman. Boatman had been greedy, Jolene thought. Marlow House and some money wasn't enough for Boatman; she had to have it all. It wasn't as if Boatman had spent all those years tending to her aunt's estate—making sure Marlow House was properly cared for—Clarence had done that. Perhaps he had overstepped the line by redirecting some of Brianna Boatman's money, but did that sin warrant his death?

Pulling over to the side of the road, Jolene parked the car and looked ahead blankly.

"What am I going to do?" she asked aloud. "Why can't I have some of Danielle Boatman's luck and find a priceless neckless hidden in my floorboards?" It was then Jolene remembered the conversation she'd had at the museum with Ben after his radio interview. The gold coins—*did they still exist?*

BILL JONES FLIPPED through his clipboard as he finished his cup of coffee. He shoved the now empty breakfast plate to the edge of the table and waited for the server to bring his bill. Looking through his job orders, he rearranged the pages, placing them in a specific order to schedule his day. The next house he was going to was on the north side of town. The first house was one located on the same street as the Hemming house. There was a bathroom faucet to replace; he had already picked up a new one.

Looking at the order, Bill paused a moment and looked up, staring absently into space. The work order made him think of the Hemming house—and of the gold coins that might be hidden there.

Adam is full of it, he thought. He had known Adam most of his life, and there was no way he wasn't just as curious as Bill about the possibility of hidden treasure. From what Bill had since read after that fiasco with the Missing Thorndike, if Bill did happen upon the hidden gold—like when he was doing repairs at the rental—he could legally claim the gold under Oregon's treasure trove laws. At least, he was pretty sure he could. Hell, he didn't need Adam to do this. He didn't need Adam at all.

"Hey, Carla, bring me my check!" Bill shouted to the server. He smiled to himself. *I think I need to go check out Ian's rental, make sure nothing's broken.*

THIRTY-SIX

"Sally set me up?" Jack sounded heartbroken. Walt had just repeated most of what Danielle had told him about what she had learned through her dream hop with Emma. The two old friends sat up in the attic on the sofa while Sadie napped by their feet and Max perched on the windowsill, tail swishing back and forth, as the cat stared out the window.

"From what Danielle overheard, I don't think Sally knew they were going to kill you. Just use you to get on that boat."

"But wouldn't she have known when I never came back and they did?"

"I'm afraid they may have gotten rid of Sally."

"What do you mean?" Jack asked.

"We all thought you and Sally ran off together. When I went looking for you at her place, she was gone."

"They killed her?" Jack asked.

Walt shrugged. "That would be my guess. I never saw her again."

Jack let out a weary sigh and leaned back in the sofa. "I suppose that answers most of the questions. What happened to me, why I was on the boat."

"I still wonder what happened to our money. If they took you the way they said they were going to, at the motel—you wouldn't have taken the money with you when you went to meet Sally, would you?"

Jack let out a snort. "Hardly. Always thought Sally was a fun girl, but I'd never trust her around my wallet. No, that money's probably still across the street at George's. Unless someone else has found it since that time, which is entirely possible considering how long it's been."

"You already said you moved it. The question is, where to?"

"I remember I was going to bring it here, but then I wanted to go to Sally's—which was obviously a stupid idea. I moved it. Somewhere safe. Hidden."

"Where?"

"I don't remember."

Walt chuckled. "Well, we can't use the money now anyway."

"I would like to know who was behind it all. Who knows, maybe when I move on, I'll find out."

"Does this mean you're ready to move on?" Walt asked.

"I think so." Jack looked at Walt. "What about you? You could go with me. See what's on the other side. A new adventure."

Walt smiled. "I don't think so. You go ahead. I'll catch up later."

Jack studied Walt for a moment. "It's that little doll, isn't it?"

Walt frowned and looked away. "What are you talking about?"

Jack laughed. "I see how you look at her. I

remember how you used to look at Eva. Not so different."

Walt stood. "Oh, shut up." He walked to the window.

"Hell, not different at all," Jack scoffed.

Walt turned from the window and looked at Jack. "What do you mean?"

"You never had a chance with Eva. She always saw you as a brother; that was never going to change. And with Danielle. Well, isn't it obvious? I don't see you as having much of a chance with her either, but for an entirely different reason."

"THAT WAS A DELICIOUS BREAKFAST," Hillary said as she dabbed the corners of her mouth with a cloth napkin.

Danielle stood up and began to gather the dirty dishes off the dining room table. "Yes, it was. Thank you, Ian and Lily."

Ian stood up and started helping Danielle clear the table. "Considering all the meals I've mooched, I figure I owed you."

"Ian makes a mean waffle," Lily said as

she popped her last bite of bacon into her mouth. She then stood up and snatched the pile of dirty dishes from Ian. "You should go get that file for Dani to see."

"What file?" Danielle asked.

"Ian's been doing his own research on the *Eva Aphrodite*," Lily explained.

Curious, Danielle looked to Ian, her hands now full with dirty dishes.

"On the passengers and crew," Ian explained. "We know they were murdered. What we don't know is, was someone on that ship the real target—were the others collateral damage? Or was it a home invasion at sea?"

"I love a good mystery!" Hillary said. "What have you discovered?"

Ian flashed Hillary a smile and then looked at Danielle. "Okay, I'll run across the street and get the file with my research so far. It's a good excuse to get out of doing the dishes, anyway!" he added with a laugh as he dashed from the room.

———

KURT CROUCHED in the far corner of the

closet, holding his breath, praying the tenant didn't come into the bedroom or open the closet door. He had been so careful at first, looking out the front window every few minutes, preparing to escape out the back door the moment he saw the man with the dog returning from across the street. But then he got distracted in one of the bedrooms, and just as he stepped into the hallway to check the window again, he heard someone open the front door. He managed to duck in the bedroom just as the man came inside. Kurt had one thing to be grateful for: the man hadn't brought the dog back with him. If he had, Kurt was fairly certain he'd be in deep trouble by now.

IAN COULD NOT REMEMBER where he had left the research folder. He swore it was on the kitchen table, but when it wasn't there, he went to look in the living room. Just before he reached the living room, the doorbell rang.

When he answered it, he found a nicely

dressed, older woman standing on his front porch.

"Yes, how can I help you?" Ian asked.

"Hello, you must be Ian Bartley," she said, extending a hand in greeting. "I'm Jolene Carmichael from the Frederickport Historical Society."

Ian accepted her hand, yet paused a moment when he remembered why he recognized the name. She was the one Danielle had mentioned—the widow of Clarence Renton's business partner—the one who had been snarky to Danielle.

After the brief handshake, he asked, "How can I help you?"

"The historical society has been considering a historical home tour. This house is one of the oldest in Frederickport and—"

"I'm just renting the house," he interrupted. "You'd need to speak to its owner, Marie Nichols."

"Yes, yes. Of course, we will. I was just wondering if it might be possible—if it's not too much trouble, if I could look around inside?"

Ian frowned. "I'm not sure why."

"The interior of the house may not even be suitable for a historical home tour—considering any modern renovations it's had over the years."

"I don't think it's been changed much."

"Oh, wonderful! If I could just look around—see if it's what we're looking for, then we can contact Marie Nichols and see if she'd be willing to cooperate."

"You do know I'm renting the house. I don't intend to move out any time soon."

"Oh, this would not infringe on any of your renter's rights, I promise you! No, no. And who knows, if you just let me look around, it's entirely possible I'll discover this won't work for what we have in mind."

"How long will this take?"

"Were you on your way out?" she sounded hopeful.

"I was going back across the street. I just came over here to pick something up."

"It should only take—oh, maybe twenty minutes—you could go ahead and go. I'd be happy to lock up for you. I hate to be an imposition."

Ian arched his brows at the request.

Knowing who she was, he wasn't worried about letting her poke through the house, but he certainly wasn't going to leave her alone while he went back across the street. "I tell you what. You go ahead and have a look around. I need to get some things together anyway." He opened the door wider and stepped to the side, letting her come in. He watched curiously as she scurried off and started her inspection.

Just as Ian reached the living room, the doorbell rang again. Before answering the door, he glanced around the room, searching for the file. It was nowhere in sight. Returning to the front door, he opened it. Standing on the front porch was Bill Jones, toolbox in hand.

"Hi, Bill. What can I do for you?"

"I need to check your GFI switches."

Ian frowned. "GFI?"

"You see, before you moved in, I replaced a bunch of GFI switches in this house. Well, it seems there was just a recall, and I need to make sure none of the ones I put in here are part of the recall. I don't want your house to burn down."

Ian opened the door wider and stepped aside. "No, we don't want that."

Bill smiled and walked into the house. "If you were heading out somewhere, I can lock up for you. This will probably take a while."

"Yeah, well…maybe," Ian mumbled as he closed the front door. "I'm looking for something, and then I'll be heading back across the street, and—"

Bill walked off in the direction of Ian's bedroom, not waiting for Ian to finish his sentence. Ian was about to tell Bill not to be surprised when he ran into Jolene, who was wandering somewhere in his house. Instead, he shrugged and started back to the living room. He hadn't seen the file in there the first time he had looked, but he remembered another place he wanted to check.

A few moments later, Ian stood in the living room, scanning the bookshelves, looking for the end of a file he may have inadvertently stuck in between a couple of books, something he occasionally did. The doorbell rang again.

"What the hell is this, Grand Central Station?" Ian muttered. Just as he stepped away from the bookshelf to answer the door, he noticed the end of a folder sticking out from between two books.

"There you are!" Ian laughed as he snatched the folder from its place on the shelf. He quickly flipped through it to see if it was what he was looking for. Just when he was confident it was the correct folder, the doorbell rang again.

"I'm coming already!" Ian grumbled. Setting the file down on the coffee table, he hurried toward the front door. When he opened it, Adam Nichols was standing on the front porch.

"Adam? What are you doing here?"

Adam nodded toward Bill's truck. "I noticed Bill's truck out front. Is there a problem?"

"That's what he's checking."

"What do you mean?" Adam frowned.

"The GFI switches."

"What GFI switches?" Adam asked.

"The recall." When Adam still did not seem to comprehend, Ian said, "He probably didn't bother telling you about it." Ian opened the door wider and stepped aside. "Come on in; he can explain it to you."

Just as Adam stepped into the house, a bloodcurdling scream came from the spare bedroom.

THIRTY-SEVEN

A few minutes earlier

W*ho keeps ringing that doorbell?* Jolene wondered. Whoever it was, she hoped he or she would keep Bartley busy while she went through the house. While she knew finding the hidden treasure—if it was still here—was a long shot, she wanted to have a look around; perhaps she could convince the historical society to sponsor periodic home tours, which, of course, she would volunteer to oversee. With the tenant out of the house for a few hours before and during the tour, she would have an opportunity to inspect the rooms, searching for likely hiding places. She remembered Danielle Boatman had found the Missing Thorndike tucked behind some boards in the attic across the street.

Going to the closet, Jolene opened its door slowly, cringing when it started to squeak. She didn't want Ian Bartley to hear her opening the closet doors and wonder what she was doing. After she opened the closet door wide enough to slip into, she opened her purse and pulled out her iPhone to use as a flashlight.

KURT HELD HIS BREATH, his heart beating rapidly, when the closet door slowly opened. The last thing he expected to see was an elderly woman sticking her head into the dark and narrow space. A curtain of overcoats, hanging on the center of the overhead rod, helped conceal him from the intruder on the opposite end of the closet. From the darkness, he watched as she groped at the panels of the weathered wooden floor.

He had surmised this room was used as a guest room, since the only thing in the closet were the jackets blocking him from the woman—and the boxes he noticed shoved on the overhead shelf. From what he knew about the house, it was rented by a bachelor —who he assumed was the man he had seen leave earlier with a dog before returning alone.

The doorbell had rung several times since he had taken refuge in the closet, and he assumed this woman was one of the people who had just arrived. He wondered if she had been a recent guest and had returned to look for something she might have lost in the closet. *An earring perhaps?* The last time he spent a weekend away with a girlfriend, she complained about losing an earring in the motel. The women he knew seemed to always be losing earrings.

When she turned on the flashlight app of her iPhone, he held his breath, praying she wouldn't point that thing in his direction. He was tempted to grab the end of the nearest overcoat and pull it to one side to better conceal himself, yet was afraid the movement might catch her attention.

He watched as she knelt by the opening,

iPhone in one hand while the other hand fidgeted with a loose board.

She's not looking for a lost earring, she's about to pull that floorboard up, he thought. Mesmerized, he watched as she eagerly tugged at the weathered panel, dislodging it. He could swear he heard her make a gleeful cackling sound. Almost in a frenzy, she yanked up one board after another and then reached down into the opening and pulled up a box, which she quickly opened.

He could not contain his gasp when her greedy fingers dipped into the pile of gold coins, lifting them out of the box while they spilled from her fingers. The moment she heard his gasp, she let the rest of the coins drop as she quickly snatched up the iPhone and directed its beam toward him.

Jolene screamed.

WITHOUT PAUSE, Ian bolted from the doorway, heading for the sound of the scream. Adam followed close on Ian's heels. He was so intent on following his tenant, he failed to see Bill dart into the hallway from the master bedroom. Bill had also heard the scream. Bill and Adam collided. Ignoring the two men behind him, Ian swung the door open to the guest bedroom.

"What are you doing here?" Adam hissed under his breath to Bill.

Before Bill could reply, Ian's loud, "What the hell?" turned Bill's attention—and Adam's—to what Ian was now staring at.

Wild eyed and frantic, Jolene crouched on the floor in front of the partially opened closet. She clutched to her bosom an armful of gold coins as she looked from the man still hidden in the closet back to the three men peering in at her from the now open doorway.

Ian walked into the bedroom, with Adam and Bill following behind him.

"They are mine!" Jolene shouted. "Mine, mine, mine!"

Adam pushed around Ian and approached Jolene, staring into the closet. He could see the hiding place revealed by the now removed floor panels.

"Marlow's missing gold," Bill said.

"Damn, I knew I should have checked that closet first."

Adam pointed to the box. "Those aren't yours! Those were hidden in my grandmother's house! They belong to her!"

"I'll be damned," Ian said as he approached Jolene and the gold. "Those were here all this time?"

Hugging the gold to her chest, Jolene glared at Adam. Shaking her head furiously, she shouted, "Stay away! I claim these under Oregon's treasure trove laws!"

"What are you talking about?" Adam said as he reached down and attempted to snatch the coins from her grasp. She swatted him away and shouted an obscenity.

ACCORDING TO HEATHER DONOVAN, someone had broken into Ian Bartley's house. What Brian didn't understand was, why had she waited so long to call the police? It had been over an hour since she had seen the man slip into Ian's back door. Apparently, she had been jogging at the time. Her reason for not calling sooner was that she thought the man was probably a friend of Ian's but, after thinking about it for a while, decided she should probably call the police.

When Brian arrived at the scene, there were three vehicles parked in front of Ian's house. He recognized the truck; it belonged to Bill Jones, the handyman who worked for Adam Nichols. If Brian wasn't mistaken, the car parked behind the truck belonged to Adam. He didn't recognize the third vehicle. Ian's car was parked in the driveway.

Brian didn't notice the open front door until he was halfway up the walk. By that time, he could hear the shouting coming from inside the house. By the colorful expletives and number of different voices he heard, it sounded like a riot. Pausing a moment, he called for backup before going inside. He didn't know what he was facing.

By the sound of it, Brian imagined he was walking into a dangerously volatile situation, possibly with weapons drawn and blood spilled. What he found was something entirely different, more like a scene from a slapstick comedy.

Adam Nichols was playing slapsy with Jolene Carmichael, who kept yelling, "Mine, mine," while she hugged what appeared to be a pile of gold coins, many of which had already fallen from her grasp and landed on the floor around her.

Bill Jones was attempting to snatch some of the coins from the floor while Adam kicked his hand away while shouting at Jolene to let go of his gold. Meanwhile, Ian stood calmly on the sidelines, iPhone in hand, while he recorded the mayhem.

Brian's authoritative shout for everyone to quiet immediately silenced the group, which turned to him—including Ian, who now aimed the iPhone's lens at the officer and continued to record. When Brian realized Ian was recording him, he gestured for him to stop. Reluctantly, Ian complied, turning off the video app and tucking his phone into his back pocket.

The quiet didn't last long. Soon everyone was talking again, this time directing his or her words to Brian. In their competition to be heard, their volume increased, and soon they were shouting more at each other than trying to explain to the police officer what was going on.

Once again, Brian shouted to be quiet. He looked at Ian, the calmest of the group, and told him to explain what was going on.

"To be honest, I'm not really sure," Ian admitted.

Jolene started to say something, but Brian immediately hushed her and turned his attention back to Ian.

"First, Jolene Carmichael here"—Ian gestured toward the woman, who was now stumbling to her feet while snatching the fallen coins from the floor and returning them to the booty in her arms—"stopped by, asking to look around the house. She said the historical society was considering putting this house on some historical home tour."

"What home tour? No one's ever mentioned that to me," Adam piped up. Brian immediately hushed him and looked back to Ian again.

"I was in the middle of looking for some papers, so I told her to go ahead, have a look around. And then Bill stopped by, saying something about GFI switches needing to be looked at."

"GFI, my ass," Adam snapped, glaring at Bill. Bill snapped back, and soon the two were arguing. Once again, Brian hushed them and turned his attention back to Ian.

"I told Bill to go ahead, do what he needed to do, and I went back to looking for my papers. That's when Adam stopped by and asked why Bill was here. The next thing I know, someone is screaming bloody murder, and I run in here and find Mrs. Carmichael in my closet. It's pretty obvious to me her story about the home tour was just a ruse to get in and look for the treasure they've been talking about, and apparently she found it."

"It's mine!" Jolene screeched.

"It's not yours," Adam shouted back. "It was found in my house!"

"Technically it's your grandma's house," Bill muttered.

"Shut up, Bill," Adam snapped.

"This wouldn't have happened if you had just listened to me!" Bill countered.

Adam turned to Bill. "And that's why

you're here—GFI, my ass. You were treasure hunting!"

"If you hadn't gotten greedy—" Bill started to say.

"What do you mean greedy?" Adam asked.

"Get real, Adam, I know you. You were going to keep the treasure for yourself!"

"It's in my house!"

"Your grandmother's house!" Bill shouted back.

"It doesn't belong to either of you! I found it first!" Jolene yelled in a shrill voice.

Again, the three started screaming at each other while Ian and Brian watched on and exchanged glances.

Taking a deep breath, Brian expelled a frustrated sigh and yelled, "Shut up, and I swear if anyone says another word, I'm going to shoot him!"

Everyone got quiet. The silence was broken a moment later when someone said from the doorway, "I don't think shooting anyone would be a terrific idea. Too much paperwork."

They all turned to the voice. It was Chief

MacDonald, an amused expression on his face. Next to him stood Joe Morelli. His expression was more confusion than amusement.

The chief stepped into the room and surveyed the scene. As he approached Jolene—who still clung protectively to her treasure—Adam and Bill stepped back, making room for the chief. When MacDonald reached Jolene, he looked around her to the closet. With one hand, he gently pushed her aside so he could have a closer look at where she had discovered the coins.

MacDonald stuck his head into the closet and looked at the missing floorboard and the box half full with gold coins and several pieces of paper. He turned his gaze to the side and paused a moment before asking, "Who are you?"

THIRTY-EIGHT

I t was crowded in the interview room, but Chief MacDonald thought this was the best place to gather the principal parties. They had each been interviewed separately, but he wanted to bring them all together to discuss the gold's fate.

He had sent Bill Jones home. Technically, Bill hadn't broken any laws, and the chief figured he and Adam could work out their differences later. The man he had found hiding in the closet—Kurt Jefferson—was in lockup. The chief would deal with him later.

Both Danielle and Marie Nichols had been called down to the station. Joe had picked up Marie, while Danielle came down to the station with Lily.

Sitting around the room were Marie, Adam, Jolene, Ian, Danielle, and Lily. While Lily was not directly a principal party, the chief let her stay, considering her relationship to Danielle and Ian, and the fact that they both insisted she be there. Also in the room was Jack Winters. The only ones who knew he was there were Danielle and Lily, although the chief suspected he might be. Sitting on the center of the table was the box of gold pulled from its hiding place under the floor-boards from the Hemming house.

"Technically speaking, Jolene is right—she could, under the right circumstances, claim the gold under Oregon's treasure trove laws," the chief explained.

Jolene glared at Adam. "I told you that."

"I said under the right conditions," the chief reiterated.

"How is that even possible?" Marie asked. "Someone can really come onto my property and start ripping up my floorboards and take whatever they find?"

The chief nodded. "Yes, especially considering a tenant of your father left the treasure there. It never belonged to your family. The treasure trove laws in Oregon are rather liberal in regards to finders keepers."

"I'll get a lawyer—" Adam began, but was quieted by his grandmother, who reached over and grabbed hold of his hand, giving it a gentle squeeze.

"Does this mean I can take it?" Jolene asked.

"No. I'll let the courts handle this. But I suspect they'll decide the rightful owner of the gold is Danielle."

All heads turned to Danielle who blurted, "Me?"

With a nod, the chief walked to the table and pulled a plastic bag from the box. It held a small ledger book and a handwritten letter the chief had carefully slipped into the bag after initially examining the contents of the box.

"What's that?" Jolene asked with a frown.

"You were so focused on the gold coins, you ignored these," the chief explained.

"I remember now," Jack said from the corner, where he stood watching the scene unfold. Danielle glanced to him. "When I moved the box, I put my will in it." He laughed. "I was a little drunk when I wrote the will, but I was annoyed at Walt for implying I wasn't capable of keeping the money in a safe place. I figured when I took it over to Marlow house, he would find my will inside and feel guilty for thinking I was a piker."

"The amount of gold found in the box matches what's recorded in the ledger. If one were to read the ledger, they would assume the business was nothing more than a tour boat—there's no mention of moonshine. All very legal. The owners of the business—and the gold—are listed as Walt Marlow and Jack Winters. The document in the plastic bag is the last will and testament of Jack Winters— where he leaves all his worldly possessions to Walt Marlow. George Hemming witnessed the will—it has his signature."

"What does this mean?" Adam asked.

Marie reached up and took her grandson's hand. "It means, dear, the gold belongs to Danielle."

"No…" Adam groaned.

Jolene shook her head furiously and

jumped to her feet. "That's impossible! I found it; it's mine!"

"You can try fighting it in court," the chief said with a shrug. "But Winters left all his worldly possessions to Marlow. Marlow left all his worldly possessions to Brianna Boatman's mother, which went to her and she left all her worldly possessions—aside from specific amounts to several charities—to Danielle Boatman."

Adam started to say something but was again silenced by his grandmother, who squeezed his hand. After a moment, he looked at Danielle and said, "Okay, but I expect a steak and lobster dinner out of you. Several."

Danielle flashed Adam a guilty smile.

"This isn't fair!" Jolene ranted, turning her wrath at Danielle. "Why you? You get everything! Your aunt's estate, your cousin's, this, and even the real estate that should belong to our law firm! It was my family's money! It should be mine!"

Jolene was still screaming when Joe and Brian came into the interrogation room and removed her.

"What was that all about?" Adam asked. "I'm the one who should be crying like a baby."

Marie was pleased to see he was smiling.

"After they started digging into Renton's affairs, many assets from the law office were liquidated to pay off his debts—which included money he embezzled from my aunt's estate. I'm afraid Renton's law firm didn't do a very good job protecting their own assets— or Jolene's. I feel bad about it, but—"

Marie interrupted Danielle, "You had nothing to do with that."

"I suppose," Danielle reluctantly agreed.

"Who was the guy in the closet?" Ian finally asked. "I figured that's why you wanted me here."

"I thought you should be here in case you felt you had a claim to the gold since you were renting the property. As for the guy we found hiding in your closet, he's another treasure hunter," the chief explained.

"DO YOU WANT TO PRESS CHARGES?"

the chief asked Ian. Adam had already taken Marie home, and the chief had returned to his office with Ian, Lily, and Danielle. Jack, who had gotten bored, had vanished after they left the interrogation room.

The chief sat at his desk, while Danielle and Ian sat in the chairs facing him, and Lily perched casually on Ian's left knee.

"Does he have a record?" Ian asked.

"Nothing. He has a diving and salvage company in Astoria. I suspect he heard Paul's interview with Ben and, like the others, wondered if the gold was still in the house."

A knock came at the office door. They all turned to the open doorway. Heather Donovan stood there, wearing a sheepish smile as one of her hands twirled the tip of her right pigtail.

"Come on in, Heather." The chief waved her in. "Heather here was the one who called us about your break-in. She saw him sneak in your back door. At first she thought it was someone visiting you and then—"

"I lied," Heather blurted out.

"Excuse me?" the chief said.

"I knew who it was, I recognized him—

Kurt Jefferson. I know him because I hired him to do some diving for me."

The chief frowned. "What kind of diving?"

"I hired him to put the jewelry back on the *Eva Aphrodite*."

"You?" Danielle gasped. "You were responsible for the box getting on the boat?"

"I was trying to get rid of all this bad karma. But I blew it today. I saw Kurt going into Ian's house, and I knew why he was there. But I just didn't want to deal with it. And then I realized if I ignored it, then my karma would never get straightened out."

The chief stood up. "Maybe we should go back to the other room. There are more chairs there, and you can explain it to us."

Another knock came at the door. It was Joe. "Sorry to bother you, but Jolene refuses to leave."

"Jolene Carmichael?" Heather asked.

"Yes."

Heather turned to face the chief. "I think you should have Mrs. Carmichael join us. She's dealing with some pretty messed-up karma too, and this might help her understand."

———

THE CHIEF, Danielle, Lily, Ian, Heather, and Jolene were back in the interrogation room. Joe and Brian quietly watched and listened from the adjacent room, through the two-way mirror. Jolene kept muttering, "I don't know why I'm here."

Heather stood up and took a deep breath. She looked around the room. "As many of you know, my great-grandfather was a very bad man. He killed a young boy after that boy found some of the stolen gems from the Thorndike necklace. What you don't know is Harvey Crump was not the only person he ever killed."

Everyone but Heather remained seated, their attention riveted on her.

"Ephraim Presley, my great-grandfather, was friends with Anthony Taylor. Some of you know Taylor as the husband of Eva Thorndike, who, with Ephraim, stole the gems from her necklace."

"What does any of this have to do with me?" Jolene asked.

Heather faced Jolene. "Your grandfather, Ralph Templeton, was also a very bad man."

"What are you talking about? He was a wonderful man!"

"No," Heather said calmly. "He had financial troubles and tried to get Walt Marlow to finance a business deal with him. He had already been embezzling from the family business and was facing possible financial ruin."

"That's not true. Walt Marlow wanted to go into business with him. I read Ethel Pearson's diary."

"No. Your grandfather needed his brother's support, and unfortunately, his brother believed Walt was having an affair with his wife. He wasn't. Your grandfather knew that. He knew his sister-in-law was really having an affair with Anthony."

"So? Why is this important now?"

"Because your grandfather decided the solution to his problems was to murder his brother and sister-in-law. After all, Thelma had brought a considerable fortune to the marriage, and she had no family. If both

Howard and Thelma died—everything would go to your grandfather."

"Wouldn't someone have been suspicious had the boat not sunk with everyone dead on board?" Lily asked. "I can't believe they knew there was going to be a storm."

Heather looked at Lily. "The plan was to sink the boat after killing everyone. The storm —that was a gift. They watched the boat sink. The storm didn't come up until they were back at shore. Like I said, a gift. No one ever suggested foul play. As for the inheritance, Ralph Templeton understood it would take a while before he could claim it since there were no bodies; but that didn't really matter, because in his brother's absence he would have control of the estate. He also hoped that with his brother gone, he could approach Walt about his deal, but Walt wouldn't even talk to him. He was too upset after both his yacht and business partner went missing."

"How do you know all this?" Ian asked.

"I found more than the emerald in my grandfather's trunk. I just never told any of you. I found Ephraim's detailed confession about the murders, along with some of the jewelry taken off the passengers. I think he initially wrote that to protect himself should Ralph Templeton ever suspect he knew who had paid for the hit."

"How would Ephraim be privy to all that was going on with Ralph and Walt?" Lily asked.

Heather smiled. "Ephraim had his own spies. He liked to keep tabs on anyone who he saw as a threat."

"I'm assuming Ephraim and Anthony helped carry out the murders," Danielle said.

Heather nodded. "Ralph knew Anthony wanted to get rid of Thelma. If the rich widow he was courting found out he had been carrying on with Thelma at the same time, it would end their relationship. So Ralph blackmailed Anthony while providing a financial incentive. He told Anthony that Thelma was a liability for both of them—and with her gone, they could both profit."

"Monsters..." Lily muttered.

"I don't believe it," Jolene protested.

"Anthony arranged everything. He was supposedly the only one who knew the true identity of the person behind the hit. Ralph naturally wanted it that way to protect himself. What Ralph didn't know was Anthony had spilled it all to Ephraim, who then documented—in detail—the series of events, including the location of the wreckage and the fact that Anthony mysteriously went missing not long after the *Eva Aphrodite* disappeared."

"When you hired the diver to put the jewels back on the boat—you wanted to return them, like you did with the emerald," Danielle said.

Heather smiled at Danielle and then looked to Jolene, her expression now somber. "The only descendent I was able to identify attached to the jewelry was you, Jolene. And while you inherited the estate through your grandfather, I didn't think it was right returning the jewelry to you. After all, your grandfather was the one who had those poor people murdered."

Jolene suddenly stood. "It's all lies!" she shouted.

THIRTY-NINE

Alone with the chief in his office, Danielle slouched down in the chair, her head leaning against its backrest as she stared up at the ceiling. "What now?"

"Jolene could fight you in court for the gold coins, but I don't think she will."

Danielle lifted her head and looked at the chief, who sat behind his desk. "Why wouldn't she? From what I heard, Joe and Brian had a heck of a time prying those gold coins out of her fingers before they brought her down here this morning."

"For one thing, Jolene knows enough about the law to realize it's legally yours. And for another, I don't think she'd welcome that kind of publicity."

"You mean because of her grandfather?" Danielle asked.

With a nod he said, "The story will come out in the paper, but it'll die down and people will forget. But if she takes this to court, the horrific deeds of her grandfather will be amplified for everyone to see. I've known Jolene for a long time. She wouldn't want that."

"What about Thelma's jewelry? If the gold legally belongs to me, I would think Thelma's jewelry would go to Jolene."

The chief leaned forward, resting his elbows on the desktop. "I agree."

"It's obvious Heather doesn't, considering what she tried to do with them."

"True. But it's really not Heather's call. If Ralph was still alive and went on trial for his part in those murders and was convicted, his brother's will would be overturned, and Jolene wouldn't have inherited through her grandfather. Yet since she's the next living relative and wasn't involved in the murders, she'd probably inherit through her father, who would have been the next in line to inherit his uncle's estate back then, had his father been convicted for the murders."

Danielle sat up in the chair. "Even if there was a trial now, I can't imagine someone of Ralph Templeton's stature ever being convicted on a letter written by someone like Ephraim Presley."

"Agreed."

"I don't know about the statute of limitations on these things, but couldn't the families of the victims sue her grandfather's estate? Even without Ralph being formally convicted of the crime; look at OJ. He got off on the murder charges, but the victim's families still managed to sue him in a civil court."

The chief shrugged. "If the victims' families of the *Eva Aphrodite* could sue, it wouldn't get them anything."

"I thought Ralph Templeton left Jolene a fortune?"

"He did. But it's all gone."

"I sorta heard that, but I wondered if it was really true, if she really lost it all."

"Like I said, I've known Jolene for a long time. My wife was a close friend with her daughter. They went to college together; she's an attorney in New York. We still keep in touch. She and her mom have always had issues."

"I heard Jolene moved back to New York to be with her daughter after her husband died."

"That's what Jolene claimed. I know she had money coming in from the law firm and did her own thing in New York. From what I understand, all that stopped when Clarence was arrested."

Danielle stood up. "I guess that explains why the woman hates me."

"There is one more thing I think you should be aware of." The chief stood. "Your neighbors have made it perfectly clear to the city council that they don't want that wreckage left on the beach. Even the historical society has backed off."

"What does that mean?"

"There's been talk that you should be the one to pay for having it removed, not the taxpayers, since Walt Marlow owned the yacht."

"I suppose I could argue Jolene should pay for cleanup, since her grandfather was the one responsible for sinking it."

"Perhaps. But Jolene doesn't have any money, and I'm sure it won't take long before everyone realizes that gold will probably be going to you."

"Me and Uncle Sam. The IRS loves me these days."

"On the bright side, I doubt they can make you pay for it."

———

INSTEAD OF TURNING into her driveway, Danielle impulsively continued down the street. She parked near Chris's house. Getting out of her vehicle, she glanced up at the sky. Gray clouds blocked the afternoon sun. Pulling the front of her sweater tightly closed to ward off the damp chill, she slammed the car door shut and walked down the sidewalk to the opening leading to the beach. Once there, she looked out to the *Eva Aphrodite*—and beyond it to the ocean, its waves breaking along the shoreline.

"They're gone," a voice said.

Danielle looked abruptly to her right. Jack stood next to her.

With a shiver she asked, "Are you sure?"

"Yes. I can feel it. They've moved on. All they wanted was for the world to know Ralph Templeton was the one responsible."

Danielle looked curiously at Jack. "How did you know that? I didn't see you there when Heather told us who was behind the murders."

"Lily." Jack smiled.

"Lily? I don't understand."

"When she got back from the police station, she came up to the attic and told Walt and me everything. I had just finished telling Walt what I'd heard at the station before she arrived."

An image of Lily, seemingly alone and talking to herself in the attic, flashed through Danielle's mind. She couldn't help but wonder where Ian had been when Lily was up there, but the picture made her smile.

"If anything could convince me to stick around, it's that little doll Lily." Jack let out a low whistle in appreciation. "If I was alive, I'd give that Evan guy a run for his money."

"You mean Ian?" Danielle corrected.

"Yeah, him too. She's one hotsy totsy." Jack sighed and stared out to the ocean.

"Does this mean you're ready to move on?"

"Yes. I've already said goodbye to Walt." Jack looked from the ocean to Danielle and smiled. "I tried to get him to go with me."

Danielle glanced at Jack. "And?"

Jack chuckled. "I think you know. He's not going anywhere. At least not yet. He has his own hotsy totsy keeping him here."

Danielle scowled and looked back to the sea. "Don't be silly."

Jack laughed and then grew serious, glancing over to Chris's house and then back to Danielle. "Walt tells me you have a boyfriend."

"He said that?"

"Not boyfriend exactly, just said you were sort of involved with someone, that the guy lived there." Jack nodded to Chris's house. "Walt told me he could see spirits too."

"Yes, he can."

"Too bad I can't stick around and meet him."

They were both silent for a few more minutes, each looking out to sea, when Danielle said, "It would be nice if you could put that thing back before you leave."

"What do you mean?" Jack asked.

"It's going to be a pain—for someone—to get rid of that boat."

Jack looked over to the boat and shrugged. "I suppose if I did it once, I should be able to do it twice."

"While that would be nice, I doubt you'd be able to. Plus, it would probably just freak everyone out." Danielle considered the possibility for a moment and then chuckled. "Although from a marketing perspective, the mystery of the wreckage magically appearing and then disappearing would be gold for tourism."

"Why wouldn't I be able to?"

"Moving something like that requires a lot of energy. From what you've told me, it sounds as if you never really harnessed your energy those years you were on the *Eva Aphrodite*, not until you brought the boat up. Probably took all your reserves—stored up from the last ninety plus years."

"I don't imagine it'll require as much energy. After all, it's not like I'm bringing it up from the bottom of the ocean again." Narrowing his eyes, Jack studied the wreckage, a sly smile forming on his lips.

"What are you doing down here?" a second male voice called out. "It's cold."

Danielle turned toward the street and saw Joe Morelli walking toward her. When she looked back to Jack, he was gone.

"Hi, Joe," Danielle greeted him when he reached her side. Shivering, she wrapped her arms across her body, warding off the chill. "I could ask the same of you."

"I had to drop something off at Ian's." He shivered and glanced briefly to the sky. It was even grayer than it had been when he had left the station fifteen minutes earlier.

"After all that happened this morning, I just had to stop. Kept thinking of all those poor people who were murdered so senselessly. Some people can be pretty damn evil."

Burying his hands in his coat pockets to ward off the cold, Joe gazed out to sea. "Yes, they can. But maybe you should go in now. It's freezing out here; looks like a good storm's brewing."

"In a minute, *Dad*," Danielle teased.

Joe retorted with a comment, but Danielle didn't hear him. Instead, she was distracted by laughter. She looked to the *Eva Aphrodite* and spied Jack standing on the top deck, his arms outstretched as he looked up into the sky, laughing and shouting to the universe. The wind started to howl.

"See what I mean," Joe said, protectively wrapping his arm around Danielle's shoulder in an effort to provide warmth, while attempting to nudge her in the direction of her car.

"Just a minute, Joe." Mesmerized, she watched Jack.

With a frown, Joe's gaze followed Danielle's. "What are you looking at?"

"I thought I heard something." The wind intensified, loosening strands of her dark hair from the confines of her braid. They slapped against her face as she attempted to push them away with one hand.

"It's just the wind. Looks like it's going to be a big one." Joe, his arm still wrapped around her shoulders, looked up to the dark sky. The wind intensified. When he looked back to the wreckage, his eyes widened, not believing what he was seeing. The massive hull rocked slightly as it inched its way toward the ocean.

"It's moving!" Joe shouted, dropping his arm from Danielle so that he could grab his phone.

Still focused on Jack and the *Eva Aphrodite*, she glanced briefly to Joe. "What are you doing?"

"I need to call someone. It's moving," Joe said in a panic.

Danielle laughed. "What do you think you're going to do to stop it?"

Lightning flashed across the dark sky, followed by a loud clap of thunder.

"That was close," Joe said, dropping the hand clutching the cellphone to his side. He looked back to the ship and silently watched as it slid toward the ocean. What he didn't see was Jack, who stood atop the upper deck, hooting enthusiastically while urging the *Eva Aphrodite* on her final voyage.

They could hear nothing but the wind's howl. Rain began to fall; it soaked their hair, their clothes. Silently transfixed, they stood motionless, watching the *Eva Aphrodite* return to the sea. Instead of sinking as one might expect it would, the battered hull stayed afloat, drifting slowly away from the shore.

Raindrops clung to Danielle's eyelashes. The storm's intensity increased. Her clothes now drenched, she made no effort to find shelter. Instead, she watched Jack, who stood proudly aboard the top deck of the departing ship. He faced her and, with a flourish, gave her a final salute before vanishing.

FORTY

The first thing Lily did the next morning was call Craig Simmons, the landscaper, who happened to be Joe's brother-in-law. He was the same landscaper Danielle had used to get the yards in order when they had first moved into Marlow House nine months earlier. The previous day's storm had left behind debris, including several downed tree limbs, one of which hung precariously from a tree not far from the front entry.

Looking out the attic window, Walt by her side, Danielle thought that if it hadn't been for the dislodged shrubbery scattered across the front yard, one might never guess there had been a recent storm. The clear blue sky boasted not a single cloud, and the sun seemed somehow brighter than normal.

Together Danielle and Walt watched the unusual heavy traffic on the street. They understood what it was about. Word had already gotten out that the mysterious ghost ship had vanished during the storm. Although, considering Joe's interview on Paul's radio show, they all knew it hadn't vanished exactly. According to Joe's eyewitness account, the sudden storm the previous afternoon had somehow dislodged the wreckage and pushed it back to the sea, where it mysteriously stayed afloat until it disappeared from view. Of course, by that time, Joe had made a call to the Coast Guard to let them know what had just happened.

"I was wondering where you were," Hillary called out from the attic doorway.

Danielle turned to her and smiled. "Hi. I was just watching all the commotion from up here, better view."

"Do you mind if I join you?" the woman asked as she made her way toward Danielle, without waiting for an answer.

"I saw you walking back up the street," Danielle said when Hillary reached the window, taking Walt's place. Annoyed, Walt quickly moved out of the way and took a seat on the sofa before summoning a cigar.

"I had to see for myself. It's really gone. Amazing," Hillary said in awe. She paused a moment and took a deep breath. "I smell it again. Reminds me of my second husband."

"That smell comes and goes in Marlow House. I believe the previous owner used to smoke a cigar," Danielle said, stifling a giggle.

"There must be a hundred people down on the beach. Are you going down there?" Hillary asked.

"I was down there with Joe when it took off yesterday. So I already saw it. I'm not big on crowds."

"Just lucky someone didn't get hurt! Imagine if that thing had taken off and someone was standing behind it."

"Fortunately, no one was hurt." Danielle smiled.

"But if it's still out there—floating around —it could be a danger."

"We don't have to worry about that," Danielle told her.

"We don't?"

"Joe Morelli, the officer who was with me yesterday, gave me a call a little while ago. I guess the Coast Guard already located it. Doesn't sound like it's going anywhere."

"Did it sink?"

Danielle nodded. "From what I understand, it's in pretty deep waters. They're just leaving it there. The *Eva Aphrodite*'s final resting place."

"Oh look! A police car just parked out front." Hillary pointed out the window toward the street. It was Chief MacDonald, and he was walking toward Marlow House.

"Yikes, I better warn him about that tree limb!" Danielle said as she darted from the room.

FIVE MINUTES LATER, Danielle sat alone in the parlor with Chief McDonald.

"I came to apologize to Walt," MacDonald told her.

"For thinking he was a mass murderer?" Danielle teased.

"Pretty much," he said sheepishly.

"He's up in the attic right now, watching all the commotion. Seems like everyone in town is here, even more than when the *Eva Aphrodite* showed up. And this time, there's nothing to see."

"It solves a big problem and saves the taxpayers some money."

"I thought you were going to make me pay?"

"Hey, I never said I was going to make you pay," he said with a laugh. "I was just letting you know what some people were saying."

"Yeah, right," Danielle grumbled, feigning annoyance. She then smiled and said, "But you can thank Jack for taking her back to sea. Well, you could thank him if he hadn't already moved on."

"They found where she landed, by the way."

"Yeah, Joe called me about a half an hour ago and told me. Without Jack to bring her back up again, I imagine she'll stay put this time."

"Speaking of Jack…" The chief stood up and reached into his pocket. He pulled out Jack's Masonic ring and handed it to Danielle. "I wanted to give you this."

Standing briefly, she took the ring and then sat back down. Looking at the Masonic emblem, she rolled the ring between her fingers. "Jack's ring."

"I figured legally it belongs to you, and I thought Walt might want it since Jack was his best friend."

Smiling softly, Danielle studied the ring in her hand. "Thanks, that's sweet. But doesn't the will have to go through probate or something?"

"You don't see me turning over the gold coins right now."

Danielle laughed.

Grinning, the chief said, "I figured it wouldn't hurt to go ahead and give this to you. Not sure what's going to happen with everything we found in the box Heather left on the ship. The court will have to figure that one out. As for Jack Winters, I already did some checking, and it looks like he didn't have any family."

"No, he didn't," Walt said when he appeared in the parlor a moment later.

"Hi, Walt. Look what the chief brought." Danielle held up the ring for Walt to see.

The chief looked to where he imagined Walt might be standing. "I wanted to apologize, Walt, for thinking you might have killed those people."

"Tell the chief there's no hard feelings. I understand he was only worried about you and Lily. It'll be comforting to know you have friends looking out for you when I'm gone."

WHEN WALT SHOWED up in Danielle's room that evening to say goodnight, he found her already under the sheets and blankets. But the light on the nightstand was on, and she was sitting up, leaning against the headboard, waiting for him.

"What did you mean earlier today when you said it'll be nice knowing I have friends looking out for me when you're gone?"

He sat down on the edge of the bed next to her. There was no dip in the mattress; it was as if he wasn't even there.

"Just that. When I'm gone, I want to know you and Lily will be okay."

"Is that why you're sticking around? Because you're not sure we'll be okay on our own?"

Walt smiled and swung his legs up onto the bed. Without thought, Danielle scooted to the other side of the mattress, making room for Walt. They lay side by side—Danielle tucked under the sheets and blankets, wearing her pajama bottoms and T-shirt, while Walt, stretched out atop the bed linens, wore his blue pin-striped suit. They both leaned back against the headboard.

"You are both helpless women," he teased.

Danielle let out a snort.

"That's not very feminine, Danielle. We will not get you married off if you go around snorting."

Danielle giggled. "Since when did you decide I needed to get married off?"

"Don't you want to get married?"

Danielle shrugged. "I already was."

"Don't you want to get married again? Have children?"

Danielle looked over at Walt. "What's this all about?"

"I just want to see you happy."

Danielle smiled. "I am happy."

"Do you miss Chris?"

"Chris?" Danielle studied Walt for a moment. "Sure. He's a good friend."

"Have you talked to him much since he's been gone?" Walt asked.

"Yeah."

"How often?"

"Every day…Walt…why did you tell Jack I was involved with Chris?"

He turned to Danielle, studying her for a moment. "Aren't you?"

Danielle shrugged. "I guess…sort of. He's a good friend."

"Has he kissed you again?" Walt said, thinking of the brief New Year's kiss.

Danielle groaned and scooted down in the bedsheets, turning her back to Walt. "That is none of your business, Walt Marlow. Sheesh. I'm tired."

The light went out. Danielle stared off into the darkness. After a moment, she said in a whisper, "Walt?"

No answer.

"Walt?"

Still no answer.

Letting out a deep sigh, Danielle snuggled down in the bed and went to sleep.

———

THE SEA AIR caressed her face. Danielle opened her eyes. She stood on the deck of a ship—a yacht. Her hands gripped the railing as she looked out to sea. Glancing to her right, she spied a life preserver hanging from the railing. The words *Eva Aphrodite* arched over the top half of the ring.

Spinning around, she came face-to-face with Walt, whose blue eyes looked out at her from under the rim of a panama hat. He wore a white linen suit, and when she glanced down, she noticed the dress she wore was also white. Genteelly, he took her arm and led her down the deck.

"This is the *Eva Aphrodite*," Danielle said in

awe as she looked around, stunned at the transformation from a barnacle-encrusted hull to an elegant ship with polished wood decking and freshly painted wood chairs facing out to sea.

"As it used to be," Walt said, pausing a moment to snag two glasses of champagne from a passing waiter.

"It's beautiful," Danielle whispered. She accepted the glass Walt offered and took a sip. Pausing a moment, she looked up at him and said, "I can taste it. It tastes like champagne."

He laughed. "I suppose I'm getting better at this." He guided her to several chairs. They sat down.

Danielle took another sip of the champagne. "Amazing," she murmured.

"I thought I'd use this opportunity to let you say hello to someone—or perhaps goodbye."

Danielle looked up from her glass and noticed a young black couple walking in their direction. Dressed elegantly in the fashions of the 1920s, they were obviously lovers, the way he repeatedly leaned over to kiss her cheek while she laughed gaily, looking into his eyes with adoration.

Recognition dawned. Danielle stood abruptly. "Emma!"

When Emma spied Danielle, she grabbed the arm of the man at her side and pulled him toward Danielle and Walt. Looking up at Walt, she said, "I have to thank you again, Mr. Marlow, for inviting us."

"Please, call me Walt."

Confused, Danielle looked from Walt to Emma.

"I wanted to introduce you to my Emmett," Emma explained.

"You've moved on?" Danielle asked.

"Yes, thanks to you." Emma reached up and kissed her husband's cheek and then formally introduced him to Danielle. The four chatted a while before Emma and Emmett walked off, disappearing into one of the cabins.

"Are they really here?" Danielle asked.

"Their spirits are. I wasn't sure if I could really pull it off—it's a little tricky once they've moved on."

"Like my Christmas dream?"

Walt nodded. "If it was possible for me to bring back all your family for regular visits—I would, Danielle. But unfortunately, it doesn't work that way."

Danielle set the half-full champagne glass on the table between their chairs. "This is lovely, Walt. Your yacht was beautiful. I can't imagine how it would be to have something like this."

"Chris could afford a boat like this. I should talk to him."

Blushing, Danielle stood up. "You're funny, Walt."

"I'm not trying to be funny. I just meant he seems crazy about you, and if you two get together, he should spoil you. You deserve it."

"If you'll remember, I have money of my own—thanks to you." Danielle flashed Walt a grin and sashayed to the railing. Leaning against it, she gazed out to sea and took a deep breath. In the distance, she spied dolphins. She stood there a moment, watching them leap and dance like a water ballet, when she felt something brush over her cheek. Turning from the railing, she found Walt's blue eyes staring into hers. They were just inches apart.

His right hand reached up and cupped her face, his thumb gently caressing her skin. Unable—or unwilling—to move away, Danielle's eyes widened as he moved closer, his lips a breath away from hers. Walt hesitated, as if rethinking his bold advance. In that moment she was certain he was going to pull away, so she did the only thing she could.

Danielle leaned forward, claiming Walt's kiss while wrapping her arms around his shoulders, pulling him close.

HER EYES FLEW OPEN. Danielle was in her bed. Moonlight streamed through the bedroom window. She was alone.

"Oh crap," she groaned. Grabbing the tops of her sheets and dragging them over her head, she scooted down in her bed, hiding under the bed linens.

THE GHOST AND THE MYSTERY WRITER

RETURN TO MARLOW HOUSE IN

THE GHOST AND THE MYSTERY WRITER

HAUNTING DANIELLE, BOOK 9

A killer strikes under Frederickport Pier.

Before dawn the next morning, Marlow House's celebrity guest, mystery author Hillary

Hemingway, is busy writing about the crime for her upcoming novel—including details that only the real killer would know.

Coincidence? If so, it isn't the first time.

NON-FICTION BY

BOBBI ANN JOHNSON HOLMES

BOOKS BY ANNA J. MCINTYRE

COULSON FAMILY SAGA

Coulson's Wife

Coulson's Crucible

Coulson's Lessons

Coulson's Secret

Coulson's Reckoning

Sundered Hearts

After Sundown

While Snowbound

Sugar Rush